LIGHTS, CAMERA, MURDER!

The Kitty Karlyle Pet Chef Mysteries by Marie Celine

DISHING UP DEATH
LIGHTS, CAMERA, MURDER!

LIGHTS, CAMERA, MURDER!

Marie Celine

Severn House Large Print
London & New York

This first large print edition published 2017
in Great Britain and the USA by
SEVERN HOUSE PUBLISHERS LTD of
19 Cedar Road, Sutton, Surrey, England, SM2 5DA.
First world regular print edition published 2015 by
Severn House Publishers Ltd.

British Library Cataloguing in Publication Data
A CIP catalogue record for this title is available from the British Library.

ISBN-13: 9780727895196

Severn House Publishers support the Forest Stewardship Council™ [FSC™], the leading international forest certification organisation. All our titles that are printed on FSC certified paper carry the FSC logo.

Typeset by Palimpsest Book Production Ltd.,
Falkirk, Stirlingshire, Scotland.
Printed and bound in Great Britain by
T J International, Padstow, Cornwall.

One

'Karlyle, right?'

Kitty nodded.

'Come on,' the strange woman said in a rush. Her accent said Caribbean, but her attitude screamed New York. She grabbed Kitty's hand and pulled. 'Gretchen's antsy. Let's get you to hair and makeup.'

Kitty followed as the woman hustled off to an alcove behind the set and pointed to a styling chair in front of a large mirror with a bright string of white lights running along the top and sides. It was like something out of the movies.

It was fitting, since she was deep in the cavernous bowels of Building Two at Santa Monica Film Studios; a small semi-independent film company that occupied a small corner of property off Pico Boulevard. The fenced complex consisted of six separate buildings, mostly sound-stages by the looks of them. One taller office building stood nearest the gated entrance like a modern-day castle's keep.

'Who are you anyway?' Kitty managed to ask between breaths. She had imagined the job would involve a lot of standing around, not running around. If she'd known, she would have worn better shoes, something with traction, definitely not heels.

The woman stuck out her hand. Kitty would

have clasped it but it held a thick hairbrush. 'Fran Earhart. Hair and makeup.' She extended her arms like wings. 'Like the flyer, you know?'

'Kitty Karlyle,' Kitty wheezed. 'Gourmet pet chef.' Though things were changing fast. In what seemed like the space of five minutes, Kitty had gone from being a struggling entrepreneur running her own little gourmet pet chef enterprise, to hosting a TV cooking show!

'Cute. So, what's all that?' The young woman's eyes cut to Kitty's handbag and gear.

'My purse and my chef's satchel.' Kitty shook the bag. 'I keep my knives and accessories in it.'

'We've got plenty of that stuff on set,' Fran said with a flutter of the hand. 'You can drop your things down here.'

'Are you sure they will be OK?'

Fran pulled a face. 'Don't worry, we're not all angels around here, but no one's going to mess with your personal stuff, girl.'

'Sorry, I didn't mean to offend you.'

'You didn't.' Fran tapped the back of the chair. 'Have a seat.'

Kitty dropped her gear and did as she was told. She shut her eyes while Fran and another woman began fussing over her like a couple of mother hens. Kitty cautiously cracked open an eye. 'So, are you any relation to Amelia Earhart?'

With her golden complexion, long black tresses and full, pouty red lips, Fran Earhart didn't look a thing like the pictures of the aviator that she'd remembered seeing in textbooks, but you never know.

'Nope. Not a chromosome.'

Ooo–kay.

Fran and the other woman brushed, plucked, dabbed and smeared, and then smoothed out all the rough edges. Kitty had to admit, lying back in the chair – feeling the supple leather caress her spine, being pampered – it felt sort of good. In fact, it felt sort of great.

When she opened her eyes and saw herself in the mirror, she was flabbergasted. 'Wow.' She couldn't believe it; she actually looked glamorous.

'It doesn't even look like me!' Kitty exclaimed. 'Are you sure it *is* me?' She tugged approvingly at her fine brown hair. Just minutes ago, that same hair had looked like nothing more than a mess of spaghetti-like strands that couldn't make up their minds what they wanted to do. She'd never been very good at applying her own makeup and doing her hair. How had Fran and her taciturn partner managed it?

Gaping in the mirror, her blue eyes sparkled back at her with delight. Kitty turned to Fran. 'You are a wizard.' She could get used to this star treatment.

'Nah,' said Fran, with a laugh, 'I only helped you realize your true potential.' She played her fingers through Kitty's hair. 'You've just never realized how good you look before.'

'Ready?' Gretchen asked, sticking her head around the corner. Gretchen Corbett, the show's producer, was probably somewhere in her fifties, by Kitty's reckoning. Her toasty brown hair bore streaks of gray and fell to her prominent cheek-bones. Her face had a certain chipmunk quality that Kitty wasn't about to comment on aloud. A simple, heart-shaped gold locket hung on a slender chain atop her sweater. Her fingers toyed with it as she regarded Kitty and Fran.

Kitty gulped. 'I think so.' She still couldn't quite believe she was here at a film studio to shoot the pilot for a new TV show called *The Pampered Pet*.

It had all come about because, unknown to her, one of her clients, whose pets she cooked for – Ernst Fandolfi, a world-famous magician – was friends with the show's producer, Gretchen Corbett. Ms Corbett needed a host for a TV cooking show and Fandolfi, without even asking Kitty, had given the producer her name, saying she'd be perfect.

Kitty thought it was all perfectly insane. Which was apropos in a sense, because she'd acquired Mr Fandolfi as a client through a referral from a Beverly Hills pet psychologist named George Newhart, who'd found one of her business cards tacked up on the community board in a local health food market.

One day they could all get their heads examined together.

'Don't worry, honey. Like I said, it's only a run-through. We'll tape the first real show tomorrow.'

Kitty let out her breath. That was a relief, though that didn't seem to match what Gretchen had explained earlier during their first meeting. But then, a lot of what the producer said was sketchy.

Kitty shrugged it off and followed Gretchen

round to the stage. What else could she do? As Gretchen had so eloquently explained, the wheels were in motion. And this roller coaster was headed down the track. All she could do was hold on and try not to scream or fall out.

They reached the edge of the kitchen set, newly constructed for the show, when Kitty stopped dead in her tracks. There were two bleachers, separated by a narrow aisle, full of people not fifty feet away, whispering and waiting.

Kitty's eyes skimmed over them, her pupils growing wider by the nanosecond. 'Who are all those people?'

'That's your audience, Kitty.' Gretchen bobbed her head. 'Good crowd, too,' she said, rubbing her hands with glee. 'Nice age spread; plenty of women, young, middle-aged and elderly. The team did a good job.'

'But where did they *come* from?' Kitty couldn't imagine how Gretchen had managed to come up with two bleachers-worth of people on short notice, especially for an unknown cooking show hosted by an unknown chef in the middle of a weekday afternoon.

'Oh, we send out flunkies with clipboards who round them up off the street. It's easy. Offer them a free show, some air conditioning, some cheap pastries, soda and coffee. Toss in an inexpensive CuisineTV souvenir, in this case a potholder, and you practically can't keep them away!'

Gretchen's brown eyes darted over the faces in the audience. 'You never know what you'll get though. It's a real mixed bag out there on the streets, you know what I mean?'

Kitty nodded, hopelessly.

'Tourists, workers on breaks or playing hooky, folks on their days off. Vagrants, though, they're mostly easy to spot and we can usually keep them out,' she added, rather callously in Kitty's opinion. 'No, you never know what you'll get. We made out great today, though.' She pointed. 'Look, there are even some people with pets.'

Kitty had noticed several dogs in attendance. She had also noticed that her heart had stopped beating and her tongue – normally her friend – felt like it had been left out in the Sahara for a week to dry out. 'I don't know about this . . .' Her voice trailed off.

Fran popped up by her side. She brushed an errant lock from Kitty's face and adjusted the pink apron they'd wrapped her in. 'Don't worry, girlfriend. You'll do great.'

The look in Kitty's eyes said that she found that hard to believe.

Gretchen introduced Kitty to the director – a short and slim, fifty-something male with long hair tied back in a loose ponytail – named Greg Clifton. His hair was more gray than black and thinning in the front. He was dressed casually in blue jeans and a loose primrose polo shirt.

The director said a brief hello then went back to barking orders to his crew. Then Steve Barnhard, the assistant producer Kitty had met earlier that day, ordered everybody who belonged there to get busy and everybody who didn't to get lost.

Kitty sensed that Steve was not an animal person – not even a people person – and she vowed to do her best to stay on his good side. He had wavy ginger hair and a light trail of freckles running from cheek to cheek. With his boyish features, she guessed he was in his early thirties, close to her own age. He wore designer jeans and an oversized gray-blue turtleneck sweater. A heavy gold cross with a diamond at its center hung from his neck.

Gretchen was shuffling Kitty on to the set when she crashed into a powerful-looking man in a deep blue business suit and wide cerise tie. 'Bill!' she exclaimed. 'I wasn't expecting to see you here. I didn't even know you were in town. I thought you were in New York.'

The man in the suit brushed himself off carefully, and then smiled. He had a firm chin and striking brown eyes that matched his hair. 'When I heard you'd managed to find the perfect host for our new cooking show, I ordered the corporate Gulfstream to get ready, and headed straight out. I didn't want to miss this. Gretchen, you had better be right.'

Gretchen visibly flinched.

He turned his smile on Kitty. 'You must be the young woman Gretchen has been gushing about.'

Gretchen spoke up. 'Kitty Karlyle, this is William Barnhard, president and CEO of CuisineTV.'

'Oh, my,' said Kitty. 'I've heard all about you. Thank you so much for the opportunity, Mr Barnhard.' Barnhard? She wondered what the CEO of the network's relationship to the assistant producer might be.

He held out his hand. 'Please, call me Bill.'

Kitty shook the CEO's hand, noticing it was quite warm to the touch. She was surprised she felt anything at all, as numb as she was feeling inside.

Greg, the director, shouted for everyone to settle down and for Gretchen and Bill to get off his set. Fran ran out once more and attacked Kitty's nose with a powder puff.

'Again?' Kitty said.

'Just for luck,' Fran whispered, then ran off again.

The CEO released Kitty's hand. 'Have a good show.'

'Thank you, sir,' replied Kitty, her stomach in knots. She felt the sweat beading up over every inch of her body as she found herself under the relentless heat of the studio lights.

'Perhaps I could prevail upon you to cook for my pets sometime, Kitty?'

'Of course, I'd be honored, Mr Barnhard. I mean, Bill.'

'Wonderful. We'll talk more after the show.'

Kitty swallowed nervously and nodded. Her life had become a maelstrom of activity.

Greg yelled. 'Quiet, everyone. It's show time!'

A thin young woman in an ecru pantsuit, whom Gretchen identified as the assistant director – or AD for short – strode out in front of the audience and coolly began explaining the show's premise. Kitty knew there was no way she was going to remain that calm under fire.

'You heard the man, it's show time,' said Gretchen. 'Now get out there.' She gave Kitty a push. Kitty found herself resisting.

'But I'm so nervous,' Kitty replied, digging in her heels – hard to do on a concrete floor in stilettos – and wringing her hands.

'So what?' quipped Gretchen, rather cold-heartedly. 'A little nerves will do you good, keep you on your toes,' she added, with a practically vicious smile. 'Now, get out there and knock 'em dead.'

'I don't know . . .' Kitty was having serious misgivings about the whole thing. What had she been thinking going along with this?

She scanned the kitchen set. A fancy, professional, six-burner, stainless-steel Viking range, double-door refrigerator and other appliances gleamed like jewels. There were racks of top-of-the-line Le Creuset cookware to the right of the sink, which itself sat beneath a window with a painted backdrop of a garden in bloom. Built-in bookshelves lined with cookbooks written by famous chefs framed the far side.

It all looked like a lovely, cozy, yet high-end home kitchen – if you ignored all the bright lights overhead, thick cables strewn across the stage floor and dozens of people moving in dozens of directions at once.

'Trust me, you've got what it takes, honey. Hook them, reel them in, and then club them silly!' she said with ruthless pleasure, all the while making clubbing motions as if she was bludgeoning baby seals in the Arctic.

'You're going to be a star, honey. National exposure on cable stations everywhere.' The producer hooked a finger under Kitty's chin. 'You'll be in every house in America!'

Why did it sound like such a bad thing when the producer said it? wondered Kitty, her stomach churning enough to make butter out of her breakfast.

Gretchen spread her arms wide. 'The audience is going to love you. They'll eat you up, the same way their pampered pets will be eating up your dishes.' She snapped her fingers in front of Kitty's nose. 'Why, we could even do a deal with one of the big pet food manufacturers to brand a specialty line of foods.'

She slapped a hand against her forehead. 'Why haven't I thought of this sooner? I can picture it now. Pretty pink cans, Kitty Karlyle's CuisineTV brand gourmet pet food – for breakfast, lunch, and dinner.'

Kitty could practically see the dollar signs appear in Gretchen's eyes as she said, 'I can't wait to tell Bill all about it. He's gonna flip!'

The assistant director, Julie McConnell, interrupted Gretchen's soliloquy. 'It's time for Kitty to go on, Gretchen.'

'Right.' Gretchen gave Kitty's apron one last tug. 'Just remember to smile, Kitty. And tell the viewers in the bleachers how cute their pets are, they eat that stuff up. Though some of the dirty beasties have been peeing all over the studio floors,' she added with a scowl. 'We may need to think about a special section for audience members with pets down the road.'

Kitty nodded and tried to speak but Gretchen cut her off. 'Your audience awaits.' The producer pointed to the overhead TV monitor, on which Kitty saw row after row of filled seats with a handful of pets scattered among them. A sea of eyes was watching the stage. Waiting for her.

Gretchen waited until the AD gave her the signal, then shooed Kitty to the edge of the set. 'Just be yourself,' she advised. 'And don't forget to smile.'

Gretchen paused, a hand on each of Kitty's shoulders, her nails digging in like talons. 'Don't forget to make eye contact with the audience – and the camera!' she instructed. She turned to Julie. 'Where the devil is camera three?'

'Some sort of technical glitch, the cameraman's working on it. It shouldn't be long.'

'David again?'

Julie nodded once.

Gretchen cursed like a sailor with a losing poker hand. 'I swear, I'm gonna kill him!' Her eyes burned with fury. 'Tell him to get it fixed right away!' She turned to her new star. 'We'll have to make do.'

Too bad. For a fleeting moment, Kitty thought she might get a reprieve, if only briefly, from her pending ordeal.

'Like I always say,' Gretchen said, giving Kitty a final push that sent her under the spotlights, 'lights, camera, murder!'

'So here she is,' said Julie. 'Ladies and gentlemen, let's hear it for the host of CuisineTV's brand-new cooking show for pets, *The Pampered Pet*! Your host, Kitty Karlyle!'

The audience dutifully applauded as coached by the assistant director and the flashing applause signs. A couple of the dogs barked too. Who knew they could read?

Kitty was barely breathing and her ears were buzzing like there were seashells taped to each as she stood center stage and said hello to the audience. 'Thank you all very much for coming,' Kitty squeaked and felt her cheeks heat up. She nervously cleared her throat. Greg, the director, scowled and made throat-slashing motions.

Oops. Kitty tensed up and started again, more firmly. 'Thank you, again, for coming to the show. I'm Kitty Karlyle and I love preparing delicious meals for pets. After all,' she said, reading somewhat stiffly from the teleprompter, 'they deserve the best, don't they?'

This brought what appeared to be a spontaneous eruption of applause. Then Kitty noticed the applause signs were flashing again.

She swallowed and wet her lips. Where was a sinkhole when you needed one? 'Today, we will be cooking for man's best friend, the dog. And I'll be making one of my favorite dishes – to cook, that is, not eat. I call it Kitty's Pooch Pot Pie.' Kitty heard chuckles from the audience. That was a relief. Hosting a cooking show was going to be hard enough to pull off without adding having her jokes fall flat to the list of her troubles.

'The pets I've made this dish for have loved it. So if you are a dog owner, I'm confident your pet will love it, too.'

A Dalmatian, contained on a leash by a frumpy, middle-aged woman in the third row, let out a mournful howl.

Kitty paused. 'Well, it sounds like somebody's hungry. How about it, big boy, are you hungry?'

She had gone off script. Kitty ignored the look of irritation that the director was aiming her way. He'd just mimed hanging himself. Kitty thought it a bit melodramatic.

As if trained for the role, the Dalmatian howled once more. That brought a burst of applause from the audience. Kitty beamed. And she noticed with some satisfaction that the applause signs hadn't even come on.

Kitty felt her muscles starting to loosen up. Maybe soon she'd start breathing again. A third camera operator quietly rolled his rig up to join the other two already filming, catching Kitty's eye. He winked at her and Kitty couldn't suppress grinning back.

Kitty crossed in front of the kitchen island she'd been standing behind – putting a barrier between herself and the audience – and motioned to the dog. 'What do you say, ma'am?' she said to the woman in the black dress and pillbox hat. 'Do you think your companion would like to come on down and assist me?'

The startled woman pointed a finger at her chest. 'Oh, dear. You mean me?'

'Yes, ma'am,' replied Kitty. 'What's your name?'

'I–I'm Agnes Whimsey,' the woman replied, sounding a touch nervous. She patted her dog's head. 'And this is Charlie.' The dog licked her hand.

'Pleased to meet you,' answered Kitty. 'Do you think Charlie would like to come down and keep me company? You know, I normally do all my pre-cooking and prepping for my clients' pets at my home. My cat and dog – that's Barney and Fred – are always around. I guess they keep hoping I'll drop something they can claim for their own.'

'Well . . .' Mrs Whimsey replied. She glanced at her dog. 'I suppose it would be all right.'

'What do you say, everybody?' Kitty asked. 'Should we get Charlie down here?' The audience hooted. Greg, the director, threw his arms up in despair and marched around in tiny circles next to his chair. Yeah, he definitely had a tendency to overdramatize.

Mrs Whimsey unhooked the leash from Charlie's collar. Kitty called out, 'Come on, Charlie, boy!' and clapped her hands. The dog glanced at Mrs Whimsey, and then ran down the steps toward Kitty, jumping into her arms like a long lost friend.

Kitty began preparing the Pooch Pot Pie, explaining each step to the audience, while Charlie weaved in and out of her legs, looking expectantly up at the countertop and licking his chops.

When the beefy pot pie was done and Charlie had licked the stainless steel bowl clean, Kitty once more thanked everyone in the audience for coming and said goodbye with a wave. The audience gave her a hearty round of applause. Kitty figured she could get used to that, too.

The aroma of the pot pie lingered and Kitty's stomach grumbled like an incipient volcano, reminding her that she hadn't had a bite since morning. She was going to need to get something to eat soon. She was beginning to feel faint, especially under the glare of all the hot lights.

As the audience thinned and streamed out the exits, Kitty returned Charlie to Mrs Whimsey.

'You did splendidly,' said Mrs Whimsey, as she clipped Charlie's leash back on his collar.

'Thank you,' Kitty replied. 'I only hope my producer thinks so. Speaking of which . . .' She looked around. Gretchen was nowhere in sight. She caught Steve by the arm as he passed. 'Where's Gretchen? I don't see her anywhere.'

Steve shrugged and waved to Bill Barnhard, calling for him to wait up.

'Nice job, Kitty,' said the director, coming up and giving Kitty a pat on the back. 'You even managed to follow most of the cues. You had me worried there when you went out in the audience like that, though. But, hey, it worked out great. You've got good instincts.'

'I really did OK, then?' Apparently he'd forgotten all about his over-the-top, behind the camera antics. This guy was complicated.

Greg smiled. 'Hey, you did better than a lot of the so-called professionals I've seen pass through here.'

'Thank you. That's so nice to hear. To tell you the truth, I'm relieved.' She let out a deep breath. 'And I'm equally relieved it's over. What did Gretchen think?'

Greg scratched his wide nose. 'I don't know. Come to think of it, I haven't seen her. Usually she's breathing down my neck when I shoot.'

As Greg ambled away, Fran came up and gave Kitty a hug. 'You did great, girlfriend.' She fluffed

Kitty's hair. 'Looked great on camera, too. If I do say so myself,' she added with a giggle.

'Excuse me,' said a soft-spoken young blonde woman in khaki shorts and a T-shirt. She held out a pen and a small notebook. Her legs were long and tanned. A typical California girl by the looks of her – the kind the Beach Boys used to write songs about. She reminded Kitty vaguely of someone, but she couldn't place whom.

'Yes?' Kitty asked.

'May I have your autograph?' She shyly pushed the notebook and pen toward Kitty.

'My autograph?' Kitty couldn't believe this girl was actually asking for her signature. 'It's not like I'm a celebrity or anything.'

'Sure you are,' Fran replied. 'Ms Karlyle will be happy to give you her autograph.' She grabbed the pen and notebook and thrust them at Kitty. 'Whom should she make this out to?'

'Jennie. Jennie Levin,' the young lady answered.

Fran nudged Kitty in the ribs and Kitty bit her lip as she thought. No one had ever asked her for her autograph before. What should she write? Finally, she wrote, *To My Number One Fan, Jennie. Warmest Wishes, Kitty.*

Kitty handed the notebook and pen back to the girl, who read the inscription and smiled. 'That's wonderful. Thank you. I'll bet your husband is really proud of you.'

'Thank you,' said Kitty. 'But I'm not married.'

'Boyfriend, then? You must have someone special in your life?'

Kitty fidgeted. She wasn't used to celebrity, yet

alone used to strangers asking her about her personal life, her love life at that.

'Yes, there is someone special in my life.' Her fiancé, Jack Young, meant the world to her. She'd met him about six months ago, when Jack was working as a detective for the Los Angeles County Sheriff's Department and Kitty had found herself embroiled in some nasty business involving a rock star client. At the time, she'd thought Jack was planning to arrest her. Now, he was planning to marry her.

'That's nice,' said the young woman. 'We all need someone special in our lives.'

Kitty agreed and, a moment later, the young woman walked off – after telling Kitty how wonderful she was – autograph in one hand, kitschy free *The Pampered Pet* – CuisineTV embossed potholder in the other.

'Even if Jennie isn't my number one fan,' Kitty said, holding her finger up after the young woman had departed, 'she is fan number one.'

Fran giggled. 'You've got to start somewhere. Besides, don't be coy. You have plenty of fans, Kitty; Gretchen for one. That lady thinks you have star potential.' Fran spread her arms overhead.

'I wouldn't be so sure about that.'

'What do you mean?'

'I mean, I haven't even seen Gretchen since we started taping.' Kitty looked around the nearly deserted soundstage. 'I'm beginning to get the feeling that she was so disgusted with my performance that she couldn't even stomach sticking around for it to end.'

Her television career could be over before it had even begun. Maybe that was a good thing.

Fran frowned. 'No, that can't be.' The lines around her mouth deepened. 'Though, now that you mention it, I haven't seen her lately either.' The makeup artist shrugged. 'Oh, well,' Fran said, a smile returning to her face. 'Gretch will show up sooner or later. She always does. That lady never stops.'

A cute young man with wavy chestnut hair and eyes the color of pale jade-green porcelain stepped up. He was easily a foot taller than either of them. He pushed a pair of thick, black-rimmed glasses up his nose that gave him an air of boyish cuteness.

'Hi, David,' Fran said.

'David? David Biggins?' Kitty said with surprise, as old memories flooded in.

'That's right. I didn't think you'd remember.' He hugged Kitty warmly. 'It's good to see you, Kitty. You look terrific.'

'Thank you.' Kitty noticed that he was even more handsome when he smiled. Fran arched her eyebrows, batted her long lashes, and made goo-goo eyes behind David's back for only Kitty to see. Real mature.

'You two know each other, I take it?' Fran's brow arched into an exaggerated question mark.

David answered. 'We went to high school together.'

'Newport High,' added Kitty. 'It's so nice to see you again. But what are you doing here? You weren't dragged in off the street like all those other poor people who were promised

me, Kitty Karlyle. I wanted to talk to you and hear what you thought about the show.' She paused, waiting for a reply. 'Miss Corbett?'

Kitty hovered outside the door. Was Gretchen gone or was she simply so disgusted and disheartened by Kitty's performance that she didn't even want to see her face?

There was only one way to find out for sure. 'I may as well get this over with.' Kitty tried the doorknob. It wasn't locked. She slowly pushed open the door. The room was practically dark, the blinds pulled shut. 'Miss Corbett?'

Kitty stepped into the room, trying to remember if there was a light switch somewhere. Her fingers explored the nearest wall. She tripped over something at her feet and landed in a sprawl against the desk. Her hands touched something soft and clammy.

'What's going on?' a gruff voice demanded. A flashlight flicked on and flashed toward her.

That's when Kitty noticed Gretchen lying prone in front of her on the floor. The producer was sprawled on her stomach, her body spread out with her arms akimbo, and her fingers curled up as if she'd been clawing at the rug.

The producer's face, twisted in Kitty's direction, was a pale death mask pressed against the floor. Her vacant, half-open eyes seemed to stare beseechingly at Kitty. Or was it accusingly?

And was that one of Kitty's kitchen knives sticking out of Gretchen Corbett's back?

Two

'Ohmygod!' Kitty leapt to her feet and scrambled as far away from Gretchen's body as she could.

The security guard stepped into the room and flipped the light switch. He was young, with a bristly black crew-cut and a pasty white face – kind of spooky looking; almost as scary looking as the corpse on the floor.

Gretchen's last words to her came back as if to haunt her. 'Lights, camera, murder,' mumbled Kitty. She suddenly felt chilled to the bone and hugged herself for warmth.

'What'd you say?' The guard was leaning over Gretchen and now turned his attention to Kitty.

'Nothing,' Kitty answered quickly.

The guard shoved his silver flashlight back in its holster. He reached for the radio clipped to his shirt and pressed the send button. 'Manny, this is Brad. I need some backup.'

'What's the trouble?' squawked Manny. 'Vending machine on the fritz again? I've told you a hundred times, man, you gotta—'

'No. Be quiet and listen, Manny. This is serious. Get an ambulance here, pronto!'

'Did you say ambulance?' The metallic voice sounded skeptical.

'Yeah,' he shot Kitty a hard look. 'And you'd better call the police.' He looked back at the body on the floor. 'I think she's dead.'

'Dead!' Manny's shriek blasted through the receiver. 'What are you talking about? Who's dead?'

'Gretchen Corbett,' replied Brad. 'And I think I've got her killer right here.'

'Hey!' Kitty stamped her foot. 'Not so fast, buster. I'm no killer!'

Manny let out a string of invectives and promised to call the cops right away.

The security guard clipped his radio to his shirt. His eyes narrowed as he said, 'You're that dog lady, aren't you?'

'Actually, I'm a gourmet pet chef,' Kitty answered. She had backed up to the doorway and was desperate to leave.

'Yeah,' Brad said, nodding. 'I saw a couple of minutes of your show. Good stuff. I've got a dog of my own, you know.'

'Oh, thank you.' She glanced at the knife in Gretchen's back. The heart-shaped locket Gretchen had been wearing now stuck to the back of her lifeless neck. The chain must have gotten twisted around in the struggle. 'I–I didn't kill her. She was like that when I came in. You've got to believe me.'

The security guard twisted his lips and frowned. 'I guess we'll find out soon enough.'

David Biggins stuck his head in the door. 'What's going on?'

'David!' cried Kitty in surprise. 'I thought you'd gone.'

'Hi, Kitty.' He nodded to the guard. 'I forgot my jacket,' he said with a lopsided grin, dangling a tan windbreaker on his index finger. 'I came in through the side door with Brad.' The guard glanced over his shoulder and frowned.

It was then that David's eyes fell to the body on the floor behind the guard's legs. 'What the . . .' He fell back against the door. 'Is that Gretchen?'

Kitty nodded. 'Yes, I found her like that. I came looking for her. I wanted to see how she liked the show. But when I came in,' Kitty waved helplessly toward the corpse, 'there she was.'

'Wow,' was all David could say.

The sound of multiple sirens penetrated the room.

'I think we'd better all step outside. We don't want to contaminate the crime scene,' stated the guard. 'But don't wander off,' he added, directing his look toward Kitty.

It wasn't long before a posse of police officers and technicians showed up and started asking questions. 'Oh, brother,' said one middle-aged officer, peeking into the room and scratching his head, 'show business is one tough racket.'

'Tell me about it, Sarge,' clucked his partner.

Three paramedics arrived. 'Where's the victim?' asked the lead medic, his hands gripping a medical kit. The other two bore a stretcher.

One of the police officers jerked his thumb toward the open door. 'In there, but you aren't going to need that. A one-size-fits-all body bag will do the trick.'

'Yeah, and be careful what you touch,' said the one called Sarge, 'this is a crime scene.'

The paramedics wordlessly shoved past the officers. Kitty could see one checking Gretchen's pulse and, though she knew it was practically impossible, she prayed that they would find one.

One of the paramedics shook his head. 'Game over,' he said. He and his partners stepped back out into the hall and waited. A couple of plain-clothes detectives arrived next, escorting a young, harried looking man in black trousers, white shirt and a skinny black tie. He looked like he belonged in some eighties era new-wave band. Kitty overheard someone mention he was the medical examiner.

'In here?' one of the detectives asked a uniformed officer at the door.

The officer nodded and the three new arrivals swept into Gretchen's office. Kitty heard one of them let out a long, low whistle. 'Who found her?'

'I–I did,' answered Kitty. She shivered as she watched the man in the skinny black tie check the area surrounding the knife wound, a dour look on his face.

'That's right,' added the security guard. 'I was coming by on my rounds when I spotted this lady,' Brad said, with a jerk of his head, 'right there next to Miss Corbett.' His eyes narrowed in on Kitty.

'What about him?' The detective pointed in David Biggins' direction.

'I'm David Biggins,' said the young man. 'I came back for my jacket.' He held it up for proof.

'Your jacket was in Miss Corbett's office?'

'No, back behind the set. I was coming up the hall,' he said nervously, 'when I saw Kitty and Brad here.'

Brad nodded. 'That's right, Detective. It's just like he said.'

The detective straightened his knees and dusted himself off. 'I'd like a word with you, Miss—'

'Karlyle. Kitty Karlyle,' she said shakily.

'I'm Detective Leitch. Let's talk, Miss Karlyle,' the detective ordered, his voice flat and hard. He had on a brown business suit – all business by the looks of him – and sported a military-style crew cut. His face was pockmarked around the cheekbones, but pleasant, and his hazel eyes looked like they never missed a thing.

'Mind if I listen in?'

Kitty turned in surprise. 'Jack!' She ran to her fiancé and gave him a warm hug. 'I'm so glad you're here. This is a nightmare.'

'Calm down, Kitty,' Jack replied. Jack Young was in his thirties, with a well-balanced, muscular physique and boyish good looks. His eyes were light green and went from stern to mischievous depending on his mood. Right now, he was looking a bit on the stern side. He gripped Kitty's arms above the elbows for a second, and then released her. 'Everything's going to be fine.'

Jack turned to Detective Leitch and held out his hand. 'Good to see you again, Rick.'

'You, too, Jack.' The two men shook hands and Leitch glanced Kitty's way. 'So, you're acquainted with Miss Karlyle?'

A trace of a grin flashed across his face. 'You could say that.' He turned to Kitty. 'Kitty, this is Detective Richard Leitch. He's one of the best.'

Kitty nodded nervously and said hello again.

A tall blonde who looked like she might have just stepped off the cover of *Scandinavian Police Beat Magazine* burst on to the scene like a summer shower and interrupted the proceedings.

'Who's the victim?' she demanded loudly.

Kitty recognized that voice. This was the woman who had answered Jack's cell phone earlier.

'Gretchen Corbett, some high mucky-muck here at the studio,' Leitch offered.

The woman turned up her bottom lip and nodded once. Kitty took a good look at her and felt small in comparison. The blonde filled out her navy blue suit well; too well, in Kitty's opinion. She was standing very close to Jack, also wearing his navy suit. She was standing too close to Jack, in Kitty's opinion.

'Rick, this is Lieutenant Elin Nordstrom.' The lieutenant flashed her perfect white teeth and said hello. Her eyes were the color of blue topaz.

Kitty was suddenly feeling very unfeminine. And short. How tall was this woman, anyway? She was wearing low-heeled, black, closed-toe shoes, so she couldn't blame the woman's height on them. Kitty felt sweaty, and tired, and dirty. It had been a long day. And there was no end in sight.

She suddenly realized that Jack had been talking to her. And she very likely smelled of pet food and fear. 'Sorry, what?'

'Elin suggested we go someplace less hectic to talk.'

'OK,' agreed Kitty. Anything was better than

standing there watching while the police danced all around Gretchen's corpse.

'There's an empty office just up the hall,' offered David. Kitty noticed he looked awfully pale.

Jack eyed him up and down. 'And you are?'

David held out his hand. When Jack didn't reach for it, he ran it nervously through his hair. 'David Biggins.'

'What do you have to do with this?'

'Nothing,' David stammered quickly. 'I work here. I came back in to get my jacket is all.' He held up his lightweight jacket once more. 'I was walking by when I saw the light on and—'

Jack cut him off with a slash of his right hand. 'Fine. We'll get your statement, too. Show me this empty office.'

'You go ahead, Jack,' said Nordstrom. 'I'd like to get a closer look at the body.'

Kitty rolled her eyes. Did the woman have ice water running through those Scandinavian veins? Kitty never wanted to see the image of Gretchen Corbett lying dead on the floor with a knife in her back ever again.

Detective Leitch nodded. 'I'll give you the grand tour.' He and the lieutenant went in one direction and Jack, David and Kitty in the other. 'We're going to want your statement, as well,' he warned the security guard. 'Stick around.'

The guard promised he would.

The office up the hall was small, bare and windowless. 'It used to belong to Sonny, but he was fired last week,' David explained, pulling up one of the two chairs in front of the empty desk.

Jack seated himself behind the desk and leaned against the wall, nodding now and then to show he was listening, as Kitty and David told their stories. Jack carefully had them detail their movements throughout the evening.

As they were going over their stories for what Kitty felt was the hundredth time, the lovely Lieutenant Nordstrom strode in. She leaned over Jack and whispered in his ear.

Kitty squirmed in her chair. She couldn't make out what she was saying but she didn't like how close those pouty lips of hers were to Jack's ear.

Jack frowned and closed his eyes for a moment. When he opened them, he was looking straight at Kitty. He leaned forward, his fingers drumming on the bare desktop.

Kitty crossed and uncrossed her legs, wondering what secret the two of them had shared.

Jack's voice was even and emotionless. 'You want to tell me about the knife, Kitty?'

Three

Kitty looked nervously from Jack to the lieutenant. She could swear there was an ever-so-slight smile on the woman's smug face. Kitty attempted a smile herself but it crumbled almost immediately, like the beginnings of a failed sandcastle on the beach – a faulty construction that was more saltwater than sand.

Elin Nordstrom was looking at her as if she was a blonde cat about to pounce on a brown mouse. Kitty had seen that look in Barney's eyes every time a pigeon got within striking distance of her apartment windows. Barney was the frisky, tuxedoed stray cat that had followed her home one day. 'Why did you do it, Karlyle?' Her eyes flashed. 'Jealousy?'

Kitty practically jumped out of her chair, sending it skidding into the wall. 'What? No!'

'Greed?' Nordstrom's nose was in her face. 'Did she owe you money? Refuse your demands?'

Kitty's mouth hung open and she planted her hands on her hips.

'Maybe I should take over the questioning on this one,' Jack interjected.

This one, thought Kitty. Suddenly she'd gone from being his fiancée to *this one*.

The lieutenant pulled herself up to her full height and studied Kitty. 'Fine, Jack. See what you can get out of her. I'll check with the techs.'

With the Nordstrom woman gone, Kitty plunked back in her chair. She glowered at Jack who returned the look, which was only getting her dander up again. 'This one?' She folded her shaking arms across her chest. 'Suddenly, I'm *this one*?'

'What? What did I say?' complained Jack, gesturing with his hands. His eyes landed on David Biggins. 'How about waiting for me out in the hall?'

David swallowed, nodded silently and slid hastily out the door.

'Well?'

'Well, what?' Jack asked.

'Who is she?' Kitty's eyes jerked toward the doorway.

'You heard. She's Lieutenant Nordstrom.' Jack stood and paced the small room.

'Yes, and she calls you dear.'

'What are you talking about?' Jack stopped in his tracks and stared.

'Earlier today on the phone, when I called you. She,' Kitty said, with unhidden loathing, 'answered. And, she said "it's for you, Jack, dear."' Then the line had gone dead.

Jack waved Kitty's words away. 'Please, she calls everybody dear. It's her thing.'

'Not that I've heard so far,' countered Kitty.

'She's Swedish. Maybe it's a Swedish thing. She's my temporary boss for crying out loud. What do you want me to do?'

'Yeah, well, why doesn't she just go back to Sweden where she belongs?' Kitty muttered under her breath.

Jack leaned in. 'What?'

Kitty twisted her lips. 'Nothing.'

Jack came to the edge of the desk and sat against it. 'Listen, Kitty, now is not the time. There's a dead woman out there,' he said, pointing toward Gretchen's office, 'and the murder weapon's got your initials on it. I told you this TV show thing was a bad idea.'

The right side of Kitty's mouth turned down. Jack hadn't exactly discouraged her from trying out for the TV show but he hadn't exactly encouraged her either. She supposed part of her wanted to prove to him that she could do it; rise to the challenge. The fact that she had no interest in becoming a TV personality had taken a backseat.

'The knife?' Jack prodded once more.

'I don't know how it got there, Jack,' Kitty replied, her voice falling almost to a whisper. The monogrammed Wusthoff knife set had been a gift from her parents when she'd graduated culinary school. Those knives weren't cheap. She wondered if she'd be getting that kitchen knife back once the police were done with it. On second thought, she realized she didn't want the thing back, not ever.

'Well, you might want to start coming up with some sort of explanation,' grumbled Jack.

'What's that supposed to mean?' Kitty's voice rose as she rose once again from her chair.

'Now, calm down, Kitty.'

'Calm down? You calm down, Jack, *dear*,' Kitty said. 'Tell me, do you actually think that I might have killed Gretchen?' She glared at him accusingly.

'Of course not,' Jack quickly replied. He laid a light hand on her arm and she brushed it away. 'Look,' he pleaded. 'I can't help it. I've got a job to do. There's a woman lying dead in there and I've got to figure out who did it.' He let out a long slow breath. 'And I have to question everyone.'

'Oh really?' retorted Kitty, hands on hips. 'Well, you know what?' She wasn't waiting for an answer. 'I have nothing to say to you. How do you like that?'

'Now, Kitty—'

'No, not another word. Get somebody else to interview this suspect!'

'Please, Kitty. Try to understand.' He took her in his arms and she again pushed him away. 'I'm only doing my job.' He added under his breath, 'At least trying to.'

'I heard that. And I've heard enough from you.'

Jack leaned his head back and closed his eyes. 'I'm only trying to help, Kitty. The sooner we find Ms Corbett's killer, the better things will be for you. I'm trying to help you.'

'Well, I don't need your help,' quipped Kitty. 'In fact, I don't need anybody's help,' she thrust her chin out defiantly, 'because I'm going to find out who killed Gretchen Corbett myself. I'll prove that I didn't do it and I'll prove it without any assistance from you, Detective.' She turned her back on him.

'Oh, please,' snorted Jack. 'That's enough, Kitty. Look,' he laid a hand on her shoulder, 'go home. Get some rest. We'll talk about this tomorrow.'

Kitty twisted her neck and looked him straight in the eye, her tone mocking. If she was mad before, she was even madder now – fueled by his condescending tone. 'What, you don't want to lock me up? You're not afraid your number one suspect will take it on the lam?'

Jack rolled his eyes. 'This is crazy. You're tired. I'm tired. Let's call it a night.'

'Jack, come here, please. I need you.' That was Nordstrom's voice coming from outside in the hall.

'She needs you, Jack, dear.'

'Jack, you need to take a look at this.'

Jack looked from the door to Kitty and shrugged. 'Just a sec—'

'So, am I free to leave?' asked Kitty.

Jack waved toward the office door.

'Thank you.' She stepped into the crowded hall where David Biggins stood looking miserably by. 'Oh, David, you're still here. Detective Young has decided that we're free to leave.'

'Is that right, Detective?'

'Just give your contact information to the sergeant on your way out, Mr Biggins. We'll be wanting to take a full statement from you.' There was a tone of weary defeat in Jack's voice.

'There you are, Jack,' Nordstrom reached out and took the detective by the elbow. 'Come, take a look at this.' She began pulling Jack into the dead producer's office. 'We're about to take a look at the Corbett woman's computer files. The computer tech has cracked her password.'

The lieutenant glanced back at Kitty and David. 'Are you cutting those two loose?'

'For now. We don't need anything more from them tonight. I know how to reach them, if need be.'

Nordstrom shot Kitty a withering look. 'I don't know, Jack. She's our number one suspect. She owned the murder weapon. We should probably take her down to the station. We have not yet determined if Miss Karlyle's prints are on *her* knife.'

Kitty swallowed hard. Were her prints on the knife? Very possibly. She used it practically every day, so it wasn't going to surprise her if the police announced that they'd found her fingerprints all over the murder weapon.

The question was, what would they do next? Arrest her?

Jack looked helplessly from Kitty to the lieutenant. 'I'll vouch for her, Elin.'

'How nice of you, Jack.' Kitty resisted the urge to stick her tongue out at him. If she had any magical powers at all, Elin Nordstrom would be nothing more than a pile of ashy residue on the floor due to the smoldering look Kitty was giving her.

'And don't worry, I'm not leaving town.' Kitty looked at David. 'Neither of us are. Besides,' she said, teasingly, 'I intend to solve this murder myself.'

Jack groaned softly. It was the lieutenant's mocking laugh that piqued Kitty. 'This isn't a TV show,' scoffed Nordstrom, 'and you are a cook. Stay out of our way. Interfering in a police investigation is a serious crime.' Her eyes taunted Kitty. 'You don't want to end up in even more trouble, do you?' She turned on her heels. 'Come, Jack.'

Jack shrugged powerlessly.

Kitty bit her lip and looped her arm through David's. 'Does that offer of dinner still stand?'

'Uh, yeah, sure,' he muttered, looking confused.

Kitty smiled smugly. 'Great, let's go.' She took extra satisfaction in spying Jack twisting his head backwards – as Nordstrom pulled him along – so he could watch her leave with David.

On their way out of the studio, Kitty caught sight of Steve Barnhard sitting in his office. He was leaning back in a tall leather chair with his feet up on the desk displaying his hairy ankles. He appeared annoyed and Kitty saw why. Detective Leitch was sitting across from the assistant producer holding a small notepad and chewing on the end of his pen.

It looked like the police were questioning everyone. With luck, she wouldn't be strapped to the electric chair by breakfast with that tall, no doubt sadistic, Swede looming over her ready to throw the switch.

There might be some hope for her yet.

Four

'I'm so sorry you had to get dragged into that back there. Jack can be difficult at times.'

And hanging around Elin Nordstrom seemed to be bringing out the jerk in him. She wasn't about to say that to David though. That wouldn't be right. It seemed sort of unfaithful.

Though Kitty wasn't above telling Jack what she thought about his behavior in person the next time they were alone together, she felt it would be wrong to criticize him to a near stranger. In fact, she was planning on telling Jack what she thought the next time she got the chance. The man was going to get an earful and then some.

Kitty and David were sitting across from each other in a booth at Lester's Diner, a casual

24-hour restaurant on Hollywood Boulevard. The smell of spicy sausage hung in the air – it was a house specialty.

David grinned. 'Tell me about it.' He lowered his laminated menu. 'And that woman gives me chills.'

Kitty laughed. 'Me too.' She pulled off her earrings. They'd been bugging her all day. Usually she went with simple studs. She didn't know what had possessed her to wear the large hoops today. They'd been a distraction. She laid them on the yellow Formica table.

'Nice workmanship.' David prodded them with a finger.

'My folks gave them to me for my eighteenth birthday.'

'They sure didn't skimp.'

'You think?'

'Trust me. I know my silver. I've got a cousin down in Taos that's a silversmith in the jewelry business. It's been in her family for generations. She's a real artist. If you ever want anything, let me know.' He smiled. 'I get a family discount.'

A waitress in an above-the-knee gold skirt and clingy white T-shirt set their drinks on the table. Kitty had asked for iced tea and David ordered coffee. 'Ready to order?'

Kitty's teeth pulled at her lower lip as her eyes skimmed the menu. 'I think I need another minute.' The waitress shrugged, stuck her order pad under her apron and said she'd be back.

David poured some cream into his mug. He set his glasses next to the napkin holder. 'So that detective's your fiancé, huh?'

'Yes, that's him.'

'Have you known each other long?'

'Not really. Only a matter of months.'

'Wow,' replied David, between sips, 'that's not long. Tell me,' he said, 'is he always such a . . .' He hesitated.

'Cop?' finished Kitty.

David nodded his head. 'Yeah, cop.'

'Not always.'

'That's good.' His eyes locked in on Kitty's. 'You deserve someone who makes you happy.'

'Thanks, David.' She patted his hand across the table. 'I appreciate that. Jack's got a big heart.' Kitty thought she might have detected disappointment in David's eyes. 'How about you,' she asked. 'Seeing anyone?'

'No.' David set down his coffee. 'No one special.'

The waitress came back, took their orders and left again.

Kitty added a packet of raw sugar to her tea.

'I thought that Nordstrom woman was going to hang us both up by our thumbs until we confessed to killing Gretchen,' David said. 'Who is she, anyway?'

Kitty shrugged. 'I've never seen her before. Jack's never mentioned her.' One more thing she was definitely going to be bringing up with him. 'My guess is she isn't the new community relations officer. She's pretty though, don't you think?' asked Kitty, fishing for the male point of view.

'I guess,' said David. His shoulders moved up and down. 'Not really my type though.'

What Kitty really wanted to know was if she was Jack's type. 'Thank you,' she said to the waitress who'd brought her omelet.

David paused while the waitress laid his sandwich down in front of him. He thanked her, and then continued. 'And the way she looks at you, it makes you feel guilty of something whether you are or not.' He poured a pool of catsup on his plate. 'Do you think the police will really want to question us again?'

'I'm afraid so,' answered Kitty. 'Me, because of the knife and you, because of that.' She jerked her head his way.

'Huh?'

'That.' Kitty pointed with her fork. 'Your jacket.'

David looked puzzled.

'If you hadn't forgotten your jacket and come back for it, you wouldn't be here now and the police wouldn't be interested in questioning you.'

'Oh, right. My jacket, yeah.' David leaned forward and said softly, 'I'm glad I'm here now.'

Kitty felt herself blushing and stabbed at her eggs. There was a minute of awkward silence while they both attacked their food. 'Do you have any idea who might have wanted Gretchen dead?'

David leaned back and appeared to give the idea some thought. 'It could have been anybody,' he replied. 'You make a lot of enemies in this business.'

'Is it as bad as all that?'

David chuckled. 'You wouldn't believe the half of it. It's cutthroat in Hollywood, Kitty. That's why I stick to working behind the camera. Like my dad before me.'

'I'm beginning to wish I'd never said yes to doing the show.' She remembered David's father working as a cameraman at a local news station.

'Don't feel that way,' David said quickly. 'You were great. You've got a real knack for working with an audience.'

'You really think so?' Kitty wasn't convinced.

'Sure, I do,' replied David, a big grin on his face. 'I've seen them come and I've seen them go. You're a natural, Kitty.'

'Thanks,' answered Kitty. 'Of course, I guess it doesn't matter one way or the other now.'

'What do you mean?'

'What with Gretchen dead, I guess the show is dead, too.'

David took a big bite out of his roast beef sandwich, chewing slowly. As he finished, he said, 'Probably. The show was pretty much Gretchen's baby.' He straightened. From the look on his face, Kitty got the impression that a light bulb had come on inside his head.

'What? What is it, David?'

David scratched his cheek. 'I was just thinking.'

'Yes?'

'Well,' David said, with some hesitation, 'until you came along, the show was all set to go with Barbara Cartwright.'

Kitty's eyes grew wide. '*The* Barbara Cartwright? The one who hosted the *Holistic Health for Pets* program on the BBC?'

'That's the one.'

'I love that show. She was going to host *The Pampered Pet*? What happened?'

David pointed his fork at Kitty. 'You happened.'

'Me?'

'Yep. The way I hear it, the network was all set to go with Barbara Cartwright when Gretchen pulled a last minute switcheroo and hired you.'

Kitty wiped her lips with her napkin. 'You don't suppose Ms Cartwright could have murdered Gretchen, do you?' Kitty shook her head. 'No. Of course not. What am I thinking? She's in England.' She snapped her napkin. 'Rats.'

David was smirking. 'Nope. She's right here in LA.'

'She is? Are you sure?'

'Yep. Positive. She's staying at the Beverly Hills Hotel.'

So she could have murdered Gretchen Corbett. Barbara Cartwright must have been furious when she'd found out that she'd lost the show. She'd gone to the studio and confronted Gretchen. They'd fought and Barbara Cartwright had stabbed her. Now all Kitty had to do was prove it. Before Jack and Elin Nordstrom did. That would wipe that smug look off the lieutenant's face. 'I've got to find a way to talk to Ms Cartwright.'

David considered a moment. 'You could always ask Barnhard for her number.'

'The head of CuisineTV?' Kitty shook her head emphatically. 'No way.'

'Not Bill,' said David. 'Steve.'

'Steve?' Kitty replied, wrinkling her brow. 'Steve from the studio?'

'Steve is Bill's kid. One of them anyway.'

'I was wondering about that.' So Steve Barnhard was *the* Steve Barnhard, the son of the head of the network. Kitty should have seen that coming. What was he doing working at Santa Monica Film Studios instead of directly for his father at CuisineTV?

'Yeah. Steve should have Cartwright's number. He'd dealt with her plenty. Gretchen's relationship with the Cartwright woman was stormy at best. She foisted the woman off on Steve as much as possible.'

Kitty had a sudden thought. 'Do you think, now that Gretchen is gone, that Steve will want to bring back Barbara Cartwright and continue the show?'

David replied that he wasn't so sure. The waitress came and collected their tab. 'Steve wasn't so keen on doing the show in the first place. He's not really big on pets.' David shoved his wallet back in his pocket and stuck his glasses on his nose. 'Or cooking.'

Kitty nodded. 'I got that impression.' She got Steve's phone number from David, though he made her promise not to tell Steve where she'd gotten it. 'Steve can be a real load,' David had said. 'If you know what I mean.'

Kitty knew. But she had a murderer to catch and a reputation – hers – to salvage. It had been her knife jutting out of Gretchen Corbett's back, after all.

'And he's been even prissier lately. I hear it's

because his father's reining in his allowance. Spoiled brat.'

Kitty sensed maybe a little jealousy there. But then, who wouldn't be? She pushed such thoughts from her mind. She had more important things to worry about. Number one, she'd be calling Steve first chance in the morning, once she'd delivered to the clients on her breakfast route.

David pulled a tin of French violet pastilles from his jacket, pried open the lid and offered one of the small white pebbles to Kitty, before helping himself to one.

'Nice,' said Kitty. 'Not too sweet.'

Standing between Kitty's forest green Volvo wagon and his own silvery gray SUV in the parking lot before parting, David said, 'For what it's worth, when I saw Gretchen lying there with your knife in her back, I didn't believe for a minute that you killed her.'

'Thanks,' replied Kitty. 'I'm glad somebody thinks I'm innocent.' Now, if she could just prove it. She rummaged through her purse for her car key. 'I know you didn't kill her, too.' She stuck the key in the stubborn lock of the broken handle.

'What happened there?' David jiggled the busted door handle.

Kitty smiled. 'One of my clients doesn't know his own strength.' One of her customers, Chevy Czinski, had practically ripped the handle off earlier when she'd told him how she'd be taping a show at Santa Monica Film Studios today with Gretchen Corbett.

She hadn't thought much of it then, but now . . .

‘So, what will you do now?’ David asked, his hands thrust into his jeans.

‘I’m a pet chef. The past couple of days have been like a dream.’ A dream gone terribly wrong. ‘I’m sort of relieved it’s over.’ Well, maybe not over, with Gretchen’s corpse still fresh and the investigation only begun, but the show was over for sure. ‘My short career in showbiz has come to an end,’ Kitty said philosophically, pulling on the Volvo door, which relented but not without a goose pimple-producing squeal.

‘Hey, you never know,’ replied David, then went silent for a moment. ‘Then again, I might be out of a job myself.’

‘How do you mean?’

‘I mean Steve Barnhard is very likely to be calling the shots at the studio now.’ David grinned. ‘That man is not my friend.’

‘I hate to say it, but I’m beginning to wonder if he’s anybody’s friend.’

‘Sure you don’t want to get a nightcap?’ David’s eyes seemed to drink her in, but Kitty knew better than to succumb. ‘I know a great little bar. It’s not far from here.’

‘Sorry,’ Kitty shook her head. ‘I have to get up early.’

‘Pets to feed?’

Kitty nodded and slid behind the wheel. ‘Pets to feed.’ She demurely turned her cheek as David leaned in and gave her a peck.

Five

If the pounding on the door hadn't set Fred to barking, Kitty would have ignored it. It was simply too early in the morning to be good news or good friends. But if she allowed Fred to continue yapping, it would only set off a chain reaction of unwelcome actions.

Without a doubt, her neighbor, Mirabelle Stein, would telephone the apartment manager and lodge yet another complaint. And at the rate Mirabelle Stein seemed to be lodging them, Kitty expected the manager – who himself was always bellyaching about how overworked he was – had enough complaints about her by now to stuff a thirty-pound Thanksgiving bird.

Mirabelle Stein was the elderly widow of French-Jewish descent who lived directly upstairs from Kitty. In the beginning, Kitty had thought Mrs Stein was going to be one of those sweet little old ladies who offered you sugar cookies the day you moved in, along with a nice cup of weak hot tea served in delicate chipped white china nestled on real linen napkins.

At least, that's what Kitty had expected in the first moments of meeting Mirabelle Stein and sizing her up, when the old woman had suddenly appeared in her open door the day she was moving her boxes in.

But the tiny widow in the black frock with the white piping who smelled of rose water had instead turned out to be the Tasmanian devil of neighbors. The first words out of her denture-filled mouth that day had been something to the effect that Kitty had better not 'raise the roof' and that 'those horrible beasts of yours better behave themselves!' – all said with the wave of an arthritic finger within millimeters of Kitty's nose. She further threatened to personally see that Kitty's dog and cat were both shipped off to the glue factory should there be any slip-ups whatsoever.

Kitty had been dumbfounded. She hadn't known what to say. She also had no idea if there were any glue factories in the LA area and, if so, whether they would even want to make glue out of dogs and cats. However, wicked little old ladies – well, that was another possibility . . .

Kitty had further compounded her troubled relationship by expressing those thoughts to Mirabelle Stein. In retrospect, she supposed she should have nodded politely and kept her opinion to herself because things had gone downhill quickly from there.

If only she'd kept her mouth shut and humored the woman . . . but that window of opportunity had closed long ago.

So, now Mirabelle Stein was forever lodging complaints against Kitty. Though it wasn't just Kitty, it was all of her apartment house neighbors. Despite Kitty's best efforts to be a good neighbor, it seemed that the vast majority of those complaints had been aimed at her. She walked too loud. Her pets, Fred and Barney, were too noisy. The odors wafting from Kitty's kitchen were making Mrs Stein queasy.

Every time Kitty ran the garbage disposal, Mirabelle Stein banged on the floor in retaliation. It wasn't Kitty's fault that the garbage disposal motor sounded like a motorcycle revving up on her kitchen counter. She had asked the apartment manager, Mr Frizzell, to take a look at the appliance on multiple occasions but with no success.

Kitty had heard from one of her neighbors that Mirabelle had once been married. Everyone around the complex did call her the Widow Stein, or Frankenstein if they were feeling less kindly. There had certainly been no sign of a Mr Stein in the time that Kitty had lived in her apartment.

Kitty sometimes wondered if Mirabelle's other half might not have ended up in a glue factory himself. Kitty wasn't ruling anything out when it came to what the woman might do now or might have done in her unclear past.

Then again, having been married to Mrs Stein, poor Mr Stein might have jumped into the glue vat willingly.

So, before the banging at the door was returned by an equal banging from above, Kitty turned down the burners on the stove and wiped her hands on her apron. She went to the door and pulled it open as far as the chain allowed.

'Kitty? Is that you, girl?'

Kitty's head bounced as she tried to figure out who the stranger at the door was and how she knew her name.

'Well, you gonna let me in? I didn't catch you sleeping, did I? From the way you talked, I thought you got up with the chickens.'

The clouds in Kitty's brain suddenly cleared. 'Fran?'

'Yeah, of course it's Fran.' She pulled a pair of dark brown sunglasses from her face. Her green eyes were glossy and bloodshot. 'Gretchen's dead,' she blurted out.

'Yes, I know,' Kitty answered hesitantly.

'Well?'

'Well, what?'

'Are you going to open the door or what?'

Kitty jumped. 'Oh.' Her hands fumbled with the chain. 'I'm sorry. Come in.'

Fran strode in past Kitty and inhaled deeply. 'Umm, something smells good,' she said, one hand patting Fred on the head, the other clutching a rolled-up newspaper. Fred was a sleek black Labrador retriever. She had brought him home from an animal rescue shelter.

Fran wore tight-fitting denim jeans that ended at the ankles and a pea green turtleneck sweater. Her hair was bunched up underneath a blue-green scarf that twisted around her head. She tugged on the scarf and her long black hair billowed free.

'I'm preparing quiches.' Kitty stood at the door looking nonplussed. What on earth was the Santa Monica Film Studios' makeup artist doing at her apartment?

Fran unfurled her scarf and wiped her eyes. 'Which way is the kitchen? Though I don't think I could eat a thing. This whole murder thing's got me feeling sick, you know?'

Kitty pointed. 'Through there.'

As if understanding the conversation, Fred trotted off, leading the way, with Fran close behind. Kitty shut the front door and followed. By the time she got to the kitchen, Fran was eyeing the stovetop where different dishes were in varying stages of production.

'You always eat this good for breakfast?' Her dark eyes danced. 'Me, I pretty much stick with a piece of toast and coffee with a couple spoons of sugar.'

'Actually, no.' Kitty bent over and peered in the oven window. 'These quiches are for the Bichons.' They looked like they could keep a while longer.

'You expecting company?'

Kitty wanted to say that she hadn't been expecting anyone at all, least of all Fran Earhart. Well, if Gretchen Corbett had shown up at the door this morning, that might have been a hair more unlikely, if infinitely more Twilight Zone. Instead, Kitty replied, 'The Bichons are two dogs that I cook for. All these other dishes are for other clients' pets.'

'Ohhh,' said Fran, 'those kinds of Bichons. I thought you meant the Bichons of Beverly Hills or something.' She suddenly looked at her hands as if she'd only discovered they existed. One of them held her scarf, the other a crumpled newspaper.

She thrust the newspaper in Kitty's face. 'Have you seen this? Front page of the *LA Times*.' She rattled the paper in front of Kitty's nose, as if demanding that she take a whiff.

Fred went into game-of-fetch mode, his legs twitching, ready for action. Barney had already gone into hiding under the bed. He wasn't big on company, especially when it was loud.

'I mean, I couldn't believe it when I read about it.' Fran looked around and pulled out a chair at the breakfast table. She sat with an audible thump, the paper on her knees. Fred looked puzzled. And disappointed.

'It still doesn't seem possible. Gretchen Corbett,' Fran said, shaking her head, 'dead.' Her lips turned down. 'I hate to say it – no disrespect for the dead or anything. I mean, I liked Gretchen.' Her eyes stopped on Kitty. 'But I guess this means I'm out of a job.'

Kitty's troubled eyes stared at the upside-down paper in Fran's lap. All she could make out was a publicity shot of Gretchen. 'Could I see that?'

Fran followed Kitty's finger. 'Oh, sure.' She handed Kitty the paper.

Kitty quickly scanned the couple of paragraphs of accompanying text. She breathed a sigh of relief. It hadn't mentioned her by name at all. Only stated that the producer had been found stabbed to death in her office.

'I found the body,' Kitty confessed, her voice soft as a penitent in the confessional.

Fran lurched forward. 'You?' She snatched the paper back from Kitty. Her eyes rolled up and down the page. 'It doesn't say that here.'

Kitty shook her head. Fortunately, the reporter had only mentioned that Gretchen's body had been discovered by an employee that evening. And that the police were following up several strong leads. Maybe Jack had been able to keep her out of it – so far. Suddenly, she felt guilty that she'd been so angry with him.

'No.' Kitty checked the quiches in the oven and turned off the heat to the burners. It looked like she might be a few minutes late with her deliveries this morning. She sank into the chair opposite Fran. 'It was one of my knives that killed her.' She avoided making eye contact.

She was also preparing a special meal for Mr Cookie. Mr Cookie was an adorable cat that belonged to kindly Mr Randall, of the Randall's Department Store chain. Mr Randall's wife had met an untimely end and Mr Cookie had been poisoned as well, though he had been lucky to survive the ordeal.

Still, he'd had a sensitive tummy ever since and Kitty tried to keep his meals on the bland side. That meant he wasn't allowed any of his favorites, like Kitty's popular breakfast steak and egg burrito. She'd been experimenting with an oatmeal-based kibble and cream sauce that she hoped Mr Cookie would enjoy.

'Girl!' exclaimed Fran. There was an almost instantaneous banging from overhead that made both girls jump from their seats and look up together at the ceiling. Fran lowered her voice. 'Sorry.'

Kitty waved her off. 'That's Mrs Stein. Ignore her.' Kitty wished it was that easy. She filled Fran in on the night's events, explaining how, after the show, she had gone looking for Gretchen, only to discover her lying on her office floor dead. With one of Kitty's knives in her back.

Kitty told Fran how the security guard had discovered her there, leaning over the body and how she and David had been grilled by the police. 'I didn't kill Gretchen.'

Fran laid her hand atop Kitty's. 'Of course not,' she replied, with a comfort-implying pat.

'Thanks,' Kitty said.

'I mean, why would you murder Gretchen?' Fran snorted. 'She'd just hired you for a job that was going to make you a celebrity – make you rich, girl!'

Kitty sighed. All that money. Gretchen had offered her twenty-five hundred dollars for the pilot, then another twenty-five hundred per show. She'd also said that, if the show got picked up for a full series of twenty episodes, they would double her salary. Kitty had scrambled to do the math in her head. She was terrible at doing math in her head. Gretchen had helped her out. 'Four shows a week for five weeks, that's one hundred thousand dollars,' she'd explained.

Kitty had about fainted. In fact, she still wasn't sure why she hadn't. One hundred thousand dollars? That was worth fainting over.

She popped out of her reverie to see Fran shaking her head. 'Heck, I can think of all kinds of people that would like to see Gretchen dead. But not you.' Fran began rattling names off using her fingers. 'There's Steve. That's Steve Barnhard, of course. There's some whack-job ex she had to get a restraining order from. And she's always fighting with her daughter, Cinderella.'

'Cinderella?' interrupted Kitty.

'Her name is Cindy. I call her Cinderella because you'd think she was a princess what with the way she acts.' Fran made a disapproving face. 'Of course, that was partially Gretchen's fault. She treated that girl like she really was a princess and still the girl was always taking advantage of her, you know?'

Kitty nodded as Fran went on. 'There's poor Sonny,' said Fran, tsk-tsking. 'Gretchen let him go about a week ago.'

'Who?'

'Sonny Sarkisian. He was the studio's promo and marketing guy. At least, he was until Gretchen canned him.'

'Why did she fire him?'

Fran scratched her head. 'You know, I'm not sure. I asked her, but Gretchen wouldn't tell. It must've been something nasty otherwise she never would have cut him loose. He made the studio plenty of money from what I could tell.'

Fran eyed the coffee pot on the counter. 'Anything left in the pot?'

'What?' Kitty followed Fran's finger. 'Sure. I'm sorry. Let me get you a cup.'

'Don't bother,' replied Fran, rising and heading for the counter. She began opening and closing cabinets, found a mug and poured herself a full cup. She held out the carafe. 'Want some?'

Kitty said she was good.

Fran leaned against the counter, took a sip and appeared to be deep in thought. 'Of course, there's always Barbara Cartwright.'

'The TV host?'

Fran nodded. 'You know about her?'

'David told me. He said the same thing.' Kitty explained how she and David had gone out to get a bite to eat last night.

'Oh, you naughty girl,' Fran said, grinning. 'Didn't you say you had a boyfriend?'

'Yes, fiancé actually. Jack.'

'Well, if you ever want to switch horses, David's not only easy on the eyes, he's a good guy. Not good with money, but good with his hands, if you know what I mean.' She wriggled her brow. 'And he's really cleaned up his act from what I hear. If I didn't have a boyfriend myself . . .'

'We only went as friends.' Kitty didn't want Fran to get the wrong idea about her and David, no matter how easy on the eyes he was. And he was. 'And because I was mad at Jack and the way he was carrying on last night with that stupid lieutenant of his.'

Fran looked flummoxed.

Kitty explained how Jack had shown up at the studio with a hot, young lieutenant at his side who had all but tossed Kitty in the lockup for Gretchen's murder.

'Men,' commiserated Fran.

One word. But said with the right inflection and it just about sums it up, thought Kitty. She rose and checked her meals. She checked the stovetop clock. She'd need to get going soon.

'If you ask me, Barbara Cartwright would be at the top of my list of people who wanted Gretchen dead. She and Gretchen hated each other's guts,' Fran said, slowly refilling her mug.

'Then Barbara flies out here from London to do the new show and at the last minute Gretchen pulls the rug out from under her and replaces her with you.'

She thrust her mug in Kitty's direction. Coffee sloshed over the sides and on to the floor, though not before first splashing down on poor Fred. 'Oops, sorry about that.' Fred licked his haunches.

Kitty told her it was nothing and wiped the floor and Fred with a couple of paper towels. 'David said practically the same thing. He seems to think Barbara could be the killer, too.' She added how David had suggested getting the woman's telephone number from Steve Barnhard, who had apparently been in contact with her. 'Why did Gretchen Corbett and Barbara Cartwright hate each other so much?'

Fran grabbed a box of wheat crackers from the counter and said between crunches, 'The bad blood between them goes way back, the way I heard it. I guess they used to work together at one time and things went sour.'

Kitty nodded thoughtfully. It sounded like Gretchen had left a fair number of enemies along her trail, any one of whom might have liked to see her dead. The chiming of the doorbell stopped her thoughts.

'Oh-oh,' said Fran. 'Are we in more trouble with your upstairs neighbor?'

'No, Mrs Stein wouldn't ring the bell.' Kitty wiped her hands on her apron and headed for the door. It was sure getting trafficky for a Saturday morning. 'Banging is more her style.'

Kitty pulled open the door only to be grabbed quickly by the arm and yanked outside.

Six

'Jack!' Kitty exclaimed, breathlessly, after he'd finished kissing her. 'I wasn't expecting you.' His arms held her tightly.

He smiled. 'I thought I'd surprise you. I've missed you, Kitty.'

'I've missed you, too,' answered Kitty, enjoying the touch of his fingers through her hair, momentarily forgetting their differences of the night before. 'Are you coming in?'

'Sure.' He scratched Fred behind the ear and dropped into the blue sofa in the living room. 'So, how did it go last night?' he asked, very obviously trying to sound nonchalant.

Kitty wasn't buying the act. She hadn't known Jack Allen Young forever, but she'd certainly known him long enough. Kitty glanced at the kitchen. Fran hadn't appeared. 'Oh,' she said, playing along, 'OK. Considering the badgering I got from your Lieutenant Nordstrom.'

Jack chuckled. 'Come on, Kitty, the lieutenant was only doing her job. She's really very nice.'

'I'm sure.' Kitty grabbed her elbows. She didn't know if she was madder at Jack for his behavior or herself for acting so jealous.

'Besides, this really should be Detective Leitch's case. It was his to start with. We were only there trying to help you out because I asked the lieutenant after explaining that we were friends. And—'

'Friends?' gaped Kitty.

Jack blushed and muttered a hasty apology. 'I didn't mean that the way it sounded.' He took a breath. 'I'm here because I love you and I want to help.'

Kitty settled into the leather chair on the opposite side of the coffee table and crossed her legs. 'Thanks,' she replied curtly, her right foot bouncing. She was hardly mollified. And she really didn't think she needed any help, not from Jack or anybody else for that matter. As for Nordstrom, Kitty wished she'd never mentioned the woman. But now that she had, she couldn't help asking, 'So how long have you been working with her? I mean, you've never even mentioned her once, Jack.' Barney had come out from hiding and swatted playfully at her bobbing foot.

'Oh? Haven't I?'

As if he didn't know full well, thought Kitty. 'No,' she said, sweetly. 'You haven't.'

Jack combed a hand through his hair and shrugged. 'She's just transferred to the department. My luck, I got stuck showing her around.'

'Poor you,' replied Kitty, with very little sympathy.

'Yeah, and now Elin's been put in charge of the Corbett case.'

Elin. They were on a first name basis. It was time to change the subject. 'Speaking of which, has there been any news?'

'You mean have we caught Corbett's killer?' Jack shook his head, without waiting for an answer. 'Nope. But I do have some good news.'

'What's that?'

'I've been trying to tell you. The knife came back clean.'

'Clean as in my fingerprints are not on it?'

Jack nodded. 'There are no fingerprints at all. Whoever stabbed Miss Corbett in the back was wearing gloves, or wrapped the handle in something, or wiped the handle clean afterward.'

Kitty breathed a sigh of relief. That was good news. Maybe she wasn't going to get hauled off to jail quite yet.

'Do you think a woman could have done it?' Fran bounded into the room, mug in hand.

Jack nearly hit the ceiling. 'Who are you?' He looked quickly from Fran to Kitty.

'This is Fran,' answered Kitty. 'She stopped by.'

'Oh?'

Fran offered her hand and Jack shook it with obvious hesitation.

'Fran works at the studio.'

Jack straightened. 'Do you now?' He looked at her with interest. 'I didn't see you there yesterday evening.'

'That's because I wasn't there. I was out on a date. Like Kitty and David.' Fran grinned and shot Kitty a mischievous look.

'David and I only had a bite to eat, Fran.' Kitty turned to Jack, her cheeks pink. Was Fran trying to cause trouble? 'It was *not* a date.' She made a face at Fran who only shrugged, then sat down cross-legged on the floor, inducing Fred to lick her neck.

Jack cleared his throat rather severely as he spoke in Fran's direction. 'To answer your question, yes, it could very easily have been a woman. It would not take a man's strength to drive that knife through the Corbett woman's back. You could very easily have done it, I imagine.' He gave Fran an icy glare.

Fran made a face. 'Very funny. I don't mean me. I'm thinking more like Barbara Cartwright.' She set down her mug and wrestled with Fred. 'My money's on her.'

'The TV host?'

Kitty explained how Ms Cartwright had originally been hired to do the show that had ended up being Kitty's – at least for a day.

'We'll look into it.' Jack didn't sound like he was in too much of a hurry to do so. 'Anybody else I should know about?'

Kitty and Fran looked at one another. Kitty's eyes willed Fran to keep her mouth shut – she didn't want to give away all their secrets – and, for what Kitty figured was probably the very first time, Fran did.

Jack left shortly after and said he'd call Kitty later that day. They made plans to meet up at his place for dinner at seven. After he was gone, Kitty said, 'Thanks for not revealing any more to Jack.' She was more determined than ever to find Gretchen's killer before Jack and the lieutenant did.

'No problem. I mean, no offense – he is your

boyfriend and all, and he is cute – but I didn't like the way he was looking at me like I was guilty of something.'

Kitty laughed. 'He can't help it. It's part of his makeup.'

'If you say so.' Fran rose and dusted herself off. 'So,' she said, hands on hips, 'now what do we do?'

'I don't know about you, but I've got mouths to feed.'

Fran grimaced. 'You mean pets?' She bent at the knees and held her palm about two feet off the floor. 'Furry little critters?'

'That's right. My time in show biz might have come to a quick,' and violent, she thought, 'end, but I've still got the gourmet pet chef business. Thank goodness.'

'But what about Gretchen's murder? What about talking to Barbara Cartwright?'

Kitty sighed. 'I'm afraid reality has reared its ugly and money-hungry head. I can't afford to ignore paying customers just to go play detective.'

'Speaking of which,' goaded Fran, 'don't you want to stick it to a certain detective and his Scandinavian lieutenant?'

Kitty bristled as she grabbed the tongs and began plating up the morning's dishes. 'Fine, but first I've got to make these deliveries.'

'Great,' replied Fran, flashing a grin. 'Let's go.'

'You're coming, too?' Kitty asked, rather uneasily.

'Sure, I've got nothing else to do. Besides, with two of us, we can get the job done even quicker.'

Kitty was skeptical but agreed to let Fran tag along.

They concocted a plan as they drove out to the Fairfax District, sometimes referred to by locals as Kosher Canyon because of its historically Jewish community. Some of Kitty's favorite bakeries and fish markets were located here, so she was a frequent shopper in the area, often picking up tasty selections for her clients' pets.

First, they planned to drop off meals to a couple of Kitty's regulars near CBS Television City, one to an investment banker and his feline flock – as the client referred to his seven cats – and the other to a network executive and his pet pug. The seven cats weren't as tough as one might imagine because Kitty made it a point to serve them family style in a pair of fancy English Delftware tureens.

Mr Cookie would come next, so that meant a trip to Mr Randall's elegant old mansion in Beverly Hills. Then they would shoot out to Brentwood to serve the Fandolfis' dogs and cat, and finally Mr Czinski and his German shepherd, Buster. Chevy Czinski was a paunch-bellied, one-time star of over a dozen *Tarzan* copycat movies that had been big in Eastern Europe.

He was also something of an eccentric. He kept a Bengal tiger, a couple of lions, an elephant, an aging, poop-slinging ape and a wobbly-legged giraffe that walked around staring at the ground as if too world-weary to hold his neck up.

He was a recent client. Mr Fandolfi had referred Mr Czinski to her and the former actor had agreed to take her on. In fact, he had seemed grateful to have someone cooking up special meals for his dog.

'Let's stop at the studio first and get Barbara Cartwright's number from Steve.'

'You think he'll be there?' Kitty asked, turning the wheel.

'He's always there.'

Fran was right. Steve was there. 'That's his car – or at least one of them.' Fran pointed to a late model, black Mercedes E350 with dark windows.

Kitty couldn't help but notice there were a couple of police cruisers in the lot as well. They were a sad reminder of what had happened only last night. She was relieved not to see Jack's own unmarked sedan.

The women headed straight to Steve's office, passing Gretchen Corbett's office on the way. The door to Gretchen's office was ajar, with one lonely looking strip of sagging yellow plastic police tape blocking the way in. Kitty paused. There was no stereotypical chalk outline on the floor. Nothing really to suggest that anything unfortunate and deadly had occurred there at all.

The blinds were open and light spilled in.

'Depressing, huh?' Fran said. 'Come on.' She pulled Kitty along. Steve's door was open as well.

He was nowhere in sight. But his cellphone was. Kitty nudged Fran. 'There's Steve's phone. On his desk.'

Fran wasted no time going in and grabbing it.

'What are you doing?' said Kitty. 'What if Steve finds us here and you with his phone?'

Fran shrugged. 'He already hates me. How much worse could it get?' She began tapping on the phone. 'Here's Cartwright's contact info. Quick, jot this down.' She recited the number while Kitty wrote on a slip of paper she'd found on Steve's cluttered desk.

'I hear someone,' whispered Kitty, frantically.

'Hmm,' said Fran. 'Steve and Barbara Cartwright have been texting each other all morning.'

'Come on.' Kitty pulled at Fran's sleeve. 'I think someone's coming.'

Fran looked up from the phone's display, nodded, and dropped the phone back on the desk. Kitty stuck her head slowly out the doorway. David Biggins was standing outside Gretchen's office, hands resting lightly on the police tape.

Kitty and Fran stepped out into the hallway. 'David,' said Kitty. 'What are you doing here?'

'Huh? Oh, Steve called a meeting. Or rather, Bill Barnhard did. Isn't that why you two are here?'

Kitty couldn't help frowning. 'No, we—'

'Yeah, of course,' cut in Fran. 'No way were we going to miss it.'

David turned his eyes back to Gretchen's office. 'I still can't get over it. I mean, only yesterday Gretchen was alive and everything was different.' He turned to Kitty. 'I'm going to miss her.' He wiped an incipient tear from the corner of his eye.

'We all are,' replied Fran, laying a hand on his shoulder.

'Who would want to do such a thing?'

'You said at dinner last night that you thought

it might have been Barbara Cartwright.' Kitty rummaged through her purse for a tissue and came up empty-handed.

'Yeah,' he said, wiping his eye with his pinkie. 'It could've been.' He glanced at his watch. 'The meeting has probably started. Steve is going to have a fit if we're late. Come on.'

They walked together to the soundstage that only the day before had hosted Kitty's television debut. 'I need some coffee,' announced Fran, stopping to grab a cup at the pot set up along the wall nearest the door.

'Haven't you had enough?' chided Kitty.

Fran took a careful sip. 'Hey, I can't help myself.' She hoisted the paper cup. 'Coffee is the new water, you know.'

Kitty giggled then, realizing the solemnity of the situation, blushed and lowered her chin.

Everyone from the studio seemed to be in attendance. There had to be thirty people milling about. Bill Barnhard, dressed in a sharply creased black wool suit, was pontificating while those around him nodded like obedient sheep.

Under his breath, David said, 'He could have killed Gretchen, too.'

Kitty was shocked. 'Mr Barnhard?'

'No,' he said, with a brief toss of his head. 'Him. Steve Barnhard.'

'What possible motive could he have?'

'Don't you see?' asked David. 'His father has just anointed him the new boss around here.' He looked at Kitty.

'How is that possible?'

'Didn't you know?' answered David.

'CuisineTV owns Santa Monica Film Studios.'

Kitty hadn't known. 'So what Mr Barnhard wants—'

'Mr Barnhard gets,' finished David. 'Pretty convenient, if you ask me.'

Kitty nodded. Convenient indeed.

Fran grabbed David's arm. 'Isn't that Sonny standing beside Greg?'

She had spoken too loudly. A sudden and commanding clearing of throat brought Fran and David to a stop and a flush to Kitty's face. Bill Barnhard was glaring at the three of them.

'Is there something you would like to add to this conversation?' He was looking right at Kitty.

She shifted her weight from foot to foot and gulped. 'I–I wanted to say how very sorry I am for everyone's loss,' Kitty began uneasily. 'And–and what a pleasure it has been to work with you all – if only for one day.'

Kitty was trembling. Show business was for the birds. And like a bird, she couldn't wait to fly this coop. She couldn't wait to be out of what was a demonstrably deadly business and back to the much more pleasant, infinitely less stressful, and certainly less dangerous gourmet pet chef gig.

'Ah, Miss Karlyle, it's you.' Bill Barnhard waved her forward.

She hesitated.

'Please, come here a moment.' She did as told and he embraced her warmly. 'It's been a real tragedy.' He held her at arms' length. She fell away smelling of Clive Christian for men. 'I hadn't been expecting you this morning.'

'Well,' began Kitty, 'I hadn't been expecting me either.'

Bill Barnhard's grin held a touch of sadness. 'When I called this meeting, I told my people not to bother you.' He bobbed his head. 'I know how upsetting this whole situation must be for you. Especially seeing as how you were the one to discover Gretchen's body and all. I thought you might prefer not to be disturbed this morning.'

Kitty swallowed hard and nodded once. Where was this leading? 'Yes,' she said softly.

The CEO patted her hand. 'Believe me, I understand completely.' He looked around the soundstage. 'We all do. Don't we?' Murmurs of assent spread around the room. 'That's why I want you to take the next couple of days off before continuing our work – out of respect for the memory of dear Gretchen.'

'You mean you want to continue *The Pampered Pet* TV show?' Kitty looked confused. And she wasn't sure if she was elated or deflated. He nodded solemnly. 'With me?'

She looked around the big room. Not all of the faces looked as friendly today as they had the day before. Was it her imagination or did they suspect her of murdering their boss?

'Of course,' replied Mr Barnhard, with what Kitty expected was a well-practiced, warm smile of assurance. 'It's what Gretchen would want, don't you agree? After all, this show was her pet project,' he said. 'Pun intended.'

'But, Dad—' Steve blurted.

Bill Barnhard held up a hand. 'Uh-uh. The

show must go on, Steve. You of all people here should know that.'

'But, Dad,' Steve tried again. 'We agreed that Miss Cartwright would be best to take over hosting and—'

Bill Barnhard stopped his son before he could go any further. 'Nonsense. Kitty is our host, Steve.' He squeezed her hand. 'She's perfect.'

Kitty blushed.

Steve, on the other hand, looked apoplectic. 'Yes, sir,' he managed to spit out from between his steely jaws.

Bill clapped his hands. 'Well, it is Saturday, so I won't keep you all any longer. Thank you for coming. Enjoy the rest of your weekend, everybody.'

The CEO began to turn away, then paused. 'I'll expect to see you all at the memorial service on Monday. And I expect you all back here and raring to go on Tuesday morning.'

With that, Bill and his officious looking secretary departed, but not before Kitty noticed him exchanging heated words with Steve in the corner.

'Wow, Steve looks positively murderous,' Fran said, with unmasked pleasure.

Kitty agreed. If Steve Barnhard was capable of murder and had stabbed Gretchen in the back, then Bill Barnhard just might be next. The soundstage was emptying. Sonny Sarkisian, recently ex-Santa Monica Film Studios employee, was milling about, talking to one of the stage-hands. 'Come on,' said Kitty. 'Introduce me to Sonny.'

'Sonny?' Fran made a face. 'What on earth for?'

'Because he's here and Gretchen isn't,' Kitty answered. 'And because, a week ago, Gretchen fired him. That gives him a motive in my book.'

Fran shrugged. 'If you say so. But trust me, Sonny Sarkisian is as harmless as a slug.'

Sonny must have read the ladies' minds because he rushed to meet them when he saw the two coming in his direction. 'Fran!' he cried, squeezing her as if he expected something to pop out. 'How've you been?'

He didn't wait for an answer. 'Have you heard?' He was grinning ear to shiny ear. He had a Charlie Brown face, a cleft chin, and a nose that looked like it had stepped into a left hook. He was short, turning to fat and had almost as much hair above his eyes as he did around the ears. Above the eyebrows was another story. A dark ring of hair circled his otherwise bald head, reminding Kitty of an atoll. Albeit a shiny flesh-colored one. He was wearing loose fitting gray chinos and a pale pink dress shirt. All that was missing was the thick gold chain.

However, he had an infectiously pleasant smile. 'I got my old job back.' He turned to Kitty and grabbed her arm. 'So, you're new here.' Sonny rubbed his hands together. 'Fresh blood. That's what this place needs.' He turned to Fran. 'Aren't you going to introduce us?'

'Sonny Sarkisian meet Kitty Karlyle,' Fran replied. She was looking at Kitty when she said 'And don't say I didn't warn you.'

Sonny squeezed her hand. 'Kitty Karlyle. Nice stage name.'

'Actually,' answered Kitty, rubbing her sore fingers, 'Kitty is my real name. Well, Katherine, but everybody calls me Kitty.'

'Well, meow-meow. Good to have you aboard, kid. I mean, Kitty.' Sonny latched on to her elbow. 'Looks like you and me are going to be working together.'

'I suppose,' Kitty said with hesitation. Sonny's facial expression was suggestive of a cheap leer outside a peepshow. His large brown eyes were decidedly lupine. Either he was hitting on her or Sonny had some other sort of mental or physical issues that Fran had failed to mention. His fingers pressing against her skin felt like he'd been presoaking them in ooze.

'So, you got your old job back?' Fran said. She sounded rather dubious.

Sonny nodded. 'Yeah, Steve called me up at home and told me to get back to work right away.'

Fran glanced at Kitty. 'Well, that's good news . . .'

Kitty wrestled herself free from Sonny's grip once more. 'So sad about Gretchen, isn't it?'

Sonny pursed his lips. 'Sure, I suppose.' He didn't sound too certain. 'I mean, she was OK. Don't speak ill of the dead and all that.'

'Of course,' said Kitty, trying to slip the verbal knife in gently, 'she did recently fire you, I hear.'

Sonny chuckled nervously and shrugged. 'Yep. But all's well that ends well, right?'

'For some of us,' Fran muttered under her

breath. Kitty shot her a look and Fran took a loud sip of coffee.

'Why did Miss Corbett fire you, Sonny?'

'Oh, you know how it is. This is show business, after all.'

'What do you mean?'

'I'm good at what I do. But Gretchen didn't always like the way I did what I do.' Sonny winked. '*Capisce?*'

Kitty didn't and said so.

Sonny sighed deeply. 'Let's just say that Gretchen had some ethical issues with some of my,' he cleared his throat, 'business practices.'

'And Steve doesn't?'

Sonny smiled. 'I got my job back, didn't I?'

Kitty smiled back. 'Some people might think that's quite convenient.'

Sonny's face darkened. 'Hey,' he said, 'if you're trying to imply that I killed Gretchen just to get my job back, you're out of your mind!' His raised voice drew curious stares from the crew.

'Where were you when Gretchen was killed?' Kitty had heard that line so many times in the movies and on TV, but it sounded odd coming from her lips.

'I have an alibi,' Sonny replied. 'But I don't have to tell you. Besides,' he looked accusingly at Kitty, 'it was your knife the police found lodged in Gretchen's back, now, wasn't it?'

Kitty said yes. 'But my fingerprints weren't on it,' she explained, wondering how many more people she was going to have to explain this fact to in the days ahead. 'The knife was in my bag. Anyone could have taken it.'

Sonny looked decidedly unimpressed.

'Come on, Sonny,' cajoled Fran. 'Kitty's only trying to help find Gretchen's murderer.'

'Gretchen and I may have had our differences,' said Sonny, looking at Fran. 'But,' he said, turning to Kitty, 'that doesn't mean I killed her. And I resent the implication.'

'I didn't mean to imply that I thought you killed her. Please, Sonny, accept my apology.' Kitty gave him her best forgive-me eyes.

Sonny deflated and the smile returned to his face. 'Yeah, yeah. Sure.' Once again, he wrapped his arms around her. Kitty gritted her teeth. 'We're a team, you and me, Kitty. *The Pampered Pet* is going to be huge. Everybody is going to want a piece of this. You wouldn't believe the marketing ideas I've got. And with your piece of the deal, you'll be rich.'

Kitty worked herself free and adjusted her slacks, feeling like she'd just been manhandled. She told him what an honor it was going to be to work with him and the entire Santa Monica Film Studios staff. 'I'm sorry Miss Corbett won't be around to enjoy the show's success. It was her idea, after all.'

'That's show biz,' replied Sonny, apparently none too broken up about it. He leaned in conspiratorially. 'And, listen, if you really want to know who killed Gretchen . . .' He jerked his head to the left.

Kitty followed his move. And found herself looking at Steve Barnhard, who was locked in conversation with the show's director, Greg. 'Steve? You think Steve killed Gretchen?'

'Follow the money, right? Or in this case, the power. Look who's calling the shots now. Steve's been put in charge of the studio.'

Kitty was confused. 'But you said Steve is the one who gave you your job back.'

'Yeah, that's right.'

'It doesn't bother you that he might have killed Gretchen?'

'Nah,' said Sonny. 'I mean, what's that got to do with me?'

Seven

Kitty and Fran tried to talk to Steve about Gretchen's murder and got stonewalled. 'Later,' was all he would say. A small, dark cloud seemed to follow him when he left. No doubt he was mad, very mad.

'What a jerk,' complained Fran.

'It didn't help that you spilled coffee all over his loafers.' Kitty stuck the key in the door of the Volvo.

'Big deal,' shrugged Fran. 'One time he gets a little coffee on his shoes and he's whining.'

'He said "again?" and looked like he wanted to kill you.' Kitty got behind the wheel. Fran jumped in beside her.

'Yeah,' said Fran, pulling a tube of lipstick from her purse and studying herself in the visor mirror. She pouted. 'Instead, he fired me.'

Kitty pulled out on to Sunset. 'I'm sorry,'

she said. 'Don't worry, we'll figure something out.'

'I need a drink,' Fran declared. 'Can we stop some place?'

Kitty took her eyes off the road. 'It's still morning. Besides, I've got deliveries to make.'

They stopped first at the condominiums belonging to Kitty's Television City regulars. Andrew Keagan, a network VP, wasn't home. It was Saturday morning. That meant he was at his regular squash game. His housekeeper let them in. The pet pug, named Rosco, was happy to see her and presented no problem at all. He never was. The pug wasn't the least bit fussy, ever.

Kitty offered him a baked turkey hoagie. He got the same dish every Saturday. It wasn't the healthiest dish she could offer to an already overweight dog, but dog and owner insisted. And since they were paying . . .

Kitty Karlyle: Gourmet Pet Chef
—The Roscoe Special—

2 slices French bread, cut in half horizontally
4 thin slices of turkey breast
2 tablespoons tomato sauce
1 teaspoon spicy brown mustard
Shredded lettuce
¾ cup shredded blend of cheddar and Swiss cheese
¼ teaspoon fresh basil

The seven cats belonging to a soft-spoken banker named Warren Warfield were another matter. She'd made them her popular *California Goldie Rush*. She pulled out the menu card while waiting to be buzzed up.

Kitty Karlyle: Gourmet Pet Chef
—California Goldie Rush—

1 cup tuna, lightly browned
½ cup crushed baby carrots
½ cup finely chopped green beans
1 cup risotto, steamed
pinch kosher salt
pinch basil
1 tsp. olive oil

Warren was on the phone when he opened the door, so he let Kitty and Fran in with no questions and little fanfare. But, as Kitty began laying out the Delftware, Fran began sneezing. Big and loud, like cartoon shotgun blasts. She couldn't stop to save herself. The cats were howling and Mr Warfield came storming into the kitchen to see what was wrong.

'Sorry.' Fran rubbed her nose. 'Guess I'm allergic.'

'Perhaps you had better wait outside, miss.' Mr Warfield clutched his phone by his side and pointed to the door with his free hand.

Fran nodded and left quickly. By this time, there wasn't a cat in sight and Kitty had to coax them all out of hiding.

* * *

'Maybe you'd better wait for me in the car,' Kitty said, pulling up in front of the Fandolfis' Brentwood estate. It was their last stop and she was exhausted. 'The Fandolfis have two dogs and a cat.' The couple had no children, only the pets, who they adored to death.

'Please, one measly cat I can handle.' She threw open the passenger side door before Kitty could argue.

Kitty hoped so. After all, she had a cat herself. Thank goodness rocker, Fang Danson, and his girlfriend, Angela Evan, were in Colorado. They had an adorable pup named Benny that Kitty adored to death, and a cockatiel that Angela had named Little Rich. Rich had been the name of her deceased husband. Kitty didn't know or want to know whether she'd dubbed the bird that in honor of his memory or as some sick joke.

Fang and Angela had gone to his chalet in Colorado and taken the pets with them. That meant three weeks of not having to schlep meals over to Santa Monica and put up with Fang's wandering ways. His wandering eyes Kitty could put up with – his wandering hands were another thing altogether. Kitty couldn't figure out how Angela put up with the guy. Come to think of it, she couldn't see how he put up with the Ice Princess either.

Mrs Fandolfi, Holly, opened the door herself – a rare act of working class labor by the young woman who preferred the rare atmosphere of the upper class. She was dressed for the swimming pool in an above-the-knee blue silk robe, casually unbuttoned to the middle of her chest. From what Kitty could see of the bikini underneath, it was as itsy-bitsy as itsy-bitsy could get. 'Ah, Kitty.' She tapped her expensive Piaget watch. 'It's about time.'

'Sorry I'm late, Mrs Fandolfi.' She shot a quick look at Fran. 'I had a little trouble.'

Holly made a sour face. 'Who is your friend?' She made way to let Kitty and Fran inside. Kitty was carrying the insulated bags containing the meals for Hocus, Pocus and Houdini.

'Fran. She–she's helping me out today.' This wasn't quite true from Kitty's perspective, but there was no harm done in saying so.

Fran said, 'Hi. Don't I know you from somewhere?' She squinted.

'I don't think so,' replied Holly, with a shake of her polished and poised head. Her thick, chocolaty-brown hair was tied up in a girlish ponytail. The sunglasses kept hidden provocative, almond-shaped green eyes that, in another age, would have sent ships and their masters crashing into the rocks off someplace exotic like Gibraltar and to their ultimate death and destruction.

As if reading Kitty's mind, Holly removed the dark shades now, dangling them lightly in her long, slender fingers. Her hands were smooth and delicate, as if she'd never lifted anything heavier than a boar bristle hairbrush. Holly's fingers and toes were impeccably manicured and her nails were currently painted clementine orange. Holly had painted her lips in a complementary orange hue, and their fullness would have done Angelina Jolie proud. Kitty had no way of knowing if that fulsomeness was real or of the injected variety. There was a lot of the latter in LA.

Kitty noted the tube of Chanel Rouge Coco Shine sticking out of the pocket of her robe – expensive stuff. The color was called *Flirt* and Kitty figured that probably summed up Holly to perfection. Holly's flawless little toes wiggled in the sunlight spilling through the door like tiny aliens come to worship Earth's sun.

'You sure look familiar . . .' Fran began.

'Please come see me after you have fed the children,' Holly said airily, and headed towards the other end of the house. 'I'll be in the study.'

'Come on,' said Kitty, giving Fran a tug. 'Their food will be getting cold.'

Fran allowed herself to be dragged behind. 'I still say that lady looks familiar. I never forget a pair of eyes.'

'She's got a pair of eyes, all right.' Kitty set the food down on the counter. 'Among other things.' The intricately carved island was the size of a small aircraft carrier. Small planes could practice takeoffs and landings on it.

'Would you look at this place?' Fran ran her hands appreciatively across the marble. 'I could get used to living like this, girlfriend.'

Kitty did her best to ignore Fran while she went through her usual setup – setting out menu cards: a hearty beef stew for the dogs and broiled crab cakes for the cat. She fed the dogs first; they were always the most eager. And, though Houdini hovered, he maintained a certain aloof spirit that Kitty found rather endearing.

She washed up the dishes, leaving them to dry out atop a *The Pampered Pet* – CuisineTV embossed potholder lying near the edge of the sink. She wiped her hands on her apron afterward. 'I suppose I had better go see what madam wants.'

'If she wants a daughter,' quipped Fran, 'tell her I'm available.'

Kitty laughed. 'I'll bet you're older than she is.'

'Hey, that doesn't mean I won't call her mommy if the price is right.'

Kitty pointed a finger at Fran. 'Wait for me right here. I'll be right back. Do not,' she said sternly, 'go wandering off. I can't afford to get fired.' She was already learning that show biz was a fickle and ruthless biz. Who knew how long she or the show would last?

'Please,' replied Fran. 'You're going to be a TV star. I don't know why you're even dealing with this little business anymore at all. I'm the one who got fired.'

Kitty bit her lip. 'It still doesn't seem real to me. Besides,' she added, 'I haven't seen one cent out of Santa Monica Film Studios yet. Who knows if I'll ever get paid? I can't live on promises.'

'Fine, fine.' Fran motioned for Kitty to go. 'I'll be waiting right here, Miss Karlyle. Don't you worry about me.'

When she got back with Fran, Kitty told her what Holly had said during their conversation in the study. It was really quite strange. Holly had asked her all sorts of questions about Mr Fandolfi and about her own love life. Kitty had been quite uncomfortable and found the entire conversation baffling. She'd much rather have talked about the pets. 'I'm still not sure what the point of our conversation was.'

'That Holly is one weird chick,' opined Fran, combing her hair, or at least trying to while Kitty swerved through traffic. They were running late on their way to Chevy Czinski's house. 'Slow down, what's the rush?'

'Buster likes to eat punctually.' As for Holly, Kitty wouldn't have agreed with Fran's assessment of the woman if it weren't for her most recent conversation with the lady of the house.

'Oh, good grief. Anyway, I still think Holly looks familiar.'

'She works as Mr Fandolfi's stage assistant sometimes, Fran. You've probably seen her at one of his shows. That's how the two of them met.'

'I have caught a couple of his specials on cable. I guess that's it.' Fran gasped as Kitty cut in front of an LA Metro bus. 'So, she gets a job as his assistant and, the next thing you know, the barely legal lady lands a gig as the old magician's wife. Who does he think he is, Hugh Freaking Hefner?'

'Mr Fandolfi is really quite charming. And elegant. Too bad he wasn't there so you could meet him.'

'Maybe Holly's afraid that her husband is cheating on her or even that you might have designs on snatching him up for yourself?'

'Please, Mr Fandolfi's not the type to cheat. He adores Holly. And he's practically twice my age. He must be sixty, at least.' Not to mention that, while Kitty, with all due humility, might consider herself pretty, Holly was gorgeous. Could someone with her looks be that insecure?

'Hey, look at Holly. Mr Magician likes them young. Maybe he's got his eyes on a fresh young assistant.'

Kitty considered the idea preposterous, but had to admit it wasn't impossible.

'What I can't imagine is what she sees in someone who is nearly three times her age.' Fran answered her own question with some possibilities. 'Maybe he's got magic hands?' she quipped.

'And a million bucks or two,' Kitty threw in. Both ladies laughed. Kitty slowed as she advanced up the long, meandering, hard-packed earth drive leading to her next client's house.

Chevy Czinski resided in a log cabin that he claimed to have built by hand. Kitty had no reason to doubt him. The former Tarzan actor certainly looked like he could have done it single-handedly. While posh by the standards of an ordinary working girl like Kitty, the home was modest by Beverly Hills standards; at about twenty-five hundred square feet some of her clients had larger master bedrooms.

The cabin was nestled in a small valley, halfway up the mountains in the Malibu Canyon region of the Santa Monica Mountains. It was a long way to go for a delivery, but at this stage of her business, Kitty took what she could get. Besides, he paid well. The Volvo rolled to a stop, tires crunching over gravel. 'We're here.' Kitty's fingernails tapped the steering wheel. 'Please, be on your best behavior now.'

Fran made a face. 'You're kidding, right? This place looks more like somebody's poor attempt at a petting zoo.' Except there were no people around – the place looked forlorn and empty.

Buster appeared out of nowhere and barked in the window. Fran hit the ceiling. 'Dang it, dog. You've got some lungs!'

Kitty laughed. 'Hey there, Buster.' She saw Chevy limping down from the tiger's den. 'Here he comes. Like I said, be on your best behavior.'

'Hey!' Fran scowled but put up no further argument.

Mr Czinski's knees were so bad they squeaked. When she'd suggested knee replacement surgery, he'd replied that he didn't believe in such things. The former actor clapped his hands, setting off a muffled explosion that rolled through the canyon. 'Here, boy!'

Buster turned at the sound of his master and dropped from the car. 'How are you today, Mr Czinski?' asked Kitty as she climbed out of the Volvo and popped open the rear to fetch Buster's lunch.

The smell coming from the pens – a mixture of hay, several fruits and vegetables in various stages of decay, and a healthy dose of dung – always reminded Kitty of her visits to the LA Zoo and the San Diego Zoo Safari Park. Mr Czinski didn't like to refer to the animal pens as cages. He preferred to use the term *abodes*.

Czinski had catlike blue-gray eyes and puffy cheeks. A full head of medium-brown hair and angular features gave a hint of his once ruggedly handsome good looks. 'Fine. How about you, Kitty?' Czinski wore a blue chambray work shirt and tan cargo pocket khakis over steel-toed work boots, like he always did. There was a half-chewed cigar protruding from the pocket of his shirt. The frazzled end looked like it might have been gnawed on by a lion.

Czinski had explained to Kitty that the steel-toed boots were a necessary precaution as some of his menagerie found toes quite the delicacy. She wasn't sure whether he'd been teasing or not. Maybe it was his way of seeing that she didn't wander into any of the abodes. Not that there was any chance at all of *that* happening.

Kitty said she was doing well and introduced her friend, Fran.

'Tell me,' he said, watching Kitty prepare Buster's meal out on the wide front porch, 'how did this cooking show go that you were telling me about?'

Kitty was surprised he'd even mentioned it now. She had told him all about it the last time she had been out to his place. 'Not so good,' she admitted, setting a menu card on the front stoop.

Kitty Karlyle: Gourmet Pet Chef
—Busterlicious Beef Stroganoff—

1 ½ pounds cubed round steak
½ cup all-purpose flour
2 tablespoons olive oil

2 tablespoons butter
1 small onion, sliced
2 medium carrots, sliced
½ cup green peas
4 ounces fresh mushrooms, sliced
8 ounces beef broth
6 ounces cream of mushroom soup
Salt and black pepper
½ cup sour cream
1 ½ cups cooked egg noodles

'Not so good?' Czinski scratched his knee. 'How not so good?'

When Kitty had first explained how she'd been offered a cooking show for pets, Mr Czinski's Tarzanlike muscles, though normally buried beneath layers of fat due to years of neglect, had bulged and his face had swollen up like a red balloon. His fist had been wrapped around the door handle of her car at the time and Kitty could have sworn she'd heard her old Volvo squeal like a pig that had been snatched by the throat by some predator.

Then when she'd told him the name of the producer, he'd given the door handle a twist that broke one end loose. Looking askance, he'd said he was familiar with the studio. He'd tried in vain to reattach the handle but the bolt was broken. The door handle still dangled against the metal door like a broken wing.

Kitty had asked him if he knew anything about Santa Monica Film Studios. He stepped back from the car and looked toward his prized animals. As he'd turned back toward Kitty, there had been a hard look on his face that hadn't been there before. 'If I were you, I would stay very far away from Santa Monica Film Studios,' he had said, his Polish accent grown thicker than normal. 'You should very much stay away from that–that producer, Gretchen Corbett.' Mr Czinski had practically spat the producer's name. So Kitty would never have dared broach the subject again if he hadn't brought it up himself.

Kitty plated Buster's food in a large stainless steel dish that Mr Czinski kept near the front door as she formulated a reply. 'Well,' she said softly, 'the producer got murdered.'

'Murdered?' Mr Czinski's hand went to his chest and his face paled.

'Are you OK, Mr Czinski?'

'Yes, yes.' He shook himself. 'I'm fine. I hadn't heard, that's all. I don't get the paper and I rarely watch television.' He glanced toward his little menagerie. 'Murder is always such an awful business.'

'Mind if I use the little ladies' room?' Fran asked. She shrugged. 'Sorry, guess it's all the coffee.'

Mr Czinski nodded and gave her directions. 'If you'll excuse me, I need to go check on the animals.'

'Sure, Mr Czinski,' said Kitty, eying him curiously. The murder seemed to have hit him hard. Maybe he wasn't used to such things, living out in the country, far removed from the city and all its crimes. He did seem very happy out here with his animals. In many ways, Kitty envied him his chosen lifestyle. 'I'll wait 'til Buster is finished and then clean up.'

He nodded and trudged toward his animals.

Kitty spent a few minutes playing with Buster after he'd finished, and then picked up his bowl. She carried the dirty dog dish to the kitchen and rinsed it out in the farm-style sink. She noticed a CuisineTV potholder next to the toaster. These things were popping up everywhere. Gretchen had wasted no time promoting her newest show.

'Wow!'

Kitty turned. 'Fran?'

'Yeah,' called Fran. 'Come here, you have got to see this.'

Kitty followed the sound of Fran's voice and found her in a large, oak-paneled den with a big bay window looking out across the small valley.

'Look at all this stuff,' she exclaimed. 'Have you seen this?'

Kitty looked about. She shook her head. 'No, I've never come further than the main room and the kitchen.' And she was feeling uncomfortable doing so now. 'Come on,' she said, lowering her voice, 'we shouldn't be snooping.'

'Who's snooping?' replied Fran, waving her arms around. 'I mean, all this stuff is on display. On the walls, on the floor, on the shelves.' Kitty followed with her eyes. 'He wants people to see this stuff.' Fran picked up a stuffed lion's head and examined it at arm's length. 'You think all these trappings are real?'

Kitty nodded. There were all sorts of stuffed

animals: the male lion and its female mate, a tiger, a rhino and various exotic birds that she couldn't name. An eight-foot alligator was sunning itself in the window. Fortuitously, it was dead and stuffed. There were scores of photographs, both in color and black and white, and a dozen large movie posters in glass frames – just like at the cinema.

'What is he, some kind of weird collector?' She set the lion's head back on the trophy table and examined a four-foot movie poster on the wall. Above the poster hung a solitary elephant tusk, yellowed with age.

'No,' explained Kitty. 'He used to be Tarzan. That's him in the picture you're looking at.'

'Get out!' shouted Fran. 'This hunk?' The hunk in question was hanging one-handed from a thick, twisted vine showing a well-muscled arm, and wearing nothing but a skimpy loincloth. His other hand clutched a dangerous looking knife. Coiled on the vine next to him was an impossibly large and predacious looking snake of some sort that looked more Hollywood than natural. Its two fangs were as long and curved as sabers.

Kitty explained how Mr Czinski had once been a very big star back in Europe. 'But that was a long time ago,' she said. 'I really don't think he likes to talk about it much these days.'

'Hey, isn't that Gretchen Corbett in this picture?' Fran's fingernail pushed against the glass of a small, grainy black and white photo on the wall.

'No.' Kitty took a closer look. 'I don't know.

It could be, I suppose.' The woman in the picture with her arms around a much younger version of Chevy Czinski couldn't have been more than twenty-five years old at the time that photograph was taken.

'The picture's not that clear though.' Kitty shook her head. 'I don't think it's her. In fact, when I mentioned the meeting I was going to be having with Gretchen at the studio, he didn't say anything at all about being friends with her.' Kitty stopped and made a face.

'What? What is it?' Fran asked. She had picked the framed photograph off the wall and was examining it from every angle.

'I'm not sure,' said Kitty, rubbing her jaw. 'It's just that when I happened to mention the meeting to Mr Czinski, well, it might have been my imagination, but he seemed upset about it.' He had practically ripped the handle off her car door.

'Upset? Upset how?' Fran replaced the picture on the wall and stepped over the dead alligator toward Kitty.

'He warned me to stay away from her,' Kitty said. 'I didn't think anything of it at the time. Only that it was odd.' And since Mr Czinski was odd to begin with, that in itself hadn't made the incident seem so odd to her at the time. But now . . . 'Come here,' said Kitty, waving for Fran to follow her. 'Look what I found in the kitchen.' Kitty showed Fran the *The Pampered Pet* – CuisineTV potholder.

'So?' Fran looked unimpressed. 'It's a potholder. I saw one just like it at the Fandolfis' house this morning.'

'Me too, but I didn't think anything of it then.' The potholder dangled from Kitty's finger. 'Don't you think that it's weird that they should both have one?'

Fran appeared to give the question some thought. 'I'm not sure. Should I?'

Kitty nodded. 'Gretchen had boxes of these in her office.'

'I remember. So?'

'So they were only given out at the taping – trinkets for the audience. How did Mr Czinski get his hands on one?' And the Fandolfis for that matter?

Fran snapped her fingers. 'I thought this Czinski character looked familiar.'

Kitty groaned. 'Please, you think everybody looks familiar.'

'No, really. Come on,' urged Fran, 'let's go ask him.'

They found Mr Czinski talking to Clement, his giraffe, through the fencing of his pen.

Before Kitty could formulate a question and the proper approach, Fran burst out with 'Weren't you at Santa Monica Film Studios yesterday?' It came out more an accusation than a question and Kitty stifled another groan.

'You are mistaken, young lady.'

'No, I'm not,' asserted Fran, stepping closer. Mr Czinski backed away and walked over to the lion area. They followed him.

'I remember now,' said Fran. 'You were wandering in the hallway. You said you were lost.'

Mr Czinski puffed out his chest. 'I said you

are mistaken, young lady,' he said. He turned his back to them and unlocked the steel mesh door to the lions' abode with a long key chained to his belt. The two lions, an elderly male and female, sitting on a large flat gray rock in the far right corner, perked up at the metallic sound of the door opening.

'What about the potholder?' asked Kitty, using her friendliest tone.

'Potholder?'

'I noticed a potholder for *The Pampered Pet* in your kitchen – when I went to rinse out Buster's dish.' She didn't want him to think she had been snooping.

'I must tend to the cats,' replied Mr Czinski. 'They get quite cranky if their schedule is not adhered to.' He stepped inside. 'If you have any more questions . . .' He motioned for Kitty and Fran to cross the threshold.

Kitty and Fran looked at one another. 'No, no more questions.' Kitty figured Mr Czinski wasn't about to provide any answers anyway. And being nibbled on by a hungry lion wouldn't have been worth it even if he had been willing to provide some answers. But how did he come by a potholder from the show? And what about that picture in the den that looked like him and Gretchen in an embrace?

The two walked quickly down to the Volvo. Fran hopped in and Kitty suddenly took off on foot toward the cabin. 'Where are you going?' Fran whispered loudly.

'Forgot my bag!' she yelled, hoping that Mr Czinski heard her as well. She raced up the steps to the porch and disappeared inside the house. A minute later, she reappeared. Mr Czinski was grooming the big cats and barely glanced up as Kitty turned the Volvo around.

'What was that all about?' Fran asked. 'Your bag's right here.' She jerked her thumb in the direction of the backseat.

'I know,' answered Kitty with a sly grin. She held up her cellphone.

'Why you sly dog, you,' Fran said with a laugh. On the phone was a picture of the photograph in the den.

Eight

The Beverly Hills Hotel, located on Sunset Boulevard near Will Rogers Memorial Park, has been a southern California landmark for over one hundred years. Built in the Spanish mission design style – as popular then as it is now – it had cost its owners over five hundred thousand dollars back in 1912, a sum that Kitty considered astronomical even today.

She felt ridiculously out of place walking up the wide red carpet with Fran – almost as ridiculous as she had felt giving the keys to her beat up old Volvo wagon to the impeccably dressed valet. The lobby was a beautiful, elegantly appointed expanse that could have swallowed a couple of good-sized houses whole and had room left over for dessert. A striking, recessed, circular ceiling painted sunflower yellow with a humongous cone-shaped chandelier in milky white glass and gold filigree immediately caught her eye.

This was Kitty's first visit to the Beverly Hills Hotel. Fran explained she'd been before for several studio functions and led the way confidently to reception.

'Wait,' said Kitty, pulling Fran aside and glancing at the receptionist from behind a crystal vase of white tulips. The woman behind reception eyed them dubiously.

'What's wrong? Cold feet?'

'No,' Kitty replied, keeping her voice low.

'So, aren't we going to stop at reception to let Ms Cartwright know we're here?'

'I don't think that's a good idea,' whispered Kitty. 'She might not want to see us.'

'You've got a good point.' She looped her arm through Kitty's. 'Come on, she's staying in one of the bungalows. I've overheard Gretch talking to her.'

The women sashayed through the lobby and out the doors to the immaculate grounds like they owned the place. Kitty was struck by the beauty of the hotel's surroundings as they passed the swimming pool and roamed down a quiet lane, lush with hibiscus, bougainvillea and palm trees.

'These are the bungalows,' explained Fran. 'Nice, huh?'

Kitty nodded. 'I can't imagine how much it must cost to stay in one of these.'

'I can,' said Fran. 'A couple of grand a night.'

Kitty's mouth fell open. 'A night?' It seemed inconceivable that anyone could afford such a price, even for these gorgeous surroundings. She mentally calculated the number of pet food dishes she'd have to cook and serve to spend just one fleeting night in a Beverly Hills Hotel bungalow. The number she came up with boggled the mind.

'Now all we have to do is figure out which one of these the lovely Ms Cartwright is staying in.' Fran frowned, looking about.

A bungalow door opened to the right and a man stepped out, his back half to them. 'Hide,' whispered Kitty. She grabbed Fran by the arm and pushed her down behind a hibiscus.

Fran was looking at her like she was crazy. 'That's Steve,' Kitty said. 'Coming out of that bungalow up there.'

'Our Steve?' Fran asked softly. 'Steve Barnhard?'

Kitty nodded. 'Take a look. But be careful.' They slowly lifted their heads up over the top of the bush. Steve was talking to some woman under the covered entryway to the Mediterranean styled bungalow. Steve was buttoning the top buttons of a wrinkled butter yellow shirt.

The woman had dressed in a peach peignoir with matching mules. That woman, with the distinctive pageboy haircut with a wisp of gray in a jet-black head of hair, and the pleasantly chubby round face, was instantly recognizable. This was the famous cooking star, Barbara Cartwright. 'What's Steve doing with her?'

'From the looks of it,' quipped Fran, 'I'd say they were trying out some new recipes, like hot afternoon delight – if you get my drift.'

Kitty did. 'So, Steve Barnhard and Barbara Cartwright are seeing each other.'

'Interesting,' said Fran. Both girls ducked as Steve said his goodbyes and headed down the flagstone path in their direction.

'More than interesting,' Kitty said after Steve had passed. She rose and dusted herself off. 'It gives them both a motive for killing Gretchen.'

'You're right,' said Fran. 'They could be in this together.'

Kitty nodded. 'It sure looks that way. Let's see what Ms Cartwright has to say.'

She knocked lightly on the dark-stained wood door that looked and sounded thick enough to keep out the most stalwart paparazzi, if not an invading Saxon army. 'Ms Cartwright?'

At five foot seven, Barbara Cartwright stood eye to eye with Kitty. 'Yes,' she said, her sapphire blue eyes twinkling behind a pair of round, frameless reading glasses. She glanced over Kitty's shoulder at Fran. 'Don't I know you?'

Fran nodded quickly and beamed. 'We're with the hotel.'

Kitty did a double take.

'Oh, yes. You must be with hotel services, here about the reception I am arranging for tomorrow afternoon.'

She had a lilting Londoner's accent that Kitty found pleasant to the ear.

Fran immediately said yes and Ms Cartwright beckoned them inside. 'Wow,' she gasped, obviously awed by the lavish surroundings.

Kitty cautioned her with her eyes.

Barbara Cartwright led them through to the

sitting room, took a seat in a high-backed wing-chair and motioned for the girls to take the loveseat on the opposite side of the fireplace.

The three women eyed each other in silence. It was Barbara Cartwright who broke the ice. 'Did you have some specific questions about tomorrow's reception? It will be a quiet affair, of course. Only Gretchen's closest friends and colleagues will be present.'

'Yes, of–of course,' Kitty stammered. Her mind raced. 'Had you and Gretchen known each other long?'

'Not particularly long,' replied Ms Cartwright, crossing her legs and adjusting her peignoir. 'But I do feel she deserves some sort of memorial. Her daughter will be holding a wake at her home after the funeral. This is simply my small gesture.' She waved a regal hand through the air. 'A small *in memoriam*.'

'Certainly,' Kitty was quick to agree. So that's what this was all about. 'Tell me,' she began, 'weren't you originally to be the host of that new show that Gretchen's studio was producing?'

The shadow of a scowl passed across Barbara Cartwright's face and then was gone, replaced by a vacuous smile. She pulled her reading glasses off her nose and set them on the coffee table. 'Yes, you are correct. I had originally planned on hosting a new cookery program with Ms Corbett.'

'What happened?'

'Oh,' replied Ms Cartwright, 'it simply never quite worked out. That's show business for you. The trick is to keep more than one pot on the fire.' She beamed. 'An apropos cooking metaphor, don't you think?'

Kitty nodded.

'Who do you think killed her?' asked Fran.

Barbara Cartwright's eyebrows rose. 'Don't you think that's a matter for the police, young lady?'

'Of course,' replied Kitty, shooting Fran another warning with her eyes.

Ms Cartwright poured a cup of tea from a porcelain teapot, but offered none to Fran and Kitty. She added a teaspoon of sugar and stirred. She cleared her throat before speaking. 'Still, if I was going to consider who might have wanted to see Gretchen dead—'

'Yes?'

'Well, I suppose I'd put that wretch of an ex-husband of hers at the top of my list. And her daughter second.'

'Her daughter?' squawked Fran.

Barbara Cartwright nodded. 'I hear they'd had some sort of falling out. What was the girl's name? Cynthia, I believe.'

'Cindy,' corrected Fran.

Ms Cartwright nodded and took a sip of tea. 'Then again, poor Gretchen seemed to have a falling out with everyone eventually.'

Kitty pulled her phone from her purse. 'Do you recognize the man in this picture?' She leaned forward, holding the phone out for her to see.

Ms Cartwright put on her reading glasses and chewed her lip a moment. 'Of course, that's Gretchen,' she answered, tapping the screen. 'And that ape of a husband of hers.' She laughed.

'Or should I say ape-man. That's her ex-husband, Chevy.'

Ape-man, indeed, thought Kitty. Now things were beginning to make sense. 'Tell me,' she said, shifting gears, 'will Steve Barnhard be attending tomorrow?'

Ms Cartwright smiled, but it was a scary smile. She rose and set her teacup on the table. 'I'm very tired,' she said.

'I'll bet,' Fran said, under her breath.

'Excuse me?'

'Nothing.' Kitty waved at Fran in irritation. She knew exactly what Fran was thinking. The image of Barbara Cartwright and Steve Barnhard twisting the sheets in the middle of the afternoon was about as pleasant as being kicked in the stomach by a mule.

'Roger!' called Ms Cartwright.

A young man in a pale orange Lacoste polo shirt and jeans appeared from one of the bedrooms. 'Yes, Ms Cartwright?' he said, in a voice that oozed French. He was tall and slender, with wavy brown hair brushed to one side and clean-shaven cheeks.

'Please show these strumpets out, won't you? I've had enough of their games.'

Kitty went into shock. If strumpet meant what she thought it meant, the woman had some nerve. Who uses that word anymore, anyway?

Both women leapt to their feet. 'But, Ms Cartwright, about the reception—' Kitty began.

'Please,' snapped Barbara Cartwright, her voice now granite hard. 'I've had enough. You,' she said, pointing an accusing finger at Fran, 'are that silly hair stylist from the studio. And you,' Barbara Cartwright said, turning her wrath on Kitty, her chest heaving upward, 'are that wretched dog food person who stole *my* cookery show out from under me!' she thundered.

Kitty felt Roger closing in. 'But Ms Cartwright, I can explain—' Roger grabbed Fran and Kitty and hustled them out the front door.

'You can do your explaining to Bill Barnhard, young lady. Because that's who I am going to be calling to report your deception and invasion of my privacy. I'll have your job yet!'

'Oh yeah? Big deal!' yelled Fran as the door slammed in their faces. 'I've already been fired, so what do you think about that?' She pounded the door with her fist. 'Rats,' she hissed.

'Yeah,' said Kitty, trembling. 'I think we'd better leave before she calls hotel security.'

'Please,' scoffed Fran, 'like she'd dare.'

Kitty patted Fran's shoulder and pointed. Two men in dark suits were heading their way, walking quickly, faces set and determined.

Nine

Kitty slid her Volvo into the reserved spot located ever so conveniently near the big dumpster outside her Melrose District apartment complex – who said LA wasn't all glitz and glamour? The building was a two-story, U-shaped affair, the color of an overripe peach. Her apartment was on the first floor. 'Coming up? I have to get ready for my date with Jack, but you're welcome to hang out until then.'

'Sure, I don't mind if I do.' Fran helped Kitty carry her gear and empty delivery bags inside.

Kitty was surprised to turn the key in the lock and discover that the deadbolt was already open. 'Oh, Sylvester. It's you.'

The scrawny young man in tattered jeans and a loose navy blue Bob Dylan T-shirt was on his knees on the carpet tussling with Fred. The dog had his favorite rope toy locked in his jaws and barely gave Kitty a second look, engrossed as he was in his tug-of-war with Sylvester.

'Fran, this is my next-door neighbor, Sylvester Herman. Sylvester, this is my friend, Fran.'

Sylvester let go of the rope and rose to his feet, wiping the slobber off his hands and on to his jeans where it left a silvery trail. He held out his hand and, to Fran's credit, she shook it politely.

'Pleased to meet you,' he said, diverting a long strand of slick black hair from his face. He had a hawkish nose, pleasant green eyes and a bad case of acne that made him feel insecure though Kitty was constantly reminding him how cute and sweet he was. Sylvester was from the Midwest somewhere – some small town in Kansas whose name Kitty always forgot. He'd grown up on a farm and had a real affection for animals.

'Likewise.' Fran dropped Kitty's stuff on the sofa.

'I noticed you'd been gone quite a while and thought I'd better let Fred out.'

'Thank you,' Kitty said. 'It has been a long day.' Sylvester had a spare key to her apartment and was a godsend. He and his four roommates were members of a rock band called The Tonsils. Her pets adored them all, Sylvester especially. Thankfully, he didn't question her about the murder, though he no doubt had heard about it. The whole city had.

'Guess I'll be on my way.' Sylvester paused in the doorway, hand on the knob. 'I almost forgot, you had a couple of visitors, Kitty.'

'Oh?'

Sylvester squirmed a moment, his Converse sneakers digging into the carpet. 'Yeah. Mr Frizzell, for one.' He looked at the floor. 'He wanted the rent.'

Kitty groaned and blushed. Jerry Frizzell was the apartment manager. His cousin owned the property but Frizzell treated it like his own minor fiefdom. 'That figures.'

'Don't worry,' Sylvester replied quickly. 'Me and the guys all pitched in and covered for you.' He stuck his hands in his pockets.

'You did?' Kitty rushed over and gave him a warm hug. 'You didn't have to do that.' He reddened. She gave him a peck on the cheek. 'But thank you. And I'll pay you back as soon as I can.'

'I know you will,' he said. 'Don't worry about it. 'Bye.' Sylvester started to leave.

'Wait,' said Kitty. 'Who was the other visitor?'

'Oh, some guy by the name of David.'

'David? David Biggins?'

'Yeah, *our* David?' asked Fran.

Sylvester nodded. 'That was his name.'

'What did he want?'

Sylvester shrugged. 'He came by and knocked on the door while I was here with Fred and Barney. He seemed surprised when I answered, but seems like a friendly enough guy. He was disappointed you weren't around.'

Fran shot Kitty a suggestive look that Kitty chose to ignore.

After Sylvester had gone, Kitty put out food for Fred and Barney and offered Fran a glass of wine.

'Aren't you having one?' Fran asked, watching Kitty pour out only one glassful.

Kitty explained that she had to get showered and ready for her date. 'I'm so tired, I'm afraid that if I have a drink now I'll never get out the door.'

Fran nodded her understanding. 'What about your other beau?'

'What other beau?'

'David Biggins.' Fran fluttered her long lashes.

'Oh, please,' Kitty said with a shake of the head. 'We're just friends. *Old* friends.'

'Sure you are,' teased Fran. 'So, did the two of you hook up in high school?'

'You're bad,' laughed Kitty.

'I'm just saying. I've seen the look in that man's eyes. He's got the hots for you, Kitty. Now he's showing up at your door,' she leered suggestively, 'like a lovesick puppy.'

'Let's change the subject,' Kitty said, crossing her arms over her chest, 'before you get me in any more trouble.'

'OK,' said Fran, sitting at the kitchen table, running a finger over the rim of her glass. 'It sure was nice of that Sylvester to cover the rent for you.'

Kitty gushed on about how nice Sylvester and his roommates were.

'Have you ever thought about taking in a roommate? I noticed you have a second bedroom.'

Kitty shrugged and started loading up the dishwasher. 'Not really, I mean, I suppose it would help, but with the hours I keep and *them* running around underfoot,' she said waving at her pets. 'Who'd want me, right?'

Fran cocked her head and grinned. 'Oh, I don't know. You haven't said anything that I couldn't deal with.'

Kitty started up the dishwasher and turned. 'Are you saying you'd like to move in? Here?'

Fran tilted her head. 'Well, I did just lose my job. It doesn't exactly look like you're rolling in the dough either – no offense.' She held up her hand.

'None taken,' said Kitty, dropping into the chair across the table. 'You know, I never really thought about it. I suppose it could work.' She leaned back. 'What about your boyfriend? I thought you were living with him?'

Fran scowled, downed her merlot and helped herself to another glass. 'I was. We had a bit of a disagreement.'

'Oh? What about?'

'About his wife wanting to move back in.'

'Oh.' Kitty didn't know what else to say and found herself reaching for a glass of wine after all. 'To roommates,' she said, hoisting her glass. They drank.

'I guess I'd better go get my stuff,' Fran said, pushing back her chair.

'I'll give you a spare key then,' said Kitty. 'I've got another in the drawer. You can move in whenever you like. I've got to leave for Jack's in less than an hour.'

'Don't worry, girlfriend. It won't take me that long. My suitcase is out in the Mini.'

'I see,' Kitty said with a big grin. 'Pretty sure of yourself, weren't you, having your bags out in your car already?'

Fran smiled sheepishly. 'It's just the one.' She held up her index finger. 'But, yeah. To tell the truth, I'll be glad to get it out of the Mini. Somebody vandalized it last night outside my boyfriend, ex-boyfriend, Richie's place.'

'Did they take anything?'

'Not that I could see. Busted the passenger side window though, so I've been nervous about my suitcase being in the back all day.'

'Maybe it was kids.'

'Could be. But I think it's that crazy wife of his. She has a temper – sure was mad when she caught me and Rich together at his condo.'

'Can you blame her?'

'No, I guess not. Richie never told me he was married. Maybe I ought to go bust out one of his windows,' Fran said on parting.

Ten

Jack Young owned a smallish, nineteen-forties-era house in a working-class section of Burbank. The lot was tiny. A small, detached garage on the right side, next to the alley, occupied a good portion of what little yard there was.

The house itself was a bunker-looking, white rectangle with no curb appeal at all sitting on a side street from which Kitty could hear the hiss of traffic on nearby Victory Boulevard. The grass was brown and patchy. Jack claimed to enjoy gardening; he just wasn't very good at it. A chain link fence protected the backyard; from what, she couldn't imagine.

Jack lived there with his own black Labrador, named Libby, who Kitty generally adored as much as she adored the master of the house. Though, at the moment, the adoration was tilted more in the dog's favor. For the past couple of days, Kitty had found that the detective could be even more difficult and irritating than her most demanding clients.

Then again, maybe it was just his sudden association with the annoyingly attractive, and tall, Lieutenant Elin Nordstrom that was getting under Kitty's skin. That made her angrier still. She was *not* going to let that woman make her jealous.

Kitty vowed to be on her best behavior and put

all thoughts of murder and police business out of her mind as she rang the bell.

Before leaving, she had called her parents down in Newport Beach about the rent on her apartment. She had hated to call them up, again, for money, but as nice as it was of Sylvester and his mates to pay her debt, she wanted to be sure they got their money back as soon as possible. With a struggling band and minimum wage jobs, they were no better off than she was.

Kitty's mom had answered and, after pelting Kitty with questions about her life, Jack, and the recent murder, quickly agreed to transfer funds into Kitty's bank account. She'd also exacted a promise from Kitty to bring Jack down for dinner at the family restaurant later in the week.

That was one promise Kitty had been reticent to make considering the current strain that her relationship with Jack was under. But Mom had insisted.

Kitty rang the bell a second time and reminded herself to be on her best behavior, stick to couthie conversation, and not let anything spoil the evening.

'Oh, er . . .' Lieutenant Elin Nordstrom, in a tight-fitting pair of blue jeans and tailored white shirt, filled the doorway. Kitty rose on her tiptoes and tried looking past her annoyingly statuesque form. 'Where's Jack?'

The lieutenant smiled. She had a bottle of Spendrups beer in her hand. Kitty's dad was a beer buff, so she knew this to be one of Sweden's major brands. 'Hello, Ms Karlyle.'

Kitty held back an instinctive scowl. The way Nordstrom said hello made it sound like she was talking down to a child or pet. 'Hello.'

'Come on in. Jack's on the patio. Barbecuing.'

How gracious of you, thought Kitty, but she kept the thought to herself. She went through the side door off the small galley kitchen and found Jack grilling steaks in the chill evening air. Flames fluttered and smoke rose slowly. Libby watched with anticipation of what might come her way.

'Kitty!' Jack wiped his hands on his Moe, Larry and Curly kitchen apron and gave her a hug that she withstood more than reciprocated. 'What's wrong? Everything OK? I thought we'd have steaks.' He grabbed the neck of an open bottle of Spendrups from beside the grill and drank, his Adam's apple bobbing up and down.

'Since when did you start drinking imported beer?' She'd always known him to be a Miller man – MGD to be precise. In fact, he was normally quite insistent on Miller Genuine Draft or nothing at all.

'Oh, this?' Jack looked at the bottle in his hand. 'Elin brought it.' He tapped the label with his finger. 'I never heard of it before. But it's pretty darn good. You should try it.' He started for the kitchen door. 'Let me get you one.'

'Don't bother,' Kitty replied, her voice as frosty as the beer. 'I can't stay.' She turned on her heel. To think she'd spent an hour getting ready for this date, a nice red dress, a light cashmere jacket and heels. Fran had even done her hair for her. Kitty quickly saw that having a professional stylist as a roommate was going to have its advantages.

Jack reached for her arm. 'What are you talking about?' He looked anxious, but still managed to smile. 'We have a date.' He waved the spatula over the grill. 'The steaks are nearly done.'

At the mention of steak, Libby rose on her back legs, but nothing came her way and she settled back down. Kitty stepped over the dog. 'Why don't you share them with the lieutenant? I'm sure she must be hungry.' *For something* – she left that part unsaid.

Jack looked surprised. He took Kitty's stiff hand. 'Is that what this is about?'

His grin only infuriated her and she pulled away. 'I really can't stay.'

'Come on, Kitty. The lieutenant only dropped by to talk about the case. She and Detective Leitch had been doing some digging around and she wanted to give me an update.'

'How nice of her.' Kitty pulled her jacket tight. 'And she brought you beer.'

Jack shrugged. 'She was only being friendly. There's nothing wrong with that, is there?'

Kitty remained silent.

'I told her we were having dinner. She's not staying. Come on,' he urged. 'Fresh steaks, salad greens with honeyed pecans and goats cheese, just the way you like it.'

Nordstrom called Jack's name from inside and a moment later appeared in the doorway. 'I'll be leaving now.' Libby appeared at her side and she ran her hands over top of the Lab's head. 'I do hope my being here hasn't upset you, Ms Karlyle.

I came on official police business.' She smiled in a way that Kitty found inflammatory. 'We are working to solve Gretchen Corbett's murder. The sooner we do so, the sooner your name will be out from under a dark cloud, as they say. It was your knife that killed her, after all.'

Kitty squeezed past the lieutenant. 'My knife, not me.'

Jack ran inside after her, Elin Nordstrom hovered in the background. 'Come on, Kitty. Calm down.'

Kitty didn't like being asked to calm down. In fact, it was like putting gasoline on a fire. 'I do not need to calm down. And I do not need anybody trying to clear my name. Like I said before, I'll figure out who killed Gretchen Corbett and I don't need you or anybody else's help to do it!' she boasted, looking from one to the other.

'Kitty—'

Nordstrom laid a hand on Jack's shoulder. 'I think everyone needs to take a breath.'

'Kitty,' said Jack. 'Do not, I repeat, do not go doing anything stupid. There is a cold-blooded murderer out there and if you go nosing around, you're liable to be next.'

'I can take care of myself, Jack.' She pulled open the front door.

'Kitty—'

'Let her go, Jack,' Kitty heard the lieutenant say as she stormed out into the twilight. 'Let her continue her little investigation. What could it hurt? She won't get anywhere.'

Eleven

Kitty discovered Fran soaking in the tub when she got back to the apartment. Fred was lying on the robin's egg blue bathroom rug beside her. He was fond of shag. She could hear Barney mewling in the kitchen, waiting expectantly for his evening treat. He was a creature of habit and didn't like it when his routines varied.

The matching blue vinyl shower curtain was pushed all the way to the back wall. 'Either that was one short date or I fell asleep in here and took one heck of a long nap,' Fran quipped from behind a wall of bubbles that served to keep her at least somewhat modest.

'Yeah, I'll be with you in a minute. I have to feed Barney.' Her pets always came first and she didn't like to let them down.

Kitty reached into the pantry, grabbed a container of one of Barney's favorite kibbles – an all-natural, vegetarian blend produced by a local company out in the valley – then poured a scoopful into his ceramic dish that she kept up on the side counter. The dish was a gift from Aunt Gloria and was embellished with cute little blue kitties along the outer edge. No way she could leave Barney's bowl on the floor with Fred the food-seeking missile on the constant prowl. She stroked Barney while he ate. He liked that.

Kitty sniffed. The kitchen smelled like the La Brea Tar Pits and a brownish-black, amorphous blob rested in the sink. Either a meteorite had landed in her apartment while she was out or Fran had been cooking.

Fran appeared in the kitchen doorway, swathed in a fluffy, white, knee-length bathrobe. 'Oh,' she said, following Kitty's gaze. 'I was going to clean that up. I thought I'd try one of your recipes.' She pointed to an open, spiral bound notebook beside the cooktop.

Kitty leaned over the page. 'This is a recipe for pigs.'

'Huh?' Fran came closer. 'You cook pigs? I didn't see that listed as one of the ingredients.'

Kitty laughed. 'No, not a recipe to eat pigs, a recipe *for* pigs to eat – a Vietnamese potbellied pig to be precise.'

'I guess that explains why the ingredient list called for alfalfa,' replied Fran, chewing her lip. 'I couldn't find any anywhere. Not that I knew what I was looking for.'

'So what did you do?'

'Substituted some spinach noodles that I found in the pantry. I mean, I figured they're both green. Alfalfa is green, right?'

Kitty looked toward the slab in the sink. 'That must have tasted disgusting.'

'You kidding? You don't think I actually tasted that goo?'

Kitty opened the trashcan with her foot and dropped Fran's failure inside with a loud plop that sent Barney skittering for cover. Kitty yelled that she was sorry and Mirabelle Stein banged on her floor. It was after nine o'clock, Kitty was surprised the woman was still up.

'So,' said Fran, pulling back a chair at the kitchen table. 'What happened to your date? Jack get called away on a case?'

Kitty settled into the chair beside her, but not before pouring them each a healthy glass of Trader Joe's Chablis. She told Fran how she had found she-who-shall-not-be-named at Jack's house and how things had gone swiftly downhill from there.

Fran patted Kitty's hand. 'You and I sure aren't having much luck the last couple of days, are we?'

'You can add Gretchen Corbett to that club.'

Fran nodded. 'And Gretchen,' she said soberly. 'So, what are we going to do about it?'

Kitty sat taller. 'We,' she said firmly, 'are going to find out who killed Gretchen and why – or die trying.' She raised her glass. She and Fran toasted. In your face, Elin Nordstrom.

'Here, here,' said Fran. 'I'm with you girl.' She cleared her throat. 'But instead of this "or die trying bit", could we maybe rewrite the script to read "or break a nail trying?"'

Kitty laughed. 'Agreed.' She clamped her hands over her knees. 'We'll need to grill some suspects and check out everybody's alibis. The first order of business is to do some snooping.'

'Snooping? You mean like Nancy Drew or Scooby and the gang style?'

Kitty downed her wine and smiled her biggest smile. 'You bet.' She tilted back in her chair, feeling slightly dizzy. She wasn't used to drinking on an empty stomach. She pushed ugly memories of her spoiled dinner date with Jack from her head. 'Now, if we could only figure out where Gretchen lives – lived,' Kitty said, 'we could break in—'

'Excuse me?' Fran raised an eyebrow.

'You heard me. I mean, we'll be careful and all. Who knows, maybe we'll find an unlocked door or climb in through a cracked open window.'

Kitty pulled a small notebook from her purse, along with her Montblanc pen, and began jotting down her thoughts. 'We need to compile a list of suspects.' She pointed her pen at Fran. 'But I still think a little breaking and entering is our first order of business.'

'But Kitty, girl—'

'Uh-uh. No buts.' Kitty cut Fran off and poured them each another round. 'Here, have some more wine. We're gonna need it.'

'Much more of this and what I'm going to need is another nap,' quipped Fran, though she didn't refuse the refill and drank quickly. 'But Kitty—'

'OK, the way I see it,' said Kitty, laying her hands on the table, 'we've got lots of suspects.' She stood. 'Finish your wine. I'm going to see if I can find some tools and maybe a flashlight lying around. What do you think we'll need for picking a lock? A screwdriver? I might have one here someplace.' Her eyes spun around the kitchen. The alcohol was making her dizzy. She reached for a box of wheat crackers and grabbed a handful to settle her stomach, held the box out to Fran who declined.

'Then we'll head over to Santa Monica Film Studios and search for Gretchen's address. It's bound to be there in the personnel files, right?' She fished around in a kitchen drawer and pulled out a blue-handled flashlight, flicked it on and off to be certain it worked and waved it triumphantly in the air. 'You probably know where personnel is.' She looked Fran up and down. 'So, are you in or are you out?'

Fran rose. 'I'm in,' she said, standing and tugging the belt of her robe tight. 'But do you mind if I get dressed first?'

'Good idea,' Kitty answered. 'Maybe we should dress in black.'

'Oh, please,' said Fran, 'let's save that for Gretchen's funeral. I don't look my best in black.' She reached for her purse. 'Don't be in such a hurry. And' she said, snatching the flashlight from Kitty's hand and throwing it back in the drawer, 'you can leave your tools and your toys at home.'

'What are you doing?' Kitty said.

Fran pulled a key from her purse and a cream-colored keycard from her wallet. 'This,' she said, holding up a silver key, 'is the key to Gretchen's apartment. And this,' she held up the plastic card, 'is the card that gets us into her building.'

Kitty squealed and gave Fran a hug. 'This is going to be so much fun.'

'Oh yeah, fun,' Fran said, the skepticism clear in her voice. 'Until your boyfriend and his tagalong, the Swedish inquisitor, bust us for breaking and entering.'

Twelve

'Don't worry,' said Fran. 'I've done this a million times.'

They'd left the Volvo in a visitor spot along the perimeter and approached the luxury high-rise straight on. Kitty was duly impressed. Gretchen's condo must have cost her a bundle.

'In fact, the last time I was here was the day Gretchen got herself killed. Makes me feel kind of weird now, you know?'

Kitty did.

Fran waved the keycard in front of the door and Kitty watched as a red light on a metal box turned to green and Fran pulled open the big glass door. 'There's no security on duty after seven, so we won't have to explain ourselves to anybody.'

Kitty gulped. She was beginning to feel a wee bit nervous about this and she wasn't sure why. What could go wrong?

They rode the elevator up to the eleventh floor. 'It's this one,' said Fran, sticking the key in the lock. She punched in the alarm code, entered and closed the door behind them.

The apartment was dark and the lights of the city shone below. Kitty gasped. Gretchen had a corner unit with amazing views of Los Angeles. The place appeared to have been decorated by one of those expensive designers you see spreads about in magazines. Either that or the producer had had a flair for decorating. However, in this case, a layer of clutter seemed to have settled like dust over every available surface.

A single cracked and yellowed elephant tusk hung from two hooks on the wall over the fire-place. Kitty thought it looked more like it belonged in some smoky old hunting lodge than a chic LA condominium.

Fran seemed to read Kitty's face. 'Gretchen had good taste – mostly – but she was a bit of a slob.' She plucked a frilly pink bra by its strap from the back of a sleek leather chair facing the window. 'So, where do we start?' Fran draped the bra over a nearby lampshade, giving the light a pinkish hue.

Kitty turned in a circle. The apartment was expansive but there was a staleness in the air, as if it had been closed up for a very long time. Perhaps it was only her imagination. It hadn't been that long since Gretchen's demise.

Fran had turned on only the one lamp. Though they were eleven stories up, both women were concerned that someone might notice that the lights were on in a murdered woman's apartment and telephone the police. 'I'll take the desk,' said Kitty.

An espresso-colored desk and chair sat between two floor-to-ceiling windows, near the main sitting area comprised of a couple of chairs and a loveseat. A large, flat screen computer sat atop the desk. 'How about starting in the bedroom?'

Fran nodded and disappeared down the hall. Apparently, she knew her way around Gretchen's place pretty well. Not surprising, since she'd explained to Kitty on the way over here that Gretchen had often sent her here to pick things up for her. Plus, it seemed that Fran and Gretchen's relationship had been more than simply employer-employee. Sometimes they'd hung out together. They had been friends. That was why Fran had the key to the producer's place.

Kitty ran her hand over the computer keyboard and the screen came to life. She clicked on several directories, but there was so much to see and she didn't know what she was looking for. The computer wasn't password protected but it was still doing her no good.

Kitty moved her attention to the desk drawers, performing a perfunctory search. This was frustrating; not knowing what to look for and realizing she might not recognize something as important, even if she held it in her hands, was making this whole breaking and entering thing seem useless.

There was nothing in the top drawer but a clutter of pencils, pens, paper clips and random scraps of paper. The second drawer held files. She riffled through several – bank statements, bills, and invitations, all very businesslike.

Why couldn't Gretchen Corbett have some folder conveniently labeled *skeletons in my closet* or some such? Kitty was growing more and more disheartened. Maybe Gretchen's death had nothing to do with her personal life. It couldn't have been random – it hadn't happened on the street or in some cold, dark alley, after all – but maybe the killer was someone she did business with . . . or someone from work.

That was more likely, wasn't it? She was stabbed in her office, after all. Kitty needed to learn where everyone was at the time of the murder. Most would have been on set with her, so that let a number of people off the hook.

Kitty closed the drawer. That put Steve Barnhard, his lover – Barbara Cartwright – and Sonny Sarkisian at the top of her list. Sonny certainly had a good motive; Gretchen had fired him the week before.

She made a mental note to learn why. Sonny had been evasive on the issue when she'd pressed him about it. He was slick. Too slick. And he wasn't on the set, of course. Neither was Barbara Cartwright, to the best of her knowledge. Besides, Kitty would have recognized her if she had been. Where had Steve been?

Kitty's thoughts were interrupted by a shout. 'Hey, come here and look at this!'

Kitty hurried to the bedroom where she discovered Fran waving a rubber-banded pack of letters in the air. 'What is it?' Gretchen's bedroom had ornate French-style furnishings and an ethereal looking four-poster bed with a heavy lavender quilt. The scent of Gretchen's favored Chanel No. 5 lingered in the air like a sweet memory.

'Love letters,' replied Fran, triumphantly. 'I already opened one of them. Looks like Gretchen had a secret lover.' She fell down on the edge of the king-sized bed. 'I can't believe she never told me about this guy.'

She ripped the rubber band from the rest of the stack and the letters scattered across the comforter. 'Here,' she said, grabbing up a handful. 'You take some.'

'Who is he?' Kitty started pulling open envelopes. 'And who even writes love letters anymore?' She'd never received a single one from Jack.

'I don't know yet.'

Kitty's heart raced. This could be the first thread, the one that opened up the entire investigation. Her eyes scanned the first letter and she blushed. Lots of passion and plenty of sex talk. 'Wow,' she whispered.

She felt Fran squirm beside her. 'Yeah, "wow" is right.'

'I still don't know who he is.' Kitty threw the last letter down on the bed in frustration. All the letters had been signed only by Cam, no surname.

'Yeah, me either. I mean, who is this Cam guy? Gretchen never mentioned any Cam to me.' She harrumphed. 'Here I thought we shared everything.' She slammed a fist into the mattress.

'Maybe he's someone from her past. Here, take a look at this one.' She handed Fran one of the last letters in the bunch.

Fran's eyes scanned the wrinkled page. 'You mean they broke up?'

'It looks that way,' answered Kitty. 'And none too amicably. It looks like he was giving her the old heave-ho.' Though it was hard to say for certain what had occurred since they were only reading one side of this unhappily-ever-after love story. Yet, Gretchen must have continued to care about him. After all, she'd kept all his love letters, even when things had turned nasty.

Fran yawned.

'Come on,' said Kitty. She snatched some letters and shoved them in her purse. 'Let's get home and grab some shuteye. We'll pick this up in the morning.'

Fran nodded. 'You're keeping them?'

Kitty explained that the letters might prove useful in uncovering Gretchen's killer. 'Besides,' she said, 'who's gonna miss them? If the police had wanted them, I'm guessing they would have already taken them.' She really was only guessing. She had no idea whether the police had explored Gretchen's condo or not, though it seemed likely that they would have.

Kitty scooped up the remaining letters and closed the dresser drawer. She didn't want to leave any evidence of their having been in Gretchen's condo. There would be fingerprints, of course, and she regretted that they hadn't thought to wear gloves. She had plenty of toss-away latex gloves that she used for prepping food and should have brought some along. They would have been perfect for the job.

Kitty wandered back down the hall. 'Fran?'

'In here.'

She found Fran with her hand on the refrigerator handle and her face in the fridge. 'What are you doing?'

'I'm starved,' whined Fran, her mouth full of cold pasta. 'I've got to eat something. Especially after all that wine you plied me with. You want some? This stuff is delicious. I wonder where Gretch gets-got her take-out Italian?'

'I'm not sure this is a good idea, Fran.'

'Why not? Gretchen's dead. She's not going to mind if I eat her leftovers.' Reaching toward the back of the top shelf to grab the plastic container of raspberry lemonade standing there, Fran knocked a carton of vanilla soymilk to the kitchen floor. 'Oops.' She inspected the carton and the floor. 'No harm done.'

No, no harm done except for the minor heart attack the sound of the milk carton slamming into the tile had given her. A noise like that would have set off her upstairs neighbor, Mirabelle Stein. What if whoever lived below Gretchen heard the noise and was on their way up, or, worse still, sending the cops up to investigate?

'Good thing the carton wasn't opened yet. Maybe we should take it with us?'

'Fran!'

'What? Look at the date on this carton, it's about to expire.'

'But I think . . .' Kitty froze.

Fran made a face. 'What's wrong with you?'

'Shhh.' She held out a hand to shush Fran. 'Listen,' she whispered. Kitty held her breath. 'Did you hear that?'

Fran shook her head slowly. 'I didn't hear anything.'

'I did,' insisted Kitty. A chill went up her spine. 'It sounded like somebody was trying the door handle.'

Fran dropped the container of pasta. It fell with a dull thunk. Both girls gasped. *Sorry*, mouthed Fran.

'I'm going to go check it out,' whispered Kitty.

'Be careful,' urged Fran as she bent to scoop the take-out container from the tile.

Kitty tiptoed to the front door and peered hesitantly through the peephole. There was no one in sight. She turned the knob slowly, eased the door open and stuck her head out, half-expecting to be attacked by a mysterious, dark clad stranger.

She wasn't. But what she saw was almost as frightening.

She saw Steve Barnhard open the door to the condo up the hall, then step inside.

Thirteen

'Are you sure it was him?' Fran pressed her ear to Steve's door.

Kitty nodded. 'Now, come on. Let's get out of here. What if he finds us lurking out here in the hall?' She tugged at Fran's arm. 'Get away from there. You're going to get us both arrested, if not for breaking and entering, then for harassment or something.'

Fran pulled away and shrugged. 'So what? We have just as much right to be here as he does.'

Kitty raised an eyebrow.

'Well, maybe not quite as much . . .' Fran's voice trailed off.

The whooshing sound followed by the gentle *ping* that signaled the opening of the elevator door sent them both skittering around the corner, like mice when the lights blink on in a dark basement.

'Come on,' motioned Fran. 'We'll take the stairs.'

'Good idea,' whispered Kitty. With a cop for a boyfriend, it wouldn't do to get caught in this security building. The stairwell was dimly lit and hot. Their footsteps echoed maddeningly as they hurried for the ground-floor exit.

Kitty greedily sucked in fresh air as they hobbled back to the car.

'I had no idea Steve lives in the same building as Gretchen,' gasped Fran. 'And I can't believe Gretch never mentioned it.'

'It sounds like Gretchen was keeping more than one secret from you.'

'Yeah. Hey!' Fran slammed to a halt and pointed.

'What?' Kitty asked, wearily pushing the key into the door lock.

'Your window's busted.'

'Busted?'

'Yeah. On my side. See?' Fran pushed her hand through where the glass should have been and wriggled her fingers. 'Busted.'

Kitty marched around to the other side of the car. Bits of glass covered the passenger seat. 'Great, just great.' Ka-ching, this was going to cost her even more money that she didn't have. Would she have to telephone her mom and dad for a loan? She couldn't very well drive around with a smashed out window.

Kitty peered inside. Junk everywhere – but then there always was. And it stank like the back alley of a cheesy restaurant – but it usually smelled that way too. After all, she used the Volvo mostly for hauling around herself, her pets and her customers' meals, so it wasn't exactly going to smell like the perfume counter at Macys. She leaned closer. The glove box hung open.

'That's different,' Kitty said, reaching through the window frame. 'I know I didn't leave the glove box lying open like that.' The odds and ends she kept inside had spilled out or been pushed out on to the seat and floor. Shoving papers and miscellaneous items, such as a tangled mp3 cord, a rusty can opener and a couple of dried out lipstick tubes back inside, she pushed the glove box shut before any of the stuff could fall out again.

'First my car, then yours,' Fran griped. 'You'd think the jerks breaking into cars would at least have the sense to stick to Mercedes and Porsches and the like. There are enough of the bloody things around. And I suspect they have much better pickings than our jalopies.'

Kitty agreed. She pulled open the passenger side door and began sweeping out the broken glass. 'Give me a hand.' Together they scooped out most of the shards and tossed them in the back. They weren't sharp at all – the wonder of safety glass.

As Kitty drove, Fran hung her head out the broken window for fresh air, bits of glass still in the floor mat scrunching underfoot, as she reached in her bag for her hairbrush. 'Huh.'

'What is it?' Kitty asked, though she was too tired and hungry to care much at that point. Though it was late, there was always a lot of traffic on the streets of LA.

Fran pulled a thick, unaddressed manila envelope from her satchel. 'Nothing. I just remembered, I'm still carrying around this envelope that Gretch asked me to fetch for her from her condo the day she died.' She shoved it back in her bag. 'Guess I should have left it back in her place while we were there.'

'What's in it?'

Fran shrugged. 'How should I know? I'm no snoop.'

Kitty decided it wasn't worth bringing up the fact that ten minutes ago snooping was exactly what they had been doing.

Fran pressed her fingers against the side of the envelope. 'Papers, I'd say. Work stuff, you know? Gretch always took her work home with her.'

Kitty turned left at the light. 'Maybe it's my contract for the show.'

'Could be,' Fran agreed. 'Or it could be a script for some other show. Gretch was always balancing a hundred projects at once. It could be receipts for her accountant, for all I know.'

The road ahead was clear and Kitty turned her face to Fran. 'Only one way to find out.'

Fran looked surprised. 'You want me to open it? I was thinking maybe of giving it to the cops.'

Kitty turned her attention back to the traffic on the street. Her shoulders bobbed up and down.

'You, Miss Goody Two Shoes, want me to open it?'

'If you don't want to—'

'No,' Fran replied quickly. 'I want to. I'm just surprised *you* want to.' She pulled the thick envelope out of her purse, laid it on her lap and quickly ripped open the end. Her scream pierced the air like the shriek of a supersonic jet passing through the open windows.

Kitty jammed on the brakes. The car slid sideways across two lanes of traffic. The old Volvo bounced up the curb and slammed into a fire hydrant on the sidewalk in front of a 24-hour pharmacy. The station wagon shivered for a moment, then fell still.

A weary-looking pharmacist with a hairline that receded up his skull and thick dark-rimmed glasses sliding down his nose, one thin hand holding a white prescription bag, stared out the window at them from behind his counter. He made no move to come to their rescue. Kitty figured that was just as well.

After a couple of deep breaths, she managed to speak. 'What on earth?' Kitty shook. Neither of them seemed too hurt, more rattled than anything. At least the airbags hadn't gone off. That would have been a bother. Then again, this was one old Volvo and it might never have had airbags in the first place. Thank heaven for small blessings.

'What's gotten into you, Fran?' A sedan had pulled up alongside them and the driver, a young fellow in a black T-shirt with silver plugs in his ears the size of thimbles, asked if everything was OK. Kitty said they were fine. To prove it, she turned the key in the ignition and the beached Volvo cranked right back up. She gave the driver of the other vehicle a forced smile and a thumbs up. He shook his head, silver flashing under the streetlights, and sped off.

Kitty slowly eased the car down off the sidewalk, wincing as it scraped the curb, and back on to the street. Better to get away before the police showed up and gave her any more trouble that she didn't need.

Besides, there was no real property damage, except to her front bumper where it had bounced off the fire hydrant. She'd check that out once they got back to her – their – apartment. The stubby hydrant itself looked none the worse for wear, except for a bit more chipped red paint than it had five minutes ago.

'Uh, Kitty . . .' Fran's voice trembled.

'What?' Kitty's heart was still racing and adrenaline coursed through her body.

'You might want to take a look at this.' Fran held up a bundle.

Kitty's hand went to the overhead light, but Fran pulled it back down again. 'No,' said Fran, 'no lights. Just look.'

Kitty looked. 'Is that what I think it is?'

Fran nodded soberly. 'Money,' she whispered. 'And lots of it.'

Fourteen

Kitty could barely see straight. Fran had started counting, careful to keep the money low in her lap, out of sight of any passing vehicles. By the time they had reached the apartment, she had tallied one hundred thousand dollars.

'Ten packs of one hundred dollar bills. Thank you, Ben Franklin,' Fran gasped. 'We're rich!'

Kitty pulled a face. 'We can't keep it, you know.' She made to lock the door, realized the passenger side window was nothing but a recent memory, and so didn't bother.

Fran fondled an elaborately carved silver ring in her fingers.

'What's that?'

Fran shrugged. 'Found it at the bottom of the envelope.' She bounced the ring in her hand. 'Do you think it's valuable?'

'Not as valuable as that pile of money,' Kitty replied.

Fran frowned.

'What is it?'

'I dunno. I feel like I've seen a ring like this before. I just can't remember where.'

'Well, put all that loot away, will you?' All that cash in plain sight, money whose provenance she had no clue about, was making her sweat. What on earth was Gretchen going to do with all that cash?

Fran stuffed all the bills back in the envelope, shoved the envelope back in her bag and followed Kitty to the apartment. The minute they were inside, Fred came bounding toward them. Barney wasn't far behind. For a cat, Barney didn't like to be left out. Kitty figured Fred's companionable dog nature was rubbing off on him. Maybe she should get a second cat as a role model so Barney could see how other cats had the whole aloof thing down pat.

Sylvester appeared in the kitchen doorway, giving Kitty and Fran a start. They'd had more than enough excitement for one night. 'Oh, Sylvester.' Kitty saw Fran push her bag behind her back. Was she afraid Sylvester's x-ray vision would see right through the leather? Spot all that loot?

'What are you doing here?' Kitty struggled to keep her voice even.

Sylvester's hand held a glass of tea. He shrugged. 'Fred was barking up a storm. I'm not sure why. I knocked and since you weren't home, I figured I'd keep him company until you got back or he calmed down.'

Kitty rubbed Fred's head and he licked her hand. 'Thanks.'

Sylvester said goodnight. Kitty found Fran in the spare bedroom with the navy blue curtains pulled shut. There was a white futon along the wall under the window, a leftover from her college days. Right now, it was covered with boxes of restaurant supplies that Fran was moving to the floor.

If Kitty had to assign an odor to the bedroom

it would have to be dog. Fred had taken to sleeping on the futon. Maybe now he'd go back to using the big plaid doggie bed she'd shelled out good money for at the warehouse club – either that or Fran was going to have to get used to some cuddling.

Fran looked up when Kitty entered. 'Does that guy always come and go like that?'

Kitty nodded. 'You get used to it.'

'If you say so.' Fran punched the futon's mattress and watched the dust and pet hair billow all around. 'Don't you think it was kind of weird that he was here?'

'Not at all. I told you, he has the key. He's good with the guys.' By the guys, she meant Fred and Barney.

Fran came closer. 'What if he was looking for something? What if Fred hadn't really been barking and this Sylvester character was searching the place?'

Kitty laughed. 'For what?'

'I don't know,' Fran whined. 'Money, evidence.' She punched the futon. 'I don't know,' she repeated. 'Maybe he's the killer?' She squeezed her eyebrows together. 'Does he have an alibi?'

'You're forgetting,' Kitty replied. 'Sylvester is my neighbor. He's not a murder suspect. He didn't know Gretchen and, as far as I know, he's never been to Santa Monica Film Studios.'

'As far as you know,' Fran parroted pointedly.

Kitty tossed her hand. 'Let it go, Fran. Sylvester's harmless.'

'If you say so,' Fran said, not sounding quite ready to let go. 'But wouldn't you like to go snoop around in his place sometime?'

'Not especially.' Sylvester and his roommates may be harmless, but they were not the cleanest bunch around. That was one apartment she'd rather leave untouched.

'Yeah? And what if we did and found one of those CuisineTV potholders?' Fran plopped down on the futon, as if to emphasis her point. 'He could be the killer.'

Kitty shook her head. 'Next you'll be telling me that Mrs Stein upstairs might have stabbed Gretchen in the back.'

Fran pursed her lips. 'What do you really know about this old lady? She's obviously a little whacko and she has got a violent streak, the way you talk about her banging on the floor all the time.'

'I'm taking a bath and then getting some sleep.' This conversation was leading them nowhere. Rest was what she needed.

'What about all this,' Fran lowered her voice, 'money?'

Kitty thought a moment. 'Use it for a pillow. Maybe you'll have some pleasant dreams.'

'Very funny,' said Fran. She pushed her bag under the futon's frame.

Kitty headed down the short hall to the bathroom. 'Hey,' she called, 'you left the window open when you took your bath. Please be careful that Barney doesn't get out.' Kitty stepped into the tub and pulled down the window. 'Hmmm, I'll have to get Mr Frizzell to fix that,' she muttered, noticing for the first time that the screen was bent and hanging loose on the outside.

'No, I didn't,' cried Fran in her own defense. 'Don't go blaming me. I never even opened a window.'

After a million phone calls and endless pleading, Kitty was able to find a Vietnamese shop that was open on a Sunday and willing to replace the glass in the women's cars. Though Fran suggested using some of their newfound cash, Kitty insisted that they pay with plastic.

Kitty drove alone then to Bunny's Bakery in West Hollywood. It was almost ten o'clock; Mr Fandolfi should still be there. Like Barney, Fandolfi was a creature of habit. Holly had let slip the day before that her husband would be back in town Saturday night. That meant he would be at Bunny's Sunday morning. Mr Fandolfi's Sunday morning ritual was a medium latte and fresh blueberry bagel.

Holly rarely tagged along, apparently preferring to linger in bed a little longer than her hubby did. That meant Kitty would be able to catch him alone, which was what she wanted. That's why she told Fran to stay behind. Fran was sweet, but she could be, well, brash was a pretty good word for it.

Kitty found a spot on the street just up the road from Bunny's. The magician sat alone at a black metal table for two tucked up against the brick-clad building in the shade of an elm. He looked dapper as always in a pair of gray wool trousers and matching jacket, with a crisp white shirt underneath. A floppy dark blue paisley kerchief jutted out of his pocket. Kitty wasn't sure if it was for decoration or if a dozen more would follow if she yanked on it.

Fandolfi had intelligent black eyes and a long face. His hair had long ago conceded the battle, and what was left of his follicles he kept swept back over the top of his domed skull. His hair was as unnaturally black as his wife's skin was unnaturally tan.

He stroked the edges of his immaculate moustache. Now that she was here, she realized she needed a plan. The best thing to do was to make the encounter look like a casual encounter. She grabbed her purse, angled across the street and slowly approached from the magician's blind side.

As he lowered his cup from his lips, she strategically dropped her purse at his feet. 'Oops!'

'Ms Karlyle? Is that you?' Fandolfi scooted backward, his eyes sparkling.

'Mr Fandolfi!' Kitty waved, then bent down and snatched her purse off the sidewalk, quickly giving its bottom side a dusting off. Her smile was as broad as a navy destroyer and twice as dazzling – or so she hoped.

'Coming to indulge in a bit of sweetness this fine morning?'

Kitty nodded and let Mr Fandolfi beg her to join him.

Men could be so easy.

She grabbed a coffee and an oatmeal raisin muffin at the counter inside, then joined him on the sidewalk, leaving again for only a moment to wash up inside. 'Mmm,' she said, returning to her seat and taking a whiff of her muffin. 'Smells heavenly.'

Fandolfi agreed. 'Everything Bunny creates is to die for.'

Kitty took a cautious sip of her coffee. 'How was your trip?'

'Trip?'

'Yes, your wife said you were out of town doing a show.'

'Oh, yes.' The magician twisted his napkin around his fingers. 'It went well.' He cleared his throat. 'What about you, young lady?' He raised an eyebrow. 'How was your TV show?'

Kitty walked Fandolfi through her first day shooting the show. 'I don't know if you heard, since you were gone, but Miss Corbett was murdered the same day.'

He nodded somberly. 'Yes, I heard all about that. Such a tragedy. A dear woman.' His eyes seemed to lose focus for a moment.

'Did you know her well?'

Mr Fandolfi shrugged. 'Well enough. We were business associates more than friends. I hadn't seen Gretchen in ages. Of course, we spoke on the phone recently. That's when I recommended you to her.'

Kitty nibbled at her muffin. 'Thank you again for that.'

'Tell me, with Gretchen gone, will the show go on?'

Kitty nodded. 'That's what Bill Barnhard says – he's the head of the network.'

'I see.'

'Unless Steve Barnhard, his son, and Barbara Cartwright get their way. I think they're trying to force me out so she can take over.'

Fandolfi leaned toward Kitty and patted her hand. 'Don't you let them do that to you. Nobody deserves that show more than you.' He rolled the last bite of bagel around in his hand and then Kitty watch it disappear into thin air. 'And no one is better suited.'

'Thanks, you've been very supportive. I really appreciate it, Mr Fandolfi. You must really be a fan. In fact, I noticed you had a potholder at your house.'

The magician sat back, confused. 'Potholder?'

Kitty nodded. 'You know, one of those CuisineTV potholders with the name of the show on it.'

'Oh, yes, of course.' He scratched his chin. 'The potholder. It was a gift from Gretchen.'

'Oh?'

He cleared his throat, then laced it with the remnants of his latte. 'I forgot. I stopped by the studio on my way out of town to see Gretchen – to thank her for giving you a shot. We had made plans.'

He looked uneasy and his eyes ran up and down the street. 'At the last minute, something apparently had come up and she wasn't able to see me but had left me a note – and the potholder that you mentioned.'

'I see,' replied Kitty. What she'd like to see was that note. What had it said? Had Mr Fandolfi really forgotten that he had been to the studio to see Gretchen the day she was murdered, or had he been trying to hide that little fact?

She grabbed her cellphone from her purse and pulled up the image she'd shot of the framed picture at Chevy Czinski's house. 'Do you recognize this picture?'

'Ah, Gretchen and the ape-man.'

'Chevy Czinski,' Kitty said.

The magician nodded. 'Gretchen's first husband. She'd always kept her maiden name.' Mr Fandolfi made a show of looking at his watch, pushed back his chair and bowed. 'I'm afraid I must be off, Kitty. Holly is expecting me and she gets . . .' he paused, 'concerned when I am tardy.'

'I understand.'

'Will you be attending Gretchen's funeral?' Fandolfi inquired as he slid a tip under his saucer.

Kitty nodded and they said their goodbyes. Getting back to the Volvo, Kitty spotted a crumbled sheet of unlined paper tucked under the driver's side wiper blade. Probably another flyer for a store opening, a store closing, some band giving a concert, whatever. If you left your car on the street long enough in LA, it would be plastered with handouts from people selling something, wanting something or missing something.

Kitty snatched this one from the window, wondering which it would be. She turned the paper over. KEEP AWAY was all it read, in big orange block letters that looked like they could have been scrawled with a child's hand.

Kitty's heart skipped a beat, decided that wasn't enough, and skipped another. She looked quickly up and down the busy sidewalk. Who had left the note? And what did it mean?

Fifteen

Kitty spent the entire drive looking over her shoulder and only stopped looking as she pulled up to the gate at Santa Monica Film Studios and rolled down her window. 'Hi, Kitty Karlyle,' she said quickly. 'I know I don't have an appointment, but I was hoping—'

The guard leaned out the window of the guard shack, his head practically in the Volvo. 'You're the cat lady, right?' He was nodding and chewing his lip.

'Um, that's right.'

'Yeah, I know you. I found you standing over Ms Corbett.'

Kitty's eyes fell on his name badge. 'Oh, Brad. Right.' The pasty white face and bristle brush black crew cut. How could she forget? 'I remember you.' She smiled. 'How are you? Working the gate today, huh?' A car tooted its horn behind her. Kitty saw a black Mercedes in her rearview mirror, practically breathing down her neck. 'Listen, Brad. Mind if I talk to you for a second?'

His brow scrunched up and he looked at her somewhat dubiously. The driver of the Mercedes tooted once again. Mercedes drivers probably weren't used to being kept waiting, this one certainly wasn't.

Brad hesitated, then his hand went to an unseen button and the gate rose. 'Pull up along the side of the gatehouse over there,' he instructed.

Kitty parked, waited until the Mercedes had been waved through, and then entered the gatehouse. Brad was leaning against the built-in countertop desk. 'What do you want?'

She ran a finger through her hair and laid a flirty smile on the hapless guard. 'We–ell, Brad.' She let the well draw out like she was casting a fishing line – and she was. She wanted to take a look at the logbook of entries for the day that Gretchen was killed. The police had probably already seen it, but there was no way Jack or anyone else on the force was likely to give her any information on what it had or had not contained. Who had come and gone that day? And did they have alibis?

The answer to those questions could point to a murderer. She was trying to think of the best way to frame her question when the driver of the Mercedes, now idling several yards past the gatehouse, tooted yet again.

Brad stuck his head outside. 'What?'

The driver yelled something unintelligible.

Brad cursed under his breath. 'Just a sec—' He turned to Kitty. 'I'll be right back.'

Kitty told him not to hurry. But she did. The sign-in log was right there on the countertop and she wasted no time turning the pages back to last Friday. There were quite a few names, several that she didn't recognize and several that she did, including hers.

All in all, it seemed pretty useless. Oh well,

she thought. No harm done. Then it struck her. The one name she did not see was Fandolfi's. She looked once more, running her finger up and down the page, even jumping back to Thursday and ahead to Saturday on the off chance that the magician's name had been wrongly entered.

Nothing.

'That's weird,' she muttered.

'Huh?'

Kitty jumped. Brad stood in the doorway, hands on his hips. 'What's weird?' He eyed her suspiciously.

'Oh.' Kitty's arms fell to her sides. 'It's weird the way they have you working out here, instead of inside, like the day we first met.'

He didn't look convinced that her answer made sense, but he shrugged when he answered. 'Happens all the time. We rotate around.' He moved closer and glanced at the open logbook.

Kitty nodded. 'Well,' she pulled her purse close to her chest, 'I suppose I'd better let you get back to your duties.'

He stepped across the entry, blocking her in. 'What exactly was it you wanted anyway?'

'Oh,' Kitty tried to hide her jitters behind a broad smile. 'I was wondering if you had any ideas about who might have wanted to see Ms Corbett dead. Do you?'

'The police already asked me that.' He folded his arms across his chest.

'What did you tell them?'

He wavered a moment, then answered. 'I told them that if the cat lady didn't do it, then her kid probably did.'

Kitty nodded. 'You mean Ms Corbett's daughter, Cindy?'

Brad laughed. 'Her daughter? Why would she kill Gretchen? Heck, Gretchen gave that girl everything – and then some. Kill the goose that's laying the golden eggs?' He shook his head in disgust. 'I don't think so – the spoiled brat.' He practically spat the words out.

'I'm confused. If not Cindy, then who?'

A delivery van pulled up at the gate. Brad twisted around. 'Be right with you!' He turned back to Kitty. 'Her dimwitted son, that's who.' He stepped outside the gatehouse and laid his hands on the open windowsill of the delivery van. 'How you been, man?' he said to the driver.

Kitty squeezed out past the guard and the van and hurried to her car. Mr Fandolfi had lied about coming to the studio the day Gretchen was murdered. Why? Why would he claim to have been there when he hadn't?

And the biggest discovery yet – Gretchen had a son. A son that Brad the security guard thought could be a killer.

She couldn't wait to tell Fran what she'd learned. But first, she'd do some snooping around inside. Kitty slid through the unlocked soundstage door and headed for Gretchen's office. Maybe she could find some more clues there, perhaps even some more love letters. Letters that might explain who this mysterious lover had been. Something that the police might have missed.

There were few people about and no one paid

her much attention. Sonny was ensconced behind his desk with his door open. He waved as she passed. Sonny had wasted no time getting back to work since being given his old job back. He had certainly benefited from Gretchen Corbett's sudden demise.

Kitty hurried on to Gretchen's office and ran into Jack. 'Jack,' she cried, half scared out of her wits and half delighted. He stood just inside the doorway. 'W–what are you doing here?'

He cocked his head and wiggled his eyebrows, legs spread wide, effectively blocking her way. 'Doing my job. Looking for clues. Following up leads. Interviewing witnesses.' Her fiancé folded his arms across his chest. 'What about you, Kitty? I could ask you the same question.' His left eyebrow shot up. 'And I think I just did.'

'Well . . .'

Jack grunted, took her arm and led her back out into the hall. 'Yes?'

'I, er, came in to work on the show?' Kitty replied. She hadn't meant for it to sound like a question, but it had come out that way.

'That's funny,' said Jack, pushing her gently up against the wall, 'I heard the show is on hold until Tuesday. And, if I'm not mistaken, this is Sunday. Why aren't you out delivering meals to your hungry little pet clients?'

Kitty squeezed out from between his arms. 'I thought I'd do some food research – for the show. Besides, you know I don't do my pet chef work on Sundays. That's the one day of the week I take off.'

Jack nodded. 'I forgot. Research, huh?' He frowned. 'You're not still trying to solve Gretchen's murder, are you?'

Kitty raised her chin haughtily. 'So what if I am?'

Jack sighed. 'Leave it to the police, Kitty. We know how to do our jobs, without the aid of amateurs. Besides, you could get hurt.'

Kitty thought of the crumpled up, anonymous warning note in her purse. 'Oh, really? I must be making some progress, otherwise why would I have received this?' She pulled the paper from her purse and thrust it at Jack.

He slowly peeled the note open, his face darkening as he read. 'This is serious, Kitty. Where did you get this note? You should have given this to the police right away. There could be fingerprints. This could be evidence.'

'I found it on my windshield this morning,' Kitty said, practically boasting. She explained the circumstances to Jack, who shook his head the whole time.

'I don't like this at all,' he said, tapping the paper. 'You're getting threatening notes. What is that it's written with? Lipstick? Crayon?'

'I'm not sure. Lipstick, I think.'

'This case is a mess. You're getting threatening notes, I find out Gretchen Corbett's condo gets turned upside-down.'

'What?'

'The producer's condo. Someone or someones really did a number on the joint. They ransacked the place—'

'Ransacked?' blurted Kitty. 'But, that can't be.

All we did was . . .' All she and Fran had done was open a few drawers, poke around a little bit. They certainly hadn't trashed the place.

Jack eyed her warily. 'What do you mean, that can't be? Who is this we and what did you do, Kitty?'

'N–nothing. I mean, I'm just surprised is all.' Please, please, please let there be no fingerprints of ours, she thought desperately. 'Any idea who would do such a thing?'

Jack pursed his lips. 'We're looking into it. In fact, we may just about have this case wrapped up.'

'Oh?' Kitty's heart sank. She had been counting on solving this crime herself.

'You sound almost disappointed.'

'Don't be silly. I want Gretchen's killer found and brought to justice as much as anyone does.'

'Kitty, as much as I am not sure I want to know the answer – you didn't go breaking into Gretchen's condo, did you?'

'Don't be silly, Jack.' She smiled and squeezed his hand. Technically, she wasn't lying. They hadn't *broken* in. After all, Fran had a key.

Kitty figured a quick change of subject was in order. 'So, where is the lieutenant?' She was not going to speak the vixen's name aloud.

'Having a little talk with a person of interest,' Jack answered. His head swiveled. 'In fact, here she comes now.'

She even walks like a runway model, Kitty noticed. She silently cursed as Lieutenant Nordstrom came up the hall with a doughy looking man in his thirties who seemed to shuffle more than step. He was wearing baggy blue jeans and a wrinkled green and blue flannel shirt. His greasy black hair was slicked back from a large, lumpy forehead.

It wasn't until they got up close that Kitty realized that the man's hands were handcuffed behind him. 'Ready to go, Jack?' Nordstrom ignored Kitty. 'Teddy, here, is ready to come down to the station with us.' She nudged his shoulder. 'Aren't you, Teddy?'

He nodded silently, his expression glum. His gray eyes dull.

'I'll be right there,' replied Jack.

'Who was that?' Kitty asked once the lieutenant and her prisoner were gone.

'That's Thadeus – or Teddy, as everybody around here calls him. He's the custodian. Teddy Czinski.'

'Czinski?' Kitty coughed. Her eyes bulged. 'As in Chevy Czinski?'

'Yeah.'

'What do you want to talk to him for?'

'One of the cameramen claims he saw Teddy coming out of Gretchen's office not long before you found her. We've been wanting to talk to him for the past couple of days but he hadn't been around the studio since and he hadn't been at his place. Finally, we got word from security that he'd come in today. And since we'd found his finger and thumb print on her locket—'

Kitty interrupted. 'He killed Gretchen?'

Jack shrugged. 'Maybe.'

'But why?'

'Who knows? Why does any child hate one of their parents enough to want to kill them?'

Sixteen

Kitty's head was spinning so fast she thought it would come unscrewed. Not only did Chevy Czinski have a son, that son worked at Santa Monica Film Studios and was Gretchen's son to boot.

Did that mean that Cindy was also Chevy's daughter? Or had there been another man in Gretchen's life who'd fathered Cindy? Maybe the mysterious Cam?

And no matter what the answers, what did it all mean?

She was more confused now than ever. She'd never admit it to Jack, but this crime solving wasn't as easy as they made it look on TV shows. All she knew for sure was that Gretchen had been killed at some point during her show. That gave most people alibis. After all, like Kitty, they'd been busy with the show itself. The most likely culprit was someone not directly connected to the show then. Somebody like Fandolfi.

After getting Kitty to agree to keep her nose out of official police business for the millionth time, Jack, looking somewhat appeased, departed. He'd taken Kitty's threatening note with him and said he'd have it checked for latent prints, though he didn't sound optimistic. 'If we find Thadeus

Czinski's prints on your note, that will pretty much shut the door on his future.'

'I only got the note this morning, Jack. If Teddy was at the studio, he couldn't possibly have written it.'

Jack was already shaking his head. 'Teddy only showed up for work about twenty minutes ago.'

Poor Teddy, thought Kitty. She didn't know the young man at all, but something about him made her feel sorry for him. He looked so harmless, so innocent. She couldn't believe for a minute that he had murdered Gretchen – his very own mother.

Kitty had agreed to meet Jack for dinner. That still left her plenty of time to investigate. She'd told him that she'd keep her nose clean, but she hadn't said anything one way or the other about getting her hands dirty.

'Sorry to stop by unannounced,' Kitty said.

'That's all right,' replied Chevy, grabbing a scoop of giraffe kibble and pouring it into the large stainless steel bowl that belonged to Clement, his wobble-legged giraffe. 'I'm not much for company – human company, that is – but I make an exception for you. I do enjoy your company, Kitty.'

Kitty watched the old beast as he ambled over and lazily nosed at his bowl – Clement, not Chevy.

'So,' said Chevy, turning and heading for the front porch, 'what can I do for you?'

There was no point beating around the bush.

'I wanted to ask you about your son, Thadeus,' Kitty replied, taking up a seat in one of the comfy rockers on the porch beside the former actor.

Chevy Czinski leaned back, half-closed his eyes, and rocked back and forth several times before answering. 'Teddy is a good boy.' He sighed deeply. It was a long, tired and sorrowful sound. 'A bit slow. But he has a good heart.'

He turned and looked Kitty in the eyes. 'He would never have murdered Gretchen.'

'You know about that?' Kitty hadn't expected Mr Czinski to be aware of Teddy's current predicament and had been worrying herself sick over how to break the news. It appeared she had been worrying for nothing.

Chevy nodded glumly. 'I received a telephone call a short time ago. The police are questioning Teddy now.'

'Have they charged him with . . .' she hesitated, 'anything?' She couldn't bring herself to say the word *murder* to the young man's own father.

Chevy said that they had not. 'I've called a lawyer. He's on his way down to the police station as we speak.'

'I don't believe he's guilty either, Mr Czinski. That's why I came to see you.'

He watched her expectantly.

'You see, I'm trying to find out who killed Gretchen myself.'

'You? Isn't that a job better left to the police?'

Kitty gritted her teeth. That was exactly what Jack kept saying. 'Yes, but don't you see? Gretchen was very kind to me. She'd given me a fantastic opportunity.' She paused, her voice dropping. 'And she was murdered with one of my knives. I feel sort of responsible.'

'Nonsense. It's not your fault someone used one of your knives. If not yours, he or she,' he said pointedly, 'would have found another.'

'I suppose.'

'And now you want to know who might have wanted to see Gretchen dead?' He smiled and placed his hands on his arthritic knees. 'Like me, for instance?'

'Well . . .'

Chevy rose with some effort. 'Come, I want to show you something.' Kitty followed the ex-actor into his log cabin to the den. 'My past,' he said, spreading his arms.

'Wow,' said Kitty, though she'd seen it all before when she and Fran had been poking around. Not that she was going to mention that now. She wasn't sure how one of her clients would feel about her snooping around in their home uninvited, but she was pretty sure they wouldn't be super happy about it.

The old man fondled a stuffed lion's head lovingly. 'Gretchen and I were married then.' He pointed to a grainy photo of the two of them on safari. 'We were quite the couple.' He paused, as if embarrassed. 'And quite in love.'

'And then you had Teddy?'

'Yes, and not long after, we were divorced.' He slumped into a chair. 'I'm not sure what happened to us. It was like a candle had gone out. I'm not certain either of us can explain why, but love turned to hate.'

Kitty felt a wave of sadness wash over her. 'I'm sorry.'

He looked into Kitty's eyes. 'She stole the idea for the show from me, you know.' He shook his head. 'Gretchen was always very ambitious. She was ruthless. She'd do anything to get ahead.'

A sad smile worked its way across his face. 'I'm afraid I never had much ambition. I suppose that was one of the things that drove us apart. You see,' he said, slapping his knees, 'I'm happy just being home, caring for my pets . . .'

'I don't understand,' said Kitty. 'What do you mean she stole the show from you?'

Chevy let her question hang in the air for a minute before replying. He gazed out the window while answering. '*The Pampered Pet*. Oh, the name of the show was different. But it was my show. I'd been telling her for years that CuisineTV ought to add a cooking show for pets to their line up.'

He laughed a self-deprecating laugh. 'There was even a time when I thought I might host it myself.' He turned to Kitty once again. 'But who'd want to watch a washed up old Tarzan, eh?'

'When did you find out? About the show, I mean.'

'The day you came by and told me about your appointment. I have to confess, I was quite chuffed. I called Gretchen. We argued. I told her she had no right to steal my idea. I demanded my share of the profits. The show is potentially worth lots of money.'

'I'm not greedy. It wasn't for me.' His gloomy

eyes looked out over his pens. 'It takes a great deal of money to care for these animals. They need me.'

'What did Miss Corbett say?'

'She hung up on me. I was so angry, I went down to the studio and demanded to see her. When I confronted her, she laughed in my face and ordered me to leave.'

Kitty stood motionless. Was he about to confess to murdering his ex-wife?

'No, I didn't stab her in the back. Though I suppose that would have been ironic, eh?' In the distance, one of the lions snorted. 'In the end, I simply left.'

'Have you told the police all this? I didn't see your name in the log that security keeps.'

He seemed surprised. 'You wouldn't. I hopped the fence. I knew Gretchen would never allow me on the lot.' He straightened. 'You might not think it to look at me, but these old bones can still perform a stunt or two,' he said, with pride.

A stunt like murder? wondered Kitty.

'What about the potholder?'

'Potholder?' He looked genuinely perplexed.

Kitty nodded. 'I saw it in your kitchen the other day. It's a souvenir CuisineTV potholder for *The Pampered Pet* TV show. They were distributed to everyone in the audience the day of the taping.'

'I remember. Teddy brought it home.'

'Teddy was here?' Kitty remembered Jack saying that the young man had been missing for several days after the murder.

'Yes, he stayed with me for a night or two after his mother's death. He didn't want to be alone.

My son has a small apartment in Santa Monica. He was with me until this morning when he said he wanted to go back to work. I told him it was too soon, but he insisted. I think he simply needed something to do.' He paused a moment, reflecting. 'As do we all.'

Kitty's eyes fell on the elephant tusk above a movie poster on the wall. She'd seen it earlier, when she was here with Fran. Now she remembered seeing a similar tusk in Gretchen's condo.

Chevy noted her interest. 'That's from Bull. He was a remarkable animal.'

'You have only the one tusk?'

'Gretchen has the other. I'm not sure why, but she insisted on having it in the divorce. Perhaps simply to annoy me.' His eyes sparkled. 'Maybe I can get it back now.'

That raised an interested question. 'Who inherits? Teddy?'

Chevy shrugged. 'Teddy . . . and Cindy, I suppose.'

'Is Cindy your and Gretchen's daughter?'

He chuckled. 'Oh, no. And thank goodness for that. She's a handful and more. That girl ought to be penned up herself. From what I hear, she's always spending like there's no tomorrow.'

'But why and who's—'

The sound of a ringing phone interrupted her question. Mr Czinski raised a crooked finger, signaling Kitty to wait. She desperately wanted to know why Cindy was such a handful that Mr Czinski felt she deserved to be penned up. And just who was her father?

He fished in his trouser pocket and pulled out

an old red flip phone. He muttered a few sentences, pocketed the phone and said to Kitty, 'That's Teddy's lawyer. He would like me to come downtown now.' He rose, using the chair's arm to steady himself. 'You understand.'

Kitty did.

She stopped for gas on her way back from Malibu and, while at the station, dialed Fran's number. She answered on the first ring. The first thing that Fran wanted to know was where Kitty had been. After catching her new roommate up to speed, Kitty quizzed Fran about Gretchen's mysterious daughter, Cindy.

'What about her?' asked Fran.

'What can you tell me? What's she like? What does she do?'

There was a pause at the other end of the line. 'Not much. I've only seen her once or twice in the five years I've been working for Gretch. She didn't come around the studio much. When she did, they usually fought like a couple of jealous cats.

'And I don't know that she does anything, besides shop, that is. Always came to the studio in some fancy red Mercedes sports coupe convertible.'

'What about her father, have you met him? What's he like? Did he get along with Gretchen? Would he have any reason to want to see her dead? Heavy alimony payments, maybe?'

Fran laughed through the phone. 'Heck, girlfriend. I don't know. That's a lot of questions you're throwing at me. Gretchen didn't talk much about her exes. She barely spoke about her current boyfriends, let alone what she called her past tenses.'

Kitty asked Fran again if she thought Cindy's father, Gretchen's ex, might have some motive for wanting his former wife dead.

'They were divorced. There was bound to be some acrimony. But I'm pretty sure that's ancient history,' Fran declared.

'Maybe Cindy's father is the mysterious Cam from the letters we found in Gretchen's condo.'

Fran concurred. 'But those letters didn't look that old. Do you think maybe they had something going again?'

Kitty said she thought there might be a chance.

She could practically see Fran nodding her head in agreement as she said, 'That would make sense. There was a time when Gretchen was acting all coy-like. And happy. But whenever I asked her why, she clammed up. Like I said, Gretchen didn't like to talk much about her love life. Though she didn't mind talking about her daughter's. I know for a while there that she was pretty upset with some guy that Cindy was seeing.'

Kitty hopped back in the Volvo and started the engine. It was time to pay a visit to Cindy Corbett. Maybe she could provide some answers to this mystery. 'Do you know how to get in touch with Cindy?'

'I've got her number and her address in my phone. Gretchen often used me as a go-between. Like I said, they weren't all that mothery-daughtery.'

'Great,' Kitty replied. 'What's the address?'

'Oh, no, you don't!' Fran's voice roared playfully over the phone. 'I've been sitting home alone all morning – no offense to Fred and Barney – while you're out having all the fun. If you want this address, you're going to have to come and get it and take me with you.'
Kitty knew when she'd been beaten.

Seventeen

Fran was waiting outside the apartment when Kitty pulled up. Fran had a red scarf knotted in her hair and had poured herself into a pair of black jeggings, along with which she had chosen a loose fitting top the color of cocoa butter.
Kitty asked Fran if she had the m-o-n-e-y.
'What are you spelling for?'
'Sorry,' Kitty tittered. 'I guess I'm nervous.'
'It's in my bag,' Fran said. 'I don't feel comfortable letting it get out of my sight.' Both girls found themselves scanning the parking lot for strangers.
'Neither do I,' Kitty concurred. She didn't see anyone that looked suspicious, but then, could you really tell a cold-blooded killer from a harmless nursery school teacher, for instance?
'Besides, we might want to make a side trip to Rodeo Drive before the day is done.'
Kitty thought not. Rodeo Drive was a preposterously expensive Beverly Hills shopping district.

She planned to take the envelope to Jack's tonight and break the news of what she'd done to him over dinner, preferably after a bottle of wine, of which she would be sure he drank more than his fair share.

Knowing Jack, he was not going to take kindly to her and Fran breaking into Gretchen's apartment and snooping around and making off with a purse full of love letters. But it was time he knew. If she somehow lost all that money before then, she didn't know what would happen or what the police would do. Probably lock her and Fran up and throw the key in the Pacific Ocean.

Following Fran's directions, Kitty eventually found herself staring up at a beautiful modern, white beach house along the Santa Monica coastline. There was a white picket fenced-in garden out front, punctuated with explosions of color. She found a spot for the Volvo on the side street around the corner and they walked over.

'How are you planning to talk your way inside?' Fran asked, slinging her bag from one shoulder to the other. 'Like I told you, Cindy isn't exactly my friend.'

'Easy,' answered Kitty. 'You're going to tell her that you have something for her – from her mom.'

Fran stopped, looking perplexed. The overhead sun played off her YSL shades. 'And just what might this something be?' She placed her fists on her hips.

'The envelope.' Kitty pulled open the front gate.

Her nostrils picked up the scent of Oriental poppies.

Fran's jaw dropped. 'Not,' she glanced at the gardener on her knees at the edge of a thickly mulched flower bed in the small front garden and lowered her voice, 'the money?'

'Yep.' Kitty explained her plan. She'd thought it up on the way over. They'd tell Cindy that Gretchen had left an envelope with Fran the day she was killed, which Fran was supposed to deliver to her. 'That will get us in the door. Not only that, but we'll see whether she knows anything about the money.'

'Yeah,' grumbled Fran, 'but how will we get out the door with the money once we've shown it to that greedy little princess?'

Kitty checked on the gardener; an elderly Latino woman in a wide-brimmed straw hat and baggy white pants and shirt. She was using a pair of fine scissors to trim the flowers and paid no attention to them, keeping her focus on the job at hand. The greedy little princess apparently liked a well-kept garden. So how bad could she be?

Using Fran as a shield, Kitty pulled the envelope from Fran's bag, dumped the contents in her own purse, then pushed the empty envelope back into Fran's bag.

'We're giving her an empty envelope?' Fran asked, her voice laced with skepticism.

'We're *showing* her an empty envelope.' Kitty rang the bell. 'Cindy won't know that it's empty. And if she should get her hands on it, we won't lose the cash. You never mentioned, did Gretchen tell you why she wanted you to bring her the money? Like, what she intended to do with it or who she intended to give it to?'

'Are you kidding? I didn't even know there was money in the envelope, let alone enough to retire on, girl. I just picked up the envelope, dropped it in my purse and then forgot all about it what with the murder and all.'

Kitty made an unhappy face. 'The envelope does look awfully thin though.' Kitty reached into Fran's bag and threw some loose items from her purse into the envelope; old coupons, a compact, an ad for a nail salon.

'That ought to do the trick.' The envelope looked quite substantial now. 'Quick,' Kitty said, thrusting the envelope back in Fran's bag as she caught the sound of steps approaching.

The door cracked open and a mousy face with two inquisitive blue eyes appeared in the opening. All that was missing was the whiskers. Tiny wrinkle lines laced the corners of the woman's eyes. Kitty figured her to be in her late thirties or early forties. A fruity aroma of perfume wafted out. Kitty didn't recognize the scent.

'Yes?' Medium brown hair framed a plump round face with pale skin. If this was Cindy Corbett, she apparently didn't enjoy spending time at the beautiful stretch of beach that was mere steps from her front door – a location that people paid top dollar for. In this case, that had probably been Cindy's mom, Gretchen.

'Hey, Cindy. It's me, Fran.' Fran waved from behind Kitty's shoulder and gave Gretchen's daughter her best grin.

Cindy responded with downturned lips. 'What do you want?'

Kitty held out her hand. 'Miss Corbett? I'm Kitty Karlyle. I worked with your mother.' Briefly. She pushed as much sincerity as she could into her words. It wasn't hard; in the short time she'd known Gretchen she had come to like her very much. She may have been pushy and ambitious, but she had been terribly kind to Kitty herself. 'I'm – we're very sorry for your loss.'

Cindy leaned out the door, her grip on the burnished bronze handle, and shrugged. She wore light brown silk slacks and a tight-knitted green turtleneck sweater. She looked at Kitty's extended hand as if someone had just offered her a handful of Ebola virus. 'The funeral is tomorrow. If you like, you can pay your condolences then.'

The door began to close.

Kitty spoke quickly. 'Uh – could we speak to you for a moment?'

The door came to a stop. 'What about?'

'Well,' Kitty glanced at Fran, who looked flummoxed, then pressed on. 'Actually, your mother had something for you. We thought you might like to have it. Fran was supposed to give it to you earlier, and then, well . . .'

Cindy chewed on her lip a moment. 'What is it?'

'It's so hot out here.' Kitty waved a hand in front of her face. 'Would you mind if we come in?'

Cindy frowned as if she'd just been asked to donate a kidney, but ushered them inside.

They took up seats in a small sitting area that looked out across the front garden to the sea. The surface of the water was relatively calm, with only a few light swells slowly making their way to shore.

The glass-topped table beside Cindy held a single red rose in a delicate looking pale pink vase. A small tin of pastilles rested beside it. No doubt the rose had come from the bush Kitty spotted in the garden.

'So,' Cindy said, crossing and uncrossing her legs, her gold sandals flashing. 'You have something for me from my mother?' She extended her hand.

Fran glanced at Kitty who nodded. Fran extracted the envelope from her bag. It was looking rather sad, a bit crumpled and abused.

Cindy did not look impressed. 'An envelope?'

'Don't you recognize it?' Please say yes, thought Kitty.

'Should I?' Cindy's expression turned even more sour, which Kitty hadn't thought could be possible.

With as much innocence as she could muster, Kitty turned to Fran. 'Fran, dear, I don't think that's the right envelope at all.'

Fran looked confused for a moment as she eyed the big envelope. 'Huh?'

Kitty was shaking her head adamantly. 'No, don't you see? That envelope is unlabeled. The envelope for Cindy has her name written on it.'

'Oh,' said Fran, turning the big envelope around and around in her hand. 'Silly me.' She opened the metal tab and peered inside. 'You're right. This isn't the right envelope at all.'

Cindy folded her arms over her chest, her eyes flashed danger signals. 'Just what are you up to?'

'Up to?' Kitty feigned ignorance. 'Why, we only wanted to—'

Cindy Corbett rose. 'I think you two should leave.'

Kitty's mind raced. This wasn't going well at all. She remained seated. 'Of course. I suppose we should be going. You probably want to be alone now, with your family. Your brother, Thadeus—'

Cindy snorted. 'That simpleton?'

'And your father, Cam.'

Cindy glared down at Kitty. 'Who?' Her confusion seemed genuine.

'Your father,' Kitty gulped. 'Cam. Cameron?'

Cindy laughed like she was auditioning for the part of the evil queen in some Disney melodrama. 'I don't know who you're talking about, but I don't know any Cameron. And my dear brother, who I hear may have killed Mom, can rot in jail for all I care.' She paced the room and looked out toward the Pacific. 'And Daddy,' she said with disquieting and mocking undertones, 'would never step foot in my house.'

When Cindy turned back to the ladies, she was grinning madly. 'Daddy and I have what you might call a magic relationship.'

'Why, uh, that's nice,' Kitty said, politely.

Cindy's grin widened into a chasm of bleached white teeth and wet pink tongue. 'Yes, Daddy sends me a big fat allowance each month and I do my best to make it disappear.' She smirked.

'He doesn't live locally?' Fran asked.

Cindy Corbett pointed to the door. 'Out. And if you do have something for me from my mother, bring it to the funeral tomorrow.'

Kitty rose. 'Would you mind if I use the bathroom before I go?' What she really wanted was a chance to search the place, including the kitchen for any evidence, like one of those potholders that seemed to keep showing up everywhere she went.

'There's a gas station up the street,' Cindy replied callously. She practically threw the women out the door. 'And if you're at the service tomorrow, you'd better have my mother's envelope with you. Otherwise,' she yelled at their fleeing backs, 'I'll have my attorney all over you!'

Eighteen

'Not exactly a homerun, was it?' Fran remarked between bites of her roast beef sandwich. The ladies had stopped off for a late lunch at the Musso and Frank Grill on Hollywood Boulevard, partly to appease their stomachs, partly to lick their wounds.

'Hardly,' agreed Kitty. She wiped her hands on her napkin and took a sip of tea. 'So, where do we stand?'

'Hip deep in doo-doo,' Fran replied quickly. 'Are you sure you don't want one of these?' She swirled her mimosa under Kitty's nose.

Kitty shook her head. 'Too early for me. I'll stick to the peach ice tea.'

'And the tofu burger,' Fran teased.

Kitty smiled. 'Don't knock it, until you've tried it. They're delicious and they're good for you.' Of course, the plateful of French fries that came with it – and that she kept telling herself to stay away from, but somehow every time she put one in her mouth another popped up into her fingers as if by magic – were as delicious as they were deliciously fattening. 'Now,' she said, wiping her greasy fingers on a paper napkin, 'who wanted Gretchen dead?'

'Not me,' Fran said. She waved her nearly empty glass at the waiter. He nodded and shouted from across the courtyard that he'd bring her another. 'I wanted Gretch alive.' Fran's eyes were somewhat glassy. Kitty wasn't certain if it was the alcohol oozing out or her emotions bubbling up. 'She was more than my meal ticket, she was my friend.'

Kitty pulled her pen from her purse and wrote on the back of a napkin. 'I guess I'll have to scratch you from my list of suspects.' Kitty's eyes sparkled playfully. 'But let's think about who we can add.'

'Sonny Sarkisian.' Fran grabbed one of Kitty's fries and dipped it in ketchup. 'Princess Cindy. She's about as warm and fuzzy as a cactus. And she did not get along with her mother or her father, whoever he is.'

Kitty jotted down the names. 'I agree.' Teddy worked as a janitor. He might have been resentful of his mother's wealth, his father's as well. His half-sister, Cindy, obviously went through money like it was bottled water. Either or both of them might have wanted to see their mother out of the way so they could inherit.

'And there's Barbara Cartwright.' Kitty wrote. 'Those two were bitter enemies and it sounds like Gretchen did everything she could to keep Ms Cartwright from getting the new show.'

'Yeah,' said Fran, raising an eyebrow. 'And giving it to you. It sounds like Barbara might like to see you dead, too. I'd be careful if I was you.'

Kitty looked taken aback. Fran sounded so serious. 'Do you really think Barbara might do something, I mean, try to hurt me?'

Fran shrugged. 'I'm just saying. You've got something that she wants.' She accepted her second mimosa from the lanky waiter then leaned across the table. 'Maybe she stabbed Gretchen in the back and has got you in her sights.'

Kitty felt a chill run up her spine. Was it a potential knife plunging into her back? She rubbed her arms hard. This whole detective thing could become a lot more dangerous than she had imagined. She wolfed down a couple of fries – for courage, or so she told herself, then fanned out the napkin. 'I suppose we should add Teddy Czinski to the list.'

'I suppose,' agreed Fran. 'But it's hard to imagine him killing his own mother. I saw him around the studio once in a while, though he mostly came in after hours. He always seemed so quiet and harmless.'

'I agree, but sometimes those silent types are hiding a lot of crazy.'

'Agreed.' Fran tossed back her mimosa. 'And both children stand to inherit a chunk of change.' She polished off the last bit of her double cheeseburger. 'There's also Chevy Czinski.'

Kitty added his name to the list. 'He seems so sweet. And lonely.' She thought about him living all alone out in the mountains, just himself and his animals. 'But he did get very angry at the mention of Gretchen's name the first time I brought it up. And she did steal his idea for the cooking show.'

'So he claims.'

'So he claims,' chimed Kitty. She added another name. 'Let's not forget Gretchen's other ex, Cam.' The sun hit her eyes and she scooted her chair several inches back into the shade of a palm. It seemed so strange to be talking about murder outdoors on a day like this, plenty of sun and blue sky, enjoying an afternoon meal with a friend among the palm trees and delicious aromas spilling over from the kitchen.

Fran nodded. 'And Steve.'

Kitty agreed. 'I've got him at the top of my list. I wonder what his alibi is for the time during the taping of my show. Any ideas?'

Fran shook her head. 'I didn't notice him, in particular. Then again, I generally try to avoid him. He *should* have been on set, but I couldn't swear to it.'

'And with all the lights and so many people, I

couldn't tell you who was and wasn't there myself.' Kitty tapped the tip of her pen on the tabletop in frustration. 'I sure would like to grill him about Gretchen's murder.' She leaned back. 'What is it they say? Means, motive and opportunity? Steve had all three.'

'And he lives in Gretchen's building.'

'And is romantically involved with Barbara Cartwright. Another suspect at the top of our list.' Kitty huffed. 'I suppose there's nothing we can do until tomorrow. Steve will be at the funeral, no doubt. I'll have to try to interrogate him there.'

'Why wait until tomorrow?' Fran said. 'Let's go talk to him today.'

'How? Do you think he'll let us into his building, especially if he thinks we are trying to grill him about Gretchen's murder?'

Fran made a face and squirmed. 'Steve is so going to kill me.'

Kitty perked up. 'Why? What is it?'

'I really shouldn't—'

'Spill it, Fran.'

Fran sighed. 'I had promised I wouldn't tell anyone, *ever*,' she said. 'Oh, well.'

'Fran, you're driving me crazy with curiosity. Tell me now, what are you holding back on?' The older couple dining next to them looked in their direction. Kitty lowered her voice. 'Out with it,' she whispered.

'Steve Barnhard is a man of habits. Many habits.' Fran pulled out her phone and checked the time display. 'If he's being true to form, I know exactly where Stevie boy is.'

Kitty crossed her arms over her chest and waited.

'This being Sunday, Steve went to the shooting range—'

'Shooting range?' Kitty interrupted. Hmmm, a man with a gun hobby. Gretchen hadn't been shot, but still . . .

It could mean something.

'Hey, some people go to church, some go fire off a few rounds.' Fran waved her hand in the air. Apparently she wasn't reading the same thing into it that Kitty was. 'To each his own, right?'

Kitty nodded. 'I'm not sure I want to meet a potential murder suspect at a shooting range.' She could picture him standing there with a loaded gun in his hands while she accused him of murdering Gretchen. She shook the thought out of her head. There was no way that was going to end in a pretty fashion.

'Are you going to let me talk?'

'Sorry. Continue.'

Fran wiped her mouth with a napkin and pushed back her chair. 'You know what, you're not going to believe it anyway. You're going to have to see this for yourself. Oh, Steve is going to kill me,' she said, worriedly shaking her head.

'And if we hurry, we might just catch him in the act.' Fran stood. 'Come on, pay the bill. We've got to boogie.'

'Catch him in the act of what?' Kitty asked, reaching into her purse and pulling out enough cash to cover the meal and still leave a decent tip for their server. She threw the bills on the table and weighted them down with a saucer so they wouldn't blow away. Fran was already at the sidewalk and moving fast. 'Wait for me!'

Nineteen

Fran guided Kitty to a small street off of Melrose Boulevard in the heart of Los Angeles' Melrose District, not too far from Kitty's own apartment. The Melrose District is a funky neighborhood, noted for its alternative shops and restaurants. Kitty thought it a great place to live, though the narrow street Fran led her down was unfamiliar territory. There was a pleasant bohemian atmosphere and, with the weather near perfect by LA standards, it bustled with activity.

Fran glanced at the time. 'Come on,' she implored, 'if we hurry, we can still catch him.'

She bustled across the street, looking a bit wobbly. Probably the result of those two mimosas now stewing inside her under the hot LA sun. Kitty did her best to keep up. Though, what they were going to catch Steve doing – and plenty of lurid images came to mind – she truly had no idea at all.

But of all the tawdry, dishonest and wicked things that she'd pictured him doing, she never would have imagined seeing Steve Barnhard doing what she was about to be accosted with the sight of.

Fran paced up the sidewalk, looking right and left. Finally, she slowed and crept up to a quaint little storefront with a yellow and pink canvas awning. The sign on the awning read *Come To The Point*. Fran peeked through the tinted window, then turned to Kitty and whispered. 'Take a look.'

Kitty, rather dubiously, pressed her nose to the glass. It took a moment for her eyes to take in the interior. There were several long wooden tables spread out evenly in the middle, with padded folding chairs scattered along the lengths of them. Along the edges of the interior, shelves of goods ran from floor to ceiling. The shelves were filled with an assortment of threads, needles and various kits in paper and plastic packaging.

There, in the middle of the room, amongst a group of wizened old women, sat Steve. In tattered jeans, a loose blue T-shirt and a yellow bandana wrapped around his forehead. He held a long needle in his hand and was peering intently at whatever it was he was creating.

Kitty pulled away from the window. 'Needlepoint?' She was flabbergasted. Here she'd been expecting to see him torturing kittens, stealing food from the homeless, or tying a damsel to a railroad track – anything but this.

Fran nodded and pulled Kitty around the side of the stucco building and into the rutted gravel alleyway. 'Go figure, right? Smarmy Steve Barnhard sitting around doing needlepoint with a gaggle of grandmothers.'

Kitty couldn't help but giggle. It was rather funny. She forced herself to stop. After all, there was a good chance that Steve, embroiderer or not, was a cold-blooded killer. 'Follow my lead.' Kitty broke away from Fran and marched up the steps to the front door of the shop. She took a breath, motioned for Fran to keep up, and then stepped inside.

Careful to keep her back to Steve, she watched him out of the corner of her eye while pretending to examine various needlepoint kits held in cubbies along the wall. Actually, the one she was holding in her hand right now, featuring three playful gray kittens and a ball of lavender yarn, was rather adorable. Maybe she should take up needlepoint herself?

Holding on to the needlepoint kit, she eased her way nearer to Steve's table. Fran clung close to her side, rubbing elbows and shuffling her feet nervously. When Kitty was directly behind Steve, she took a calculated step backward, giving Steve's chair a solid jolt. 'Oh, excuse me!' she exclaimed, spinning around.

Steve spun too. 'That's all right, no harm—' His eyes froze over. 'You!' He glanced at Fran. 'And you,' he said with what seemed an extra dash of contempt. With a flurry, his hands drew his needlepoint in closer to his narrow chest, like a mother bird protecting her young.

Maybe he hadn't wanted Kitty and Fran to see what he was sewing. But it was too late for that. She caught a quick glimpse of a red and white painted lighthouse perched atop a craggy island with a bit of sea in the foreground. The scene looked vaguely familiar. Then again, it was a lighthouse and all lighthouses looked pretty much alike, didn't they?

Steve caught her looking at his project. 'What are you looking at?' he demanded. 'And what are you doing here?' His forehead was pink with rage.

Kitty hesitated before speaking. Not only was Steve her boss, his father was *The Boss*. The one who could get her fired if she said or did the wrong thing. She'd have to tread carefully, very carefully. 'Oh, hello Steve.' She faked as sincere a smile as she could muster. She noticed that Fran was doing the same, though the mimosas seemed to be having an altogether different influence on her. At least she hoped it was the mimosas flowing through Fran's veins that made her suddenly lunge forward and plant a big, wet kiss on Steve's left cheek.

'Stevie,' Fran said. 'This is a surprise.' She turned to Kitty. 'Isn't this a surprise, Kitty?'

'Yes,' replied Kitty, her eyes sending warning signals to Fran that Fran seemed unable to interpret at the moment. 'Quite a surprise.' She leaned over his shoulder. 'Are you into needlepoint? I've been thinking of taking the craft up myself.' She held out the needlepoint kit. 'I was picking this one up for my Aunt Gloria. She loves to needlepoint,' Kitty said, drawing out her words. 'So what are you making?'

Steve glowered and pushed back his chair. 'None of your business.' He headed to a small buffet table atop which an urn of coffee held center stage, with a plate of sugar cookies to one side alongside a pile of napkins and coffee stirrers in a painted jar.

Kitty made a pouty-face to show she was hurt and followed after him. What she really wanted to do was to kick him in the shin and make him tell what he knew about Gretchen's murder. 'I'm sorry,' she said quickly, as Steve poured himself a cup of joe. 'I didn't mean to pry. I know we're all on edge and I'm sure you must be very upset about Gretchen's sudden death.'

Steve snorted.

Fran helped herself to a cup of coffee and Steve warned her to keep away from him. She rolled her eyes and took a step backward.

All the needlepoint ladies were shooting looks at them. And the primly dressed fiftyish woman in the pale green pantsuit, who appeared to be running the shop, eyed them suspiciously from behind the cash register. Kitty figured it was only the prospect of making a sale that kept the woman from throwing her and Fran out of her shop.

Kitty dropped her voice to a whisper. 'Did you know that Gretchen's condo had been broken into and ransacked?'

Fran sipped loudly in the background.

'No, I didn't,' Steve answered sharply. 'How would I know that?'

'I just thought that since you and Gretchen lived in the same building and were practically next-door neighbors—'

'Who told you that Gretchen and I lived in the same building?' Steve's eyebrows drew together.

'Oh, I–I don't remember. I heard it somewhere. Probably around the studio.' She smiled. 'You know how people talk.'

'Yes,' said Steve, 'I do. And the world would be a better place if they didn't.'

His voice was hard as nails. But Kitty chose to ignore the fact. 'So, you didn't hear anything?'

'Hear anything?'

'Yes, the night Gretchen's condo was broken into. I was wondering if you might have seen or heard anything.'

Steve eyed her for a moment in silence. 'Don't you think that would be something that the police should be asking?'

'Did they?'

'As a matter of fact, they did. And I told them what I knew.' He took a small sip before speaking. 'Which was nothing. I wasn't home.'

'But I—' Kitty stopped herself. He'd certainly been home the night she and Fran had broken into Gretchen's condo. It was the next day that Jack told her about it. That meant it had to have been ransacked sometime between the time they left and whenever it was that the police had gone there. The police surely wouldn't have gone in the middle of the night unless some sort of alarm had gone off. But it couldn't have. Fran hadn't reset it. So that left the next morning.

Steve could have left his condo, but had he, or was he lying? If so, why? Because he'd broken in himself and was searching for the money or some other evidence he was afraid he might have left there that would have incriminated him?

Kitty chewed her lip. All this soft shoe was getting her nowhere. 'You don't like me much, do you?'

He smirked. 'Not even a little.'

Kitty smirked back. Two could play this game. She shrugged. 'Tough. Because you're stuck with me. You heard your father, *The Pampered Pet* is going on. With me as the host. And there's nothing you or Barbara Cartwright can do about it.'

'Barbara Cartwright?' Steve looked like a trapped rabbit getting ready to run.

'Yes,' Kitty said triumphantly, working herself up to a full head of steam. 'Fran and I,' she waved a finger at her friend, who was hovering over some woman needlepointing a life-size portrait of Ronald Reagan, 'know all about you and your affair. And you can scheme all you want, but your father wants me to host the show, as did Gretchen. So you and your girlfriend better get used to it.'

Everyone in the shop had stopped working now. 'Keep your voice down,' Steve hissed. 'You've lost your mind. Wait until my father hears about this.'

'Fine!' Kitty was shouting now. 'Wait until your father hears how you killed Gretchen – stabbed her in the back. Then broke into her home and ransacked the place looking for any evidence that you might have left behind.' Steve was dodging chairs and heading for the door.

'I know you murdered her. Means, motive, and opportunity!'

Steve cursed her out. 'What are you talking

about? I was on set watching you stumble through that farce of a cooking program.'

Kitty crossed her arms over her chest. 'Huh. Can you prove it?'

He looked ready to burst and he thrust an angry finger at Fran. If it had been a bazooka, Fran would have been rocketed out the front window. 'What about *her*? She wasn't on set. She was backstage the entire time. She's not even allowed on set while taping. In fact,' he said rather smugly, and returning his gaze to Kitty, 'I heard Gretchen and her arguing the very day she was murdered. Ask her about that, why don't you?'

'But,' sputtered Fran, looking embarrassed, 'that was nothing.' Her eyes bounced from Kitty to Steve then back again. 'Gretchen and I were friends. We argued all the time. About little things, you know? Nothing to kill anybody over.' She sounded frightened. 'She was just annoyed because I'd forgotten to order some supplies.'

Steve snorted. 'There you go. And now, if you don't mind, I've said all I'm going to say to you, Miss Karlyle.'

'You can talk to me, or you can talk to the police . . .' Kitty retorted.

'You ought to talk to a shrink!' Steve threw open the door with a flourish. He was slipping away.

'And I know all about the envelope!' Kitty yelled in desperation.

Steve froze, a quizzical yet frightened look on his face.

Kitty beamed triumphantly.

'Envelope?'

'Oh, yes,' Kitty said. 'You didn't think I knew about that, did you? It's quite a valuable little envelope, isn't it? Having any money problems these days, Steve? Daddy cutting the wallet strings?' She scratched her cheek thoughtfully. 'I wonder where that envelope could be?'

Steve chewed his lip nervously, and glanced at the needlepoint ladies before he spoke again. He had turned red as a boiled lobster. 'I don't know what you're talking about.' He pointed a finger at her. 'But you had better watch your step.'

He spun on his heels. 'Don't think that just because you've got a TV show now, that you could not be axed tomorrow. My father, you will discover, can be quite fickle.'

Before Kitty could utter another word, the door slammed after him and he hurried down the concrete steps. 'Come on!' yelled Kitty. She sure hoped what Steve had said wasn't true about Bill Barnhard being fickle. She was just beginning to warm up to the idea of having some money in the bank and hated to see it slip away so suddenly.

But she didn't have time to worry about that now. 'Come on,' she called again, as Fran slowly weaved her way between the chairs. 'I've got more questions for that man. Besides, we can't let him get away. He could be making a break for the Mexican border for all we know. We've got to stop him.'

Fran hesitated. 'You're kidding, right?'

Kitty grabbed her friend's arm, spilling her coffee all over the two of them, and dragged her out the door, dripping and complaining. She paused at the top step. 'Where'd he go?'

Fran shrugged. 'You got me. I can tell you where my coffee went, though,' she complained. 'All over me.'

'He's got to be here somewhere. Maybe I should call Jack.'

'And tell him what?' Fran replied, obviously unconvinced of the rationality of such a move. 'That you've chased a man out of a needlepoint shop after accusing him of murder?'

'He is guilty of murder,' Kitty said with no uncertainty. 'He and Barbara want this show for themselves. They know how much is at stake and they are in this together. You saw how he ran.'

Kitty was down the steps now and headed up the sidewalk. He couldn't have gone far. She stepped past the shop and started to cross between the alley and the next building. She heard a sudden roar and turned her head. A large silver SUV, with the Porsche emblem on its hood, came barreling out of the alleyway, its wheels spewing gravel and dust as it raced directly at her.

Kitty froze. She wanted to move. Knew that she *should* move. But her feet seemed to have become disconnected from her brain at the very worst of times. The SUV was barreling down on her now. Kitty heard a scream from somewhere and felt herself being pushed. Hard.

The next thing she felt was her body slamming elbows first into the side of the building across the alley as the SUV shot past.

'You OK?' Fran was huffing.

Kitty gulped, then nodded. The SUV sped down

the road and turned the corner. 'He tried to kill me.' Kitty's voice shook. She'd never in her life come so close to facing death. And it wasn't something she was inclined to want to do again. 'You saved my life.' She gripped Fran's hand. 'Thanks. I owe you.'

Fran snorted. 'What you owe me,' she said, holding out her coffee-stained blouse, 'is some clean clothes.'

The needlepoint shop owner was standing outside the shop door, shouting.

Kitty smiled and waved. 'It's OK. I'm all right.'

Fran snickered. 'I don't think that's what she's shouting about.'

'Oh?'

'I think she wants you to pay for that.' Fran looked pointedly at the ground beside Kitty's feet.

Kitty looked down. It was the needlepoint kit; three little kittens and a ball of yarn. 'Oops.'

Twenty

Kitty was still fuming when she showed up for her planned Sunday night dinner date with Jack. The man had absolutely refused to arrest Steve Barnhard, no matter how much she'd protested and, ultimately, pleaded. The jerk had nearly run her down. To make matters worse, that stupid needlepoint kit had set her back almost twenty dollars.

Shouldn't one of the perks of having a boyfriend who's a detective be that he arrest someone for you every once in a while? First Steve had left a threatening note and then he'd tried to run her down, and Jack had refused to even slap the handcuffs on the thug.

'Can we just have a quiet, romantic dinner,' Jack said, touching her cheek, 'and forget all this police business? I'd like to spend some quality time with you, Kitty.'

He had taken her to one of their favorite restaurants, Gardenia, on Ventura Boulevard, one of the valley's main drags. Gardenia was an upscale establishment with plenty of vegetarian and vegan-friendly dishes, the kind Kitty favored. If Jack had his way, they'd eat red meat and potatoes every night. They had a table for two up against the windows looking out on the wide sidewalk. Outside seating was available, but Kitty preferred to keep out of the chill.

Jack poured them each another glass of wine. 'We don't have a lot of time for romance lately. And with you starting your new job . . .' He let his voice trail off. 'Did I tell you how pretty you look?' He tempted her with a smile.

Kitty leisurely sipped her cabernet. That smile was irresistible. She had worn one of her best dresses, a scoop-necked red number that fell to the knees and clung to her in all the right places. A string of white pearls adorned her décolletage. 'Thanks. Though, you've been quite busy yourself.'

'Yeah.' Jack dipped a small slice of fresh

sourdough bread in the garlic and oil that accompanied it. 'Work's been a bear. And the lieutenant never lets up.'

Kitty couldn't hide her contempt. 'I'll bet,' she grumbled.

'What?'

'Do we have to talk about her?'

Jack looked taken aback. 'Sorry,' he grabbed Kitty's hand. 'What is it that you dislike about Elin anyway? You barely know her. I mean, I get that she can appear hard but she's only doing her job, Kitty. And she's really good at it. You can't blame her for that.'

Kitty pulled her hand free. 'I'm going to have the braised seitan with potatoes. How about you?' She wasn't going to let Elin Nordstrom spoil her dinner with Jack. Not again.

Jack studied his menu and they ordered. 'You know, I probably shouldn't be telling you this, but Thadeus Czinski confessed to killing his mother.'

'He what?' Kitty's eyes went wide as saucers.

Jack nodded. 'Yep, broke down this afternoon. It's not for public release yet, though.'

Kitty shook her head as if to get the words she'd just heard to fly back out. 'So Teddy has confessed to killing his own mother.'

'Well, not confessed exactly,' said Jack, biting at the edge of his lower lip. 'But he's not exactly protesting his innocence either.' Jack pulled a face. 'I'm not sure Teddy has it altogether, if you know what I mean. And the DA is sparring with Czinski's lawyer. Maybe they're planning on going the crazy route.'

Kitty struggled with the news. 'You mean Steve . . .'

Jack nodded once again. 'Couldn't have murdered Gretchen.'

'I was so sure,' Kitty said, sounding deflated. 'Are you certain Teddy's the killer?'

Jack shrugged. 'Elin is. And trust me, this murder has got Teddy's name all over it. His prints are all over the office.'

'He worked there,' interjected Kitty. 'He was the maintenance man. He cleaned the whole studio. Including Gretchen's office.'

'His prints were on his mother's locket. Was he cleaning that?'

Kitty pulled a face. Poor Teddy, she thought, though she'd never met him. And poor Chevy Czinski. 'He must be devastated.'

'Teddy?' Jack asked.

Kitty shook her head. 'No, I was thinking of Teddy's father, Chevy Czinski. He's one of my clients, you know.'

'So you told me.'

All through the meal, Kitty couldn't keep her mind off of Gretchen's murder and the events of the day. She often marveled at the way Jack could separate his work from his personal life. Then again, she supposed it was a survival mechanism. It was tough being a cop and dealing with criminals day in and day out. Always seeing the worst in people. Suspecting the worst. Expecting them to lie at every turn.

Kitty refused to be that sort of person. She didn't think she could be that sort of person even if she tried. That wasn't the way she was put together.

For instance, she didn't believe for a minute that Fran could have been involved in Gretchen's murder no matter what Steve might suggest. The very thought was preposterous. So what if Fran had no alibi and was practically alone backstage? Fran could never have murdered Gretchen. The two had been friends. Friends didn't kill friends, did they? Then again, children sometimes did kill parents. Kitty caught Jack staring at her. 'What?'

Jack's annoyance bubbled up. 'I asked how you enjoyed your meal.' He rested his elbows on the table. 'You're thinking about the case again, aren't you?'

'Sorry.' Kitty studied her plate. 'I can't help it.' Besides, she was personally involved in this case. Gretchen Corbett had hired her one minute and then, practically the next minute, someone murdered the poor woman using one of Kitty's knives. She couldn't simply turn a switch and shut off her thoughts the way Jack seemed to at the end of the day.

'Finished?' Jack eyed Kitty's clean plate. She nodded. 'Let's get out of here,' he suggested.

The ride back to Jack's place was cold. And it wasn't just the temperature. 'Sorry,' Kitty apologized. 'I guess I'm not feeling very romantic tonight.'

'Are you sure you don't want to spend the night?' He playfully lifted the edge of her dress. 'That's a nasty looking bruise you've got there.'

Kitty looked at the ugly purple stain on her thigh and frowned. 'I got it when Fran slammed me into a wall this afternoon. I can't complain though. If she hadn't, I'd have been flattened.' She held up her scraped elbows.

Jack whistled. 'That was some hit you took.'

She couldn't help wondering now if Jack was right. Maybe it had only been an accident. Maybe Steve hadn't been paying attention, was texting and driving, and hadn't meant to run her down at all. It sure seemed that way now that it looked like Teddy had stabbed his mom.

'Sorry,' Kitty answered, apologizing for what seemed like the hundredth time that night. 'But I've got pets to feed in the morning. Then there's Gretchen's funeral service. Would you like to come with me?'

Jack shook his head. 'I'd love to, but I'm working. I'll be attending the funeral with Elin and Teddy.'

'Teddy?'

'Yep, we're holding him but it is his mother's funeral. He asked to go.'

'Weird,' replied Kitty. 'I mean, he murders her one day, then wants to attend her funeral the next. Don't you find that odd?'

'I find a lot of things odd in my line of work.' He held the Volvo door open.

She climbed behind the wheel and gave him a light kiss on the lips through the open window as she turned the key in the ignition. The starter made a clicking sound and nothing more. Kitty turned the switch off then on again. 'Rats,' she said. 'Now what?'

'Step aside,' said Jack. 'Let me try.' He got behind the wheel and turned the key in the ignition. The Volvo made clicking sounds, but the engine refused to turn over. 'Must be the battery.' Jack extracted himself from the Volvo.

'It seems like it's one thing after another with this car.' She explained about the broken handle and the busted window.

'Don't worry,' Jack said, 'you'll be able to buy a brand-new car if this TV show works out. Heck, you'll probably be able to buy two new cars.'

Kitty wasn't sure she wanted to replace her old, dependable Volvo and said so. 'It's like a member of the family,' she explained. 'It functions well for my deliveries.'

'Deliveries? The pet chef thing?' He shook his head. 'You're not going to have to keep getting up before dawn to cook for all those pampered pooches once this show of yours takes off, Kitty. You'll be able to quit your day job. Heck, you'll be able to pay some chef to come cook for Barney and Fred if you like.' Jack laughed.

Kitty fell silent.

'What is it?'

'I don't know. I guess I just hadn't thought that far ahead.' Kitty wondered whether she really wanted to do that – quit her day job. After all, she liked her work and the animals depended on her. 'Guess I've got some thinking to do.'

'Listen, it's late,' Jack said, pulling a set of keys from his trousers, 'we don't have to make all of life's big decisions tonight.' He held out the keys. 'Why don't you take the Jeep tonight? I'll charge up the battery overnight – I've got a charger out in the garage somewhere – and we can exchange vehicles tomorrow.'

'Are you sure?' Kitty knew how much he loved

his precious red Jeep. He'd never even let her sit behind the wheel before, let alone drive it, even if he was in the passenger seat. Kitty took the keys from his hand before he changed his mind.

'Sure, I'm sure.' He patted the Jeep's hood. 'We can swap cars at Forest Lawn.' That was the cemetery where Gretchen was being laid to rest.

After a lingering kiss, Kitty headed out. Feeling worn out and beaten up, all she wanted to do was sleep. It was a beautiful Los Angeles night with the stars twinkling above, as if someone had draped a blanket of stars over the world. There was a near full moon too. Kitty skipped the freeway, deciding to take the scenic route through the Hollywood Hills. The drive would be longer, but it would do her good. If she dropped into bed now, she was afraid she'd never fall asleep. So many thoughts about this murder case were running through her head. Though, from what Jack said, it appeared this murder mystery was all but wrapped up.

No thanks to her.

Her knuckles tightened over the wheel. The cool breeze swept her hair through the open windows. While the Wrangler was nowhere near as smooth driving as her Volvo, she was enjoying the masculinity of the machine. She drove deeper into the hills, wishing she'd asked Jack to remove the convertible top.

The Mulholland Scenic Parkway offered a breathtaking view of the city. It was all Kitty could do to keep her eyes on the road as she soaked in the beauty of the sparkling city below.

Mulholland was lightly traveled at the moment, and for several minutes she seemed to be the only driver on the road until some nut shot passed her on a blind curve coming from the opposite direction. Kitty shook her head. A move like that could get a body killed.

Coming around a sharp right-hand bend and into a straightaway, she spotted some headlights coming up fast in the rearview mirror. She eased up on the gas to let them pass, thinking they'd be crazy to try on this serpentine and narrow stretch but it was better to let them go by than to stick to her bumper.

The headlights kept coming, bigger, brighter. The driver had closed in and flashed on the high beams. It was a tall vehicle, an SUV of some sort, and the glare of its lights was making Kitty's eyes water. She cocked the rearview mirror downward and felt a bump. Now what?

An oncoming van whizzed past and Kitty felt a second, harder bump. Her heart leapt to her throat. The wheel jumped out of her hand and she fought to hold her position on the road. 'What is that idiot doing?' she muttered. 'Trying to get us killed?'

She strangled the wheel of the Wrangler as she took the next bend. The SUV slammed into the rear bumper again sending a jolt that shook the Wrangler like a mini-earthquake and rattled Kitty's teeth. The Wrangler was veering out of control. Kitty swallowed hard. There had to be some way out of this predicament. To her left was a sheer drop, to her right, a solid wall of rock. Two lousy options.

Before she could come up with a plan of action to save her skin, the SUV rammed her again, catching the right corner of the bumper. The Wrangler had lost its grip and was spinning sideways now. In a moment, car and driver would be sliding over the edge. And falling.

And there was nothing Kitty could do to stop it.

Twenty-One

Kitty huddled in the soft blue cotton blanket that Jack had wrapped around her aching shoulders, clutching a paper cup of hot cocoa in her right hand. Except for the sweet scent of her drink, the overly lit room smelled like a hospital.

But then, that's where she was, sitting alone but for Jack in a small room off the main ER at the North Hollywood Hospital, where the ambulance had raced her an hour ago after being summoned by a passing motorist who'd noticed the wreck. Sirens blaring, Kitty had been hauled down the mountain and into the valley where, still strapped to the gurney, they'd hustled her inside.

She had insisted to the paramedics that she was all right, except for some cuts and scrapes, but they had been even more insistent that she be taken to the hospital and checked out by a doctor. She'd been poked, prodded and scanned and, though she felt violated, she felt even more embarrassed by some of the rather personal places the doctor and nurses had seen.

Kitty had suffered multiple contusions, but no serious or permanent damage. Jack's Jeep, she feared, had probably not been so lucky. She imagined some poor guy with a tow truck was probably out there right now trying to haul up the wreckage. The Jeep had gone over the precipice to what Kitty had been expecting to be a quick descent followed by a fiery explosion – the kind you see on TV. Instead, the Jeep and Kitty had been tangled up in some trees on the mountainside.

Kitty shivered. Thank goodness for Mother Nature. If those trees hadn't been there . . .

When the nurses had asked her whom she wanted notified, Kitty thought immediately of Jack. No way was she going to bother her parents. They'd freak big time. Her mother and father would insist on driving all the way up from Huntington Beach against her assurances that she was fine. No, she'd tell them all about it later.

To his credit, Jack had raced to the hospital, burst into the ER and cradled her in his arms. His hair was a mess, his shirt was untucked and he had slippers on his feet. He was almost as big a mess as she was. But Kitty thought he looked oh-so-adorable just then. She had smiled and savored his warm embrace.

Now they were sitting alone in a tiny alcove. Jack had fetched her hot cocoa from a nearby machine and was quizzing her about the accident.

She repeated what she'd said earlier. 'It was no accident, Jack. Steve Barnhard deliberately tried to run me off the road.' She locked eyes with him. 'He tried to kill me.'

Jack nodded once. 'Like I said, we're looking for him now. He wasn't at his condo. Elin checked there first. And he isn't answering his cellphone. But we'll find him and bring him in for questioning.'

'Bring him in for questioning?' Kitty stiffened. 'Aren't you going to throw the book at him? Arrest him for murdering poor Gretchen and very nearly killing me?'

'Are you sure—'

Kitty cut him off. 'For the last time, I'm sure it was Steve Barnhard. I recognized his SUV. Look, first the guy leaves a threatening note on my windshield. Next, he tries to run me down in broad daylight. Then he comes this close to succeeding,' she pinched her thumb and forefinger within a hair's breadth of one another. 'What more do you need, Jack?'

'Look, Kitty. I believe you and, believe me, I would love to catch the culprit that ran you off the road.' He ground his fist into the palm of his opposite hand. 'More than anything.'

He described to Kitty what he would do to just such a person should he lay his hands on him, and in no uncertain terms. Few of those terms were repeatable in polite circles. 'But help me out here. Why is Steve Barnhard trying to kill you?'

Kitty noisily slurped her hot cocoa before responding. 'I don't know. Maybe he thinks I'm getting too close to nailing him for Gretchen's murder. He and Barbara Cartwright are in cahoots. They're lovers, after all. The show could be a gold mine, so I'm told. Money and power. Those are always big on the motives for murder list, aren't they?'

'I thought you told me before that he wasn't all that into the show? That he didn't really like pets?'

'Maybe not, but if he sees big potential, what does he care? The color of the money's all the same. Or maybe he simply wants to gain Daddy's approval.'

'He's already running the show. Mr Barnhard gave it to him. That much is certain. And seeing how he's Bill Barnhard's son, my guess is that he's already loaded.'

'Maybe, but maybe he needs the money. Maybe he's got gambling debts, or he's into drugs? Have you seen those beady eyes of his?'

Jack chuckled.

'And he seemed awfully interested when I told him that I knew about the envelope.'

'Envelope?' Jack pulled his arm away and gently turned Kitty's face toward his. 'What envelope?'

Oops. 'Ooooh.' Kitty doubled over in pain. She let half a cup of hot cocoa drop from her hands to enhance the act, but grimaced for real when most of it landed on a pair of heels she'd only bought last week. A ruined pair of shoes would be worth it if her ploy worked.

Jack half-rose, a look of alarm on his face. 'What's wrong, honey? Are you OK?' He glanced around. 'Do you need help? Should I call for a nurse, or the doctor?'

Kitty grabbed his elbow and pulled him back down, clutching her stomach with her free hand. 'It's not too bad,' she said, trying to sound brave and near death all in one breath. 'I–I think I just need some rest.'

She looked up at her boyfriend with big, pouty baby eyes and matching pouty lips. 'Take me home?'

Kitty dragged herself out of bed. Or rather, she let Fred drag her out of bed. He gently gripped her left hand in his maw and practically pulled her to the floor. That dog had an alarm clock in his stomach and he apparently wasn't going to let Kitty's near death experience get in the way of his breakfast.

Kitty yawned and slipped into her pink fuzzy slippers. She couldn't be mad at Fred. Glancing at the alarm clock on the nightstand, she saw she should have been up half an hour ago and had managed to sleep right through the buzzer. Her head throbbed and her body felt like it had been run through an electric blender. Yet, as much as she yearned to, this was no time to crawl back under the covers. She had pets waiting for her. She had a funeral to attend.

She also had Jack to answer to, she realized, with growing trepidation, as she first shoveled out breakfast for Fred and Barney, then started up the coffee pot. She had managed to put him off the night before, but he was a bulldog. He was going to want to know all about that envelope she had stupidly mentioned back at the hospital.

She wasn't prepared to tell him about it. It wasn't that she planned on keeping the money. Far from it. She'd like nothing more than to turn it in. Having all that cash lying around made her nervous. But now that Steve was under arrest for murdering Gretchen, how could she explain the envelope and the love letters?

Come to think of it, Steve may have already blabbed to the police about the envelope and told them what she had said about it. She groaned and took a swig of black coffee. This wasn't going to look good for her at all.

Jack was going to have a fit. That annoyingly long-legged lieutenant sidekick of his would probably insist on throwing the book at both her and Fran. What would they be charged with? Obstruction of justice? Grand theft? Stupidity?

No, it was not going to be a good day. About the only satisfaction she could muster was when she pictured that chump Steve Barnhard's smarmy face behind black iron bars. 'Serves him right,' she muttered.

'Serves who right?'

Kitty jumped. 'Oh, you scared me.'

Fran pulled down a cup from the mug tree and helped herself to some coffee. 'Serves who right?'

'Steve.'

Fran grunted. 'Anything bad that happens to that man serves him right as far as I'm concerned.' She tossed some milk and sugar into her cup and splashed it about with a teaspoon before taking a tentative sip. She smiled appreciatively. 'Perfect.'

Fran took a step back. 'Girl, if you don't mind my saying so, you look like you've been through the wringer.' She wriggled her brow suggestively. 'You and lover boy have a late night, last night? Things get hot and heavy?'

Kitty leaned against the kitchen counter. 'Oh, they got hot and heavy all right,' she answered, 'but not the way you think.' She filled Fran in on the previous night's escapade and near death experience.

Her new roommate's eyes grew wider with each word. 'Why, that rat,' Fran exclaimed. 'I always knew there was something not quite right with Steve. And I knew he and Gretchen got along like cats and dogs.' She shook her head. 'But I never thought he'd stick a knife in the poor woman's back.'

Before Kitty could open her mouth to reply, her eyes fell on the stovetop clock. 'Oh, no, I've got to start cooking. Pets will be waiting for me.' She was going to be late and her clients were going to be furious. She had to literally get cooking.

Fran gripped Kitty's wrist. 'Before you do,' she said, 'I'd like to clear the air.'

'What do you mean?' asked Kitty.

'About what Steve said. Back at the needlepoint shop,' she added, noting Kitty's look of confusion. 'I didn't have anything to do with Gretchen's murder.' Fran's eyes pooled up.

Kitty hugged her warmly. 'I never believed it for a minute,' she answered with a smile. 'Now, let's get cooking.'

With Fran's help, albeit clumsy and

unschooled, Kitty managed to get the morning's meals in order. The woman barely knew her way around the kitchen. About the only thing Fran was good at was making a fresh pot of coffee.

Nonetheless, the meals were prepped and packaged and Fran had generously tossed her the keys to the Mini. Without it, she'd have been stranded, or delivering meals on foot. Jack still had her Volvo and she'd been unable to reach him. Of course, Jack's precious Wrangler was probably in Jeep heaven.

Kitty fretted. Jack wasn't answering at home or on his cell. He was probably stuck downtown doing police work. Hopefully, grilling Steve Barnhard and watching him sweat bullets. She'd left a message for him there at his desk.

'Swing by afterward and pick me up for the funeral,' Fran asked. 'I don't want to miss paying my respects to Gretchen.'

'Me neither,' said Kitty. 'Besides, I'll have to change.' She couldn't exactly go to the funeral in casual slacks and a chef's jacket and she didn't want to go to her clients' homes dressed in all black for a funeral service. Luckily, she had only a few meals to deliver. Her first stop was the Fandolfis.

Mr Fandolfi greeted her at the door. 'Kitty, my dear. Come in, come in.' He was all smiles. The cat, Houdini, rubbed against his legs making gentle purring sounds. 'I'm afraid Rosie is off today and so I have been relegated to the post of greeter.' Mr Houdini was a pure sable Burmese with gold eyes and a shiny coat. Fandolfi claimed that Mr Houdini was a direct descendant of two cats named Wong Mau and Tai Mau.

Kitty grinned and squeezed past with the pets' meals. 'You make a fine greeter, Mr Fandolfi, sir.'

On her first visit to the Fandolfi estate, the magician had proudly explained to her that a doctor in San Francisco had imported a cat named Wong Mau in 1930 and then bred her with a male named Tai Mau, producing what were considered the first Burmese cats.

He sniffed grandly. 'And what did you bring the children this morning?'

Kitty laid the warming bags on the kitchen counter. 'For Hocus and Pocus and,' she added, holding up her index finger, 'Houdini, my famous Viennese sausage dish. I call it *Woofgang Meowzart's Pet Symphony in B flat*.'

She handed the magician the meal's menu card.

Kitty Karlyle: Gourmet Pet Chef
—Woofgang Meowzart's Pet Symphony in B flat—

¾ cup all-purpose flour
12 ounces skinless chicken breast
2 teaspoons kosher salt
½ teaspoon freshly ground pepper
3 tablespoons extra-virgin olive oil
1 ½ tablespoon unsalted butter
6 ounces white button mushrooms, sliced
1 cup grape juice
1 tablespoon raw sugar

1 clove finely minced garlic
2 tablespoons freshly squeezed lemon juice
1 ½ tablespoons finely chopped parsley

Fandolfi chuckled with delight, rubbing the edge of the menu card under his nose. 'Marvelous, simply marvelous.'

'You know,' the magician said, placing a gentle hand on Kitty's shoulder as she prepared plates, 'I wonder if you could help me with something this morning?'

Kitty paused. 'Help you, Mr Fandolfi? Of course, you know I'd do anything for you.' He was a paying customer, after all, and a very pleasant one at that. And the one who had recommended her to Gretchen Corbett – for whatever that was worth at the moment. 'What is it you need? Did you want to request something special for the pets tomorrow?'

He shook his head. 'No, no. It's nothing like that.' He looked away a moment then his eyes cut back to Kitty. 'I've been working on a new trick, you see.' He rubbed his chin. 'Holly was supposed to help me with it. But she had to run out. It requires an assistant.'

Kitty placed Houdini's meal on the floor, waited to see that he was happy – he munched and meowed with satisfaction – then fed the pups.

'I'm afraid I don't know anything at all about magic, Mr Fandolfi. I don't think I'd make a very good assistant.' She zipped her bag shut.

'Nonsense, no special talent required. You'll do perfectly.'

Before she could say another word, Kitty found herself shuffled off to a large dark study that apparently doubled as the magician's home magic studio. The faint scent of tobacco permeated the cozy room. Kitty knew Fandolfi to be an occasional pipe smoker.

Among the heavy-framed paintings on the walls and various bibelots on the shelves, there stood out a six-foot tall, two-foot wide and deep, matte black box in the center of the room. A sleek and modern guillotine-looking device stood off to the right of it. Kitty was beginning to wonder just what she was getting herself into.

At least she didn't see a wooden backboard anywhere riddled with knife marks. Fandolfi wasn't likely to want to start throwing razor sharp knifes at her like she'd seen on the old TV shows, wherein some crazy magician throws a flurry of deadly knives within inches of his even crazier victim, leaving a knife outline of a human body gouged into a wooden backdrop.

Still, Kitty shivered. Just the thought of sharp knives brought back the memory of seeing Gretchen lying dead on the floor of her office with Kitty's very own knife protruding from her back. It gave her the chills and probably always would.

At least that ugliness was all behind her now. There was nothing left but to say her goodbyes to Gretchen this afternoon, pick up the pieces and get on with her life.

'Now, here's what I'd like you to do,' said the magician, interrupting Kitty's reverie. He gripped Kitty's shoulders and edged her toward the big black box. The Bichon yipped at her heels. 'Quiet, Hocus! Pocus!' said Fandolfi. 'Shush.' He held up a long, elegant finger. 'I must concentrate now if the illusion is to work.'

The dogs quieted down, taking up position on the Persian rug beside the large mahogany desk, and watched the action with big puppy eyes.

She ran a finger up the chrome rail of the guillotine. It was cold to the touch. 'You're not planning on chopping my head off, are you?'

'Of course not, dear Kitty. I wouldn't dream of it. Especially,' he added, curling his lips, 'before noon.'

Kitty found shallow comfort in the magician's reply. 'What exactly do you have in mind?' *And why did I agree to do this?*

'Are you familiar with the name Robert Harbin?'

Kitty shook her head no.

'He was a renowned British magician. He died some years ago.'

Kitty gulped. 'Not the victim of one of his own magic tricks, I hope?'

Fandolfi grinned. 'Nothing of the sort. Though he was quite inventive. Some of his illusions include classic big box restoration-type illusions such as the Zig Zag Girl, the Neon Light, the Aztec Lady and Aunt Matilda's Wardrobe.'

'I'm afraid you've lost me.'

'Oh, you know the type,' replied Fandolfi, deftly unlatching one side of the box and peering inside.

Kitty looked over his shoulder. It was pitch black inside. Her sense of claustrophobia was beginning to kick in, churning like an antique electric motorbike motor spewing noxious black fumes in her stomach.

Fandolfi went on. 'Lock a lovely young assistant – in this instance, you,' he said, with an acknowledging wave of the hand, 'into a box in plain view. Move a few bits about. Shuffling said young assistant's body parts in various directions which are clearly humanly impossible.' His dark eyes twinkled. 'Or appear so.'

He lofted a wide scimitar that he drew from a yellow and blue Chinese porcelain urn near the paneled wall. 'Insert a few choice blades,' he waved the blade in the air with his left hand, then turned to Kitty, 'whilst said lovely assistant squirms in mock terror.'

He thrust one of the blades into a tiny slit in the side of the box that Kitty hadn't noticed previously. It was positioned just about where she estimated her spleen to be. Weren't spleens considered vital organs? Fingers of fear reached into her heart and the terror, of which she was already experiencing pangs, was anything but *mock*.

'Then I,' he said, with a slight bow, 'put all the pieces back together again.' He withdrew the blade.

Kitty noted it was blood-free. But would it be after he stuck her in that box and tried the same thing? She hoped so. And would all the pieces go back together again? There was not one part of her body that Kitty didn't consider vital.

'*Voila!*' He took an exaggerated bow. Probably from force of habit, she figured. He patted the side of the device. 'I call this Charming Holly.

She is my own little twist on Harbin's work. Believe it or not, the idea came to me in a dream.'

Kitty believed it. If not a dream, a nightmare.

'Such a shame Holly couldn't be here herself this morning for the trial run. In fact, she helped me with the build. Holly can be quite handy, though you may not think so to look at her.'

Kitty thought of the dolled up beauty and couldn't imagine for a moment that Holly had actually wielded something so pedestrian as a hammer in her smooth, callous-free hands. Would she even know which way was up?

'Yes, a pity she could not be here this morning due to her appointment.'

Couldn't or wisely decided not to?

'What do you think?'

I think I'd rather be someplace else. Kitty bit her lip. 'Interesting,' was the best she could manage with a twisted smile. This wasn't what she'd had in mind when Fandolfi had asked for a favor.

When he'd brought up the magic trick, she'd been thinking more along the lines of holding a satin-trimmed black top hat whilst a cute little white bunny rabbit wriggled out.

He motioned her inside. Kitty's claustrophobia roared. 'If you'll place one leg here.' He watched as she gingerly moved one foot inside. 'And the other just so.' He directed her to place her other foot on the outside of an inch thick board on hinges. He instructed her in similar positioning for her arms and, finally, her head.

In answer to the skepticism on her face, the

magician told her not to worry. 'There's a breakaway section inside. You, my lovely assistant, have only to pull the steel pin once I have locked you inside and rapped twice on the box with my wand. This will be your cue. With the pin removed, you'll be able to pull your extremities about from the inside and no one will be the wiser.' He twisted the tips of his moustache. 'Are you ready?'

'I – I guess so.'

'Splendid. In you go.' With that, Fandolfi closed the side door and Kitty was instantly thrust into darkness. She gulped and struggled for breath as she heard the sound of the magician's muffled voice coming from outside the box.

After what seemed an eternity but was probably only a matter of seconds – and a couple billion beats of her racing heart – she heard the two taps of the wand on the front of the box.

It was impossible to see anything. Her hands fumbled blindly in the blackness for the pin that Fandolfi had pointed out. Sections of the box were beginning to move now and she still had not managed to release the pin. Her arms and legs were being pushed and pulled in directions they had not been designed to go.

She bit her lip. This was beginning to hurt. With a monumental effort, fighting against the searing pain in her arms and legs, she managed to get a grip and extract the stubborn pin.

Unfortunately, nothing changed. Her limbs were being pulled from her and the breakaway boards were threatening to break her bones. Finally, she couldn't help herself. She screamed.

Fandolfi grunted in surprise. And, blessedly, the bits of the box stopped moving away from one another. 'Are you all right?'

'Get me out of here,' Kitty squeaked. 'Please!'

Suddenly all the parts came together again. Fandolfi threw open the side door. 'My dear, what's happened? You look agitated. Is something wrong?'

Kitty allowed the magician to escort her out of the box and lead her to a comfy smoking chair opposite the fireplace. Her arms and legs were still shouting angrily at her and she could barely move her muscles. It seemed that none of her extremities wanted to cooperate. She stared glumly at fingernails, broken and bleeding from scratching at the boards and tugging on the pin.

Fandolfi ran for a glass of water that he held out to her. Why, Kitty couldn't imagine – what she needed was psychotherapy and a deep tissue massage – but she took it anyway. Water wasn't going to help anything. Unless it was in the form of a hot bubble bath. Still, no point in hurting his feelings, even if his magic trick had tried to kill her.

'It didn't work,' Kitty croaked after taking a sip of cold water. 'The trick, I'm sorry, but it simply didn't work. I thought I was going to die in there.'

Fandolfi straightened. 'But I don't understand. I tested it myself. As did my wife.' He peered into Kitty's eyes. 'Did you remember to pull the pin as I instructed?'

Kitty nodded. 'It was hard. I mean, I couldn't

see a thing, but I finally managed.' She shrugged. 'But nothing happened.' Nothing good, anyway.

'I don't understand.' Fandolfi appeared clearly agitated. He peered into the box. 'I simply cannot understand.' His hands fiddled around in the half-dark. 'Hmm,' Kitty heard him utter. 'That's funny.' He scratched his ear.

'What's funny?' If there was something funny about this whole business she'd like to know what. She sat up. Kitty could feel the circulation slowly coming back into her extremities.

'It's odd, that's all.' His hands played with the intricate mechanism inside. 'I mean, Holly was supposed to . . .'

Kitty leaned closer. 'Supposed to what?'

Mr Fandolfi turned and smiled her way. 'Oh, it's nothing,' he said with a wave of the hand. 'A minor glitch. I'll soon have it fixed. There are always obstacles on the way to perfection.'

Yeah, obstacles like almost tearing a person limb from limb.

'The important thing,' he said solicitously, 'is that you are all right.' He took her hand. 'You are all right, Kitty?'

Kitty hesitated only a second. In spite of what he'd put her through, the magician seemed genuinely remorseful and concerned for her welfare. 'Yes.' She put on her happy face. 'I'm OK. Just a little shook up, that's all.'

He smiled back. 'There you go. Merely a little scare.' He tapped his chest. 'It gets the heart going in the morning. Quite good for the constitution.'

Kitty shook her head. It was hard to stay mad

at a man like Mr Fandolfi. She rose unsteadily to her feet. He reached out to lend a hand, but she said she'd be OK. 'Thank you, Mr Fandolfi. It's been quite a morning.'

She gathered up her things, hurrying to make her escape before he could ask her to try another of his tricks – like that mean looking guillotine.

He walked her to the front door. 'Are you sure you'll be all right? Are you able to drive?'

Kitty assured him that she was and could.

'OK, then. See you at the funeral this afternoon?'

Kitty hesitated on the doorstep. 'That's right, you and Gretchen were friends. So you'll be attending Ms Corbett's funeral?'

Fandolfi nodded and folded his hands. 'Yes, we were dear friends.' His right shoulder rose and fell. 'Besides, she is my ex-wife.'

Kitty's jaw dropped to the ground. Gretchen Corbett was Mr Fandolfi's ex-wife? 'Then, Cindy . . .'

He smiled and answered her unfinished question. 'Is my daughter.'

Kitty was stunned. 'You told me you didn't have any children.'

He shook his head. 'No, when you asked me originally, I said that Holly and I had no children. And I hope to keep it that way. One – especially of Cindy's caliber – is more than enough.'

Kitty was inclined to agree with him but kept that opinion to herself. She didn't have kids, but if she ever did she prayed they wouldn't end up like Cindy. Hopefully, one day she and Jack would have children of their own – though probably not for some years to come. The subject of children hadn't really been discussed.

Perhaps it was time that she had that conversation with him. She wasn't even sure where he stood on the subject. Jack had not even committed to a date for their wedding. Was he ready for babies?

Kitty came back to reality as Fandolfi asked her once again if she was going to be all right and Kitty assured him, yet again, that she was.

It was only after she'd driven off, and thoughts of Gretchen's murder and the case ran through her head, that she wondered if it had been an accident or if he had really intended to kill her. After all, he may have had more to gain than she had realized. He was Gretchen's mysterious other ex-husband!

Could he have been in cahoots with Steve Barnhard? Could Fandolfi have set her up as well? Could the magician have recommended Kitty to Gretchen only to set them both up?

Maybe he had expected the young and inexperienced Kitty to fail so that the network would have no choice but to give the show to Barbara Cartwright.

But then the audience had reacted positively to Kitty's on-air personality and Steve and Mr Fandolfi may have decided that Gretchen had to go.

Kitty's head throbbed. She needed to talk to Jack.

Twenty-Two

'You really think he tried to kill you?' asked Fran.

'No, of course not,' Kitty said, though she didn't sound all that convinced – and, in truth, she wasn't sure that she was. Still, she had decided to presume that Mr Fandolfi was as harmless as she'd always suspected him to be.

'It's simply all this murder stuff. It's got me seeing killers everywhere.' And that really wasn't her nature. She vowed to think better of people from here on out. 'Besides, now with Gretchen's killer caught, there's no reason to see potential murderers behind every bush.'

Nonetheless, she'd be keeping an eye on the magician and talk her suspicions over with Jack later.

The cemetery was crowded, and not just with the dead – there were plenty of living in attendance. The sun was shining overhead and the sky was blue. Kitty was thinking it looked way too cheerful for a funeral.

Fran had parked at the end of a long line of cars, mostly shiny black limos with immaculate black tires whose hired drivers lingered in a small group near the rear. 'Gretchen must have had a lot of friends.'

'Sure,' replied Fran. 'And a healthy number of enemies. But even they wouldn't miss this.'

The ladies walked carefully – winding their

way between everything from simple granite headstones to elaborate marble monuments – to where a crowd of nearly a hundred had gathered.

'There's Mr Barnhard.' Fran stuck out her chin.

'And there's his son, Steve,' hissed Kitty, taking in a breath. Her eyes widened and her face darkened. 'What is he doing here?'

Fran heaved her shoulders. 'You've got me.' She looked at Kitty. 'The way you talked, I thought he'd be safely behind bars. Maybe getting ready to face the gallows.' She dangled an imaginary rope.

'I thought so, too,' trembled Kitty, bitterly. Suddenly, she felt threatened and vulnerable, though she told herself there was nothing to worry about with so many people present. Though, if Steve did kill her here, she realized, ironically, that it could potentially be a very short commute from *dead* to *buried*.

Kitty couldn't stop staring at Steve, standing there calm as could be, in his fancy black suit and skinny black tie, right next to his father. Beside them were Barbara Cartwright and her young assistant. There was no sign of handcuffs clasped around those scrawny wrists of Steve's.

Kitty feared the worst. Her eyes scanned the crowd for Jack.

'Who are you looking for?'

'Jack.' She twisted in a circle. 'He said he'd be here.' In her hand, she clutched the manila envelope filled with the money that Fran had taken for Gretchen but never delivered. She was going to give it to Jack now that the case was solved. Minute by minute she was getting more nervous holding on to the loot. Especially since she had no idea what it represented. It could be drug money, or mob money.

Besides, Kitty and Fran really didn't have any excuse to keep the envelope and its contents any longer, despite Fran's pleas to the contrary. She'd give the love letters to him as well. Let him worry about their disposition after that.

'Is that him over there?' Fran laid a hand on Kitty's shoulder and pulled her around.

Jack was standing off to the side under the shade of an elm. Beside him stood Lieutenant Elin Nordstrom.

Of course.

Kitty's eyes narrowed. 'Can't he ever go anywhere without her? It's like they're joined at the hip or something.' She had to admit, her lover boy did clean up pretty good, though. He was looking very handsome in a dark blue suit and tie. Even his hair looked neatly combed for once.

Fran elbowed her. 'Hey, isn't that Teddy with them?'

Kitty held the envelope over her brow, shading her eyes from the sun, wishing she'd brought a pair of sunglasses. 'I think you're right. Jack told me Teddy had asked to attend, but that was when Teddy was under arrest.' There was no reason he shouldn't be at his mother's funeral now, if Steve was locked up and Teddy was innocent. Kitty bit her lip. But Steve wasn't locked up and Teddy was with Jack, not his father. What was going on?

Teddy Czinski stood on the other side of Jack, dressed in a dark brown suit and matching tie. He looked lost and disoriented. This was all very strange.

'Maybe they let him go. After all,' Fran replied, 'you said they had Steve dead to rights for murdering Gretchen and trying to murder you next.'

Kitty nodded but was far from certain. 'So I thought. Come on,' she urged, even though the service had begun, 'I've got to find out what's going on.'

She pulled Fran in her wake around the edges of the mourners and angled her way toward where Jack and the lieutenant stood watching the proceedings.

'Kitty!'

Kitty turned. Bill Barnhard was beckoning her. Reluctantly, Kitty headed over. She couldn't afford to anger her new boss. 'Hello, Mr Barnhard.' She shot a glance at his son, Steve, who appeared to be eying the manila envelope greedily. 'Such a sad day, isn't it?'

'Yes, of course.' He added a hello to Fran. 'Gretchen was a wonderful woman. She'll be missed by all of us. Won't she, Steve?'

His son nodded, Kitty thought rather reluctantly. Kitty caught Steve and Barbara exchanging a look. She was dying to ask what the heck Steve was doing there at Forest Lawn when, by all rights, he should have been locked up downtown, but hesitated to do so in front of his father. She was itching to speak to Jack about this.

Barbara Cartwright spoke up. She was dressed primly in a black dress and heels and wore a veiled black hat. 'I'm going to pay my last respects.' She leaned forward and kissed Bill Barnhard on the lips. 'I'll only be a moment.'

Kitty stifled a gasp. Ms Cartwright had just smacked Bill Barnhard on the lips in front of Steve? Her lover? What on earth was going on? She knew this was Hollyweird, but still.

She turned to Fran who merely shrugged it off, though she looked just as baffled. The person who should have reacted the strongest, Steve, hadn't even blinked. As she stood there, with her maw gaping open as wide as a sound-stage door, Bill Barnhard said, 'This is not the time or the place, young lady. But there are some things going on with *The Pampered Pet* and your behavior toward my son that concern me.'

'Yes, Mr Barnhard?' Kitty's eyes dropped to the grass. She felt like she'd been slapped in the face.

He shook his head. 'We'll talk about this later. At the studio. Meet me there. Eight sharp.' He tapped his watch – a piece of jewelry that probably cost more than her Volvo when it was new.

Kitty quaked. Was she about to lose her job? It wasn't her fault that Bill Barnhard's son was a deranged killer. 'Yes, sir. Um, you mean eight o'clock tomorrow morning?'

'Tonight,' he said sternly. 'Please don't be late.'

Was he going to fire her tonight? Tomorrow

they were scheduled to begin filming the series in earnest. Was Barbara Cartwright about to fill her shoes?

Her head was swimming. Kitty promised she'd be there, mumbled some more condolences, made her excuses, then hurried over to where Jack, Teddy and the annoyingly statuesque Ms Nordstrom – no one should look that good at a funeral – were lingering.

Jack was smiling. 'Good morning, Kitty.' He glanced at the manila envelope in her hand. 'What's in the envelope?'

Kitty looked at the envelope and frowned. There was no point going into that now, especially in front of Nordstrom. Everything was blowing up in her face. 'Recipes,' she said curtly.

'Recipes? You brought recipes to a funeral?' He looked flummoxed. 'Why the heck would you—'

'Never mind.' Kitty dragged him by the elbow until they were out of earshot of the others. 'Don't good morning me, Jack. What on earth is going on?'

Jack looked perplexed. 'What are you talking about?'

Kitty's face was nearly purple. 'I'm talking about him,' she said in a rough whisper.

'Him who?'

Kitty aimed her gaze at Steve. '*Him*, that's who.' She spun and pointed her finger at Teddy. 'And *him*.'

'Oh,' Jack let the word roll off his tongue slowly, like a cat lazily rolling out of bed. He stuffed his hands in his pockets. 'I see.'

His grin was driving her crazy. 'So tell me so I can see, too!'

Jack sighed and reached for Kitty's hands but she pulled back and crossed them over her chest. He frowned but continued. 'Look, Kitty. There's no other way to tell you this, but Steve Barnhard's not guilty of anything.'

'What?' Heads turned their way. Kitty lowered her voice. 'He tried to kill me. Twice!'

Jack shook his head. 'Somebody may have tried to kill you, but it wasn't Steve Barnhard.'

'I know it was him, Jack.'

'He has an alibi.'

The look on Kitty's face was pure skepticism. 'What sort of alibi?'

'A dozen witnesses.' He shot a look at CuisineTV's CEO. 'Including Barbara Cartwright and Bill Barnhard.'

It was Kitty's turn to shake her head. 'That can't be. That simply can't be. He tried to run me over in the street.'

'About that,' Jack shifted uneasily. 'He said to tell you he was sorry.'

'Sorry?' Kitty was nearly apoplectic.

'Yeah, it seems the guy has a problem with his blood sugar. He explained that he'd had a couple cups of coffee at that needlepoint shop where you went to have words with him, but he hadn't eaten a thing all morning. Then you came in and got him all worked up.' Jack shrugged. 'Between getting him all tense and him being all jittery to begin with, well,' Jack averted his gaze, 'he says it was all a mistake. An accident. He was all wired up. And he apologized.'

'Apologized?' Kitty whirled at Fran. 'You were there, tell him. You saw it – he practically ran me down in the street.'

'Well . . .' Fran hemmed and hawed, avoided Kitty's pleading eyes. 'We had been pretty rough on the guy. I do remember he was reaching for a cookie when you got him sort of mad and he ran out the door.'

Kitty was stunned. 'Fran! He tried to run me off the road. I'd have been a thick, wet smear in the street if you hadn't shoved me out of his path.'

Fran hesitated before speaking, looking from Kitty to Jack and back again. 'It is a pretty narrow alleyway. Steve might not have seen you coming out. And if he left in a hurry and was really upset—'

'Fran!'

Fran wrung her hands. 'I'm not saying you didn't almost get run over, Kitty. I'm just saying it *might* have been an accident.'

Jack added, 'He seemed genuinely sorry, Kitty.'

'I'll bet he did. Sorry he didn't succeed in running me over.'

Jack stayed mum.

'And what about the threatening note he left on my car?'

'Not him.'

'Oh, please,' retorted Kitty. 'Don't tell me, he needed a cookie?'

'Listen, Kitty. I know you don't like to hear this, but his story checks out. We had the note analyzed by a handwriting expert.'

'So?'

'So the note was written by a leftie. Steve's right-handed.'

Kitty balled her hands into fists. 'He ran me off a mountain!'

Jack looked pained. 'What can I say? At the time you were involved in your accident, Steve Barnhard was at the Beverly Hills Hotel with a dozen witnesses, including Barbara Cartwright and his father.'

'Then he snuck out.' She glared at Jack.

'I don't think so, Kitty. And we checked his vehicle. Not a mark on it. He takes care of that Porsche like it's his baby, and it shows.' Jack sounded jealous. Of course, his Wrangler was nothing but a pile of scrap now.

'Then he had an accomplice. Probably his lover, Barbara Cartwright. What kind of SUV does she drive?'

'Sorry, Kitty. I told you. She was there, too. And she doesn't even have a car here in LA. Takes a rented limo everywhere she goes. That's it parked over there.' He pointed to the long line of limos down the hill.

Kitty fumed. This just wasn't possible. 'And it was no accident.' She turned and glared at Steve a moment. Something about that guy was simply too slick.

'Are you sure?' Jack's calm demeanor only angered her all the more. 'It was late. Maybe it was merely a reckless driver, or a drunk driver or a stoned one.'

Jack shrugged. 'LA's a big city, it happens. Listen, we've alerted all the body shops, looking for whoever hit you,' he said in an obvious attempt to mollify her. 'But it's a million to one shot that the vehicle will ever show up. There are a thousand places a person can go in this town alone and get work done on their car, no questions asked.'

This could not be happening. This really could not be happening. Before she lost all self-control, Kitty changed the subject; after all, this one was going nowhere. 'What about him?' She pointed at Gretchen and Chevy's son, Teddy.

'We're still holding him,' said Jack. 'I told you, Steve is a dead end. Besides, Teddy confessed this morning.'

Kitty's eyes grew wide. 'He what?'

Twenty-Three

Jack nodded. 'That's right. He's admitted that he killed his mother.'

'For real?' Jack nodded again. 'And you believe him?'

'Yes.'

'Well, I don't.'

'He confessed, Kitty. With his lawyer present. Means, motive and opportunity. Like we talked about before, Teddy works at the studio and his fingerprints are on his mother's locket.'

'But not on the murder weapon,' Kitty pointed out.

Jack could only agree. 'Let it go, Kitty. I told you the police would handle this. Look at everything that's been happening to you ever since you decided to go poking around in Ms Corbett's murder. I've been concerned for your safety.'

'That's my point, Jack. If Teddy is guilty and this case is all but closed, why would someone have been trying to run me off the road last night?'

'We don't know that's what happened.'

'*I* know,' Kitty replied fiercely. She stomped off with Fran at her heels, even as Jack called after her. Unfortunately, she bumped right into Elin Nordstrom.

'Everything all right, dear?' asked the lieutenant. 'You look rather ill.'

There were a million and one things that Kitty would have liked to say to Miss Elin Nordstrom right then but she held her tongue. 'I guess it's the funeral. I get funny around cemeteries.'

She studied Teddy, who stood placidly at Nordstrom's side, hands folded in front of him. For the first time, she wondered where his father, Chevy Czinski was. She hadn't noticed him in the crowd of mourners. She thought he'd be here. 'How are you holding up, Teddy?'

He slowly turned his dark eyes toward Kitty. 'I'm sorry.' His voice was soft as a whisper.

'Me, too,' answered Kitty. 'Is your father here?'

'I saw him earlier. He came to see me this morning. He wanted to bring me to the service. But the police wouldn't let him.'

'Oh, I see.'

'Mr Barnhard came to see me, too, and David – he's always been nice to me.'

Kitty's ears perked up. 'Steve Barnhard came to see you?'

Teddy shook his head. '*Mister* Barnhard.'

Kitty was confused for a moment. Then she noticed Teddy glancing at Bill Barnhard. '*Bill* Barnhard came to see you at the station?'

Nordstrom answered for him. 'He's quite a charming man, I must say. I was there when he arrived. He was quite solicitous. He asked that we do everything we can to make Thadeus comfortable.'

Had he now? thought Kitty. Had he now? Could she have been wrong? Could it be that Bill Barnhard was behind Gretchen's death and the attacks on her? It made sense. He was head of the studio. He and Gretchen might have had a falling out. Maybe he was the mysterious lover whose letters Gretchen kept hidden in her dresser drawer. Could his middle name be Cameron perhaps?

Maybe money was the motive? Big gobs of it. Everybody kept saying what a lot of money was at stake in this crazy business. Maybe Bill Barnhard was unhappy that Gretchen owned a piece of Santa Monica Film Studios and a big piece of *The Pampered Pet.* But was he upset enough to have murdered her over it?

She'd have to find out. She had an appointment with the CEO that night. Did she dare keep it? Did she dare refuse?

Did she dare ask him if he murdered Gretchen Corbett?

'Everything all right between you and Jack?' inquired Nordstrom, interrupting Kitty's ruminations.

'Why do you ask?'

Nordstrom was smiling like she'd just conquered America. 'The two of you appeared to be arguing. I'm concerned.'

'You needn't be.'

Nordstrom mistook or ignored Kitty's contemptuous tone. 'Let me give you some advice. You must learn how to handle men, Kitty. You must be kind to them, show them respect. Take me and Jack, for instance. Why, we're nearly inseparable all day under the most stressful circumstances imaginable, yet we get along quite,' she hesitated, 'swimmingly, I think you say in the States?'

Kitty felt like telling Nordstrom to go drown herself. 'Thanks for the advice,' she managed to spit out. 'But Jack and I are fine. He's asked me to marry him, did you know?'

Nordstrom looked down at her. 'No, I did not know.' Her eyes twinkled with what Kitty interpreted as malice. 'So, when is the date?'

Kitty bit her tongue. She and Jack hadn't set a date. Jack had proven slippery in that department. She'd bet that Nordstrom knew that and had been baiting her.

As Kitty struggled for a retort, Nordstrom spoke. 'Funeral's over.' Workers had finished lowering the coffin into the ground. 'Time to go, Thadeus.' The lieutenant motioned for Teddy to accompany her. Teddy glanced over his shoulder, looking forlornly at his mother's white coffin as he was being led away.

It was then that Kitty noticed Chevy off in the distance. He was dressed in a rumpled gray suit, white shirt and pink tie. It was the first time she'd seen him in anything but casualwear. Well, that and the loin skin he'd been squeezed into in those old movie posters she'd seen. He stopped over the earthen hole at the bottom of which Gretchen's coffin now rested, said a few words, then veered off like a tired old lion toward the vehicle that Nordstrom had escorted Teddy to, probably to have a few parting words with his son.

'Such a pity, is it not?'

Kitty turned. 'Oh, Mr Fandolfi.' He wore the crispest, sharpest black suit that Kitty had ever laid eyes on and she wondered if it belonged to his onstage collection. 'Yes, poor Teddy. You remember Fran.'

He nodded. 'This is a sad day for everyone. Gretchen may have had her faults, but she was quite a woman.'

Kitty couldn't help but notice the face that Fandolfi's current wife pulled. Apparently the current Mrs Fandolfi was no fan of the former.

'Good morning, Mrs Fandolfi.' Kitty couldn't decide whether Holly was dressed for a funeral or a night at the opera, in a clingy black dress, matching pumps and a string of pearls that looked like they could have come from the Queen of England's private Tower of London collection.

Holly Fandolfi daubed at the corner of her left eye with a silk tissue held in her white-gloved left hand. She used her right hand to pull her husband closer.

'How are you holding up, Kitty? It seems we

keep missing each other – at Bunny's Bakery the other morning and then up at the house this morning. I hear my dear husband caused you no end of anguish with one of his tricks.' She slapped his wrist and made *tsk-tsk* noises.

'I did apologize, my pet.' Fandolfi squeezed Kitty's arm. 'You are all right now, I hope?'

Though every bone in Kitty's body ached and every muscle attached to every bone screamed with every move she made, Kitty managed to say with a smile that she felt fine. She didn't want to hurt Mr Fandolfi's feelings and she really didn't want to give Holly any ammunition to use against him – assuming he wasn't a cold-blooded killer, like she'd told herself he wasn't.

'Still,' Holly said, 'after all you've been through lately, I'm surprised you're even continuing.'

'Continuing? Continuing what?'

'The pet chef business, of course.'

'Oh, but I'd never give that up.' Kitty was surprised that Holly would even suggest such a thing.

Holly looked troubled. 'But, after all you've been put through. The threatening notes, the attacks on your life . . .' Holly glanced toward the open grave. 'Aren't you concerned, Kitty? That could be you there.'

A chill ran up Kitty's spine. Was Holly actually threatening her in some way? Or was this her own weird way of trying to warn her to be careful? She couldn't possibly care about someone other than herself, could she?

Kitty laughed it off. 'Oh, I'll be fine, Mrs

Fandolfi. Besides, the police think they have the case pretty well wrapped up.'

'Oh?' said Fandolfi.

Kitty nodded. 'My boyfriend, Jack – I told you about him – is one of the lead detectives on the case. I'm not sure I should be saying this, but he told me that Teddy confessed.'

'Thadeus confessed to murdering Gretchen?' Fandolfi's eyebrows flew upward.

'That's right.'

'But you don't believe him, do you?' That was Holly.

Kitty shrugged. 'I'm not sure. I'm not sure at all.'

'If you ask me,' Fran said, 'Teddy wouldn't hurt a fly. I've known him as long as I've been working for Gretchen. That boy is a sweetheart.'

'Then how do you explain his confession?' asked Holly.

'Well, pardon my saying so,' Fran said with obvious reluctance, 'but Teddy is . . . that is, he could be considered—'

'Slow?'

Kitty and Fran twizzled around. Teddy's father, Chevy Czinski, had come up behind them. He stood with his hands in his pockets. His eyes were red and his face was pale and puffy.

'Is that the word you were looking for, young lady?'

Fran gulped. 'I–I didn't mean anything, Mr Czinski, sir.'

He managed a wan smile, even as he patted her arm. 'That's quite all right. You do not offend me or Teddy.' He smiled at each of them. 'My son has always been *special*. My ex-wife, Gretchen, gave him a job to keep him occupied. Teddy always had a difficult time finding employment.'

Fran and Kitty had said their goodbyes and were heading back to Fran's Mini when a voice called out to them. Both ladies turned. It was David Biggins. Despite the solemn occasion, Kitty couldn't help noticing that David looked quite handsome in a suit and tie. She also couldn't help noticing Jack opening Elin Nordstrom's door for her after first securing Teddy in the backseat of an official-looking sedan.

As Jack waved to her from a distance, Kitty leaned in and gave David a friendly hug. 'Hello, David.' She noted with guilty satisfaction that Jack hesitated a moment, all the while looking her way, before getting into his car and slowly driving off. 'How are you holding up?'

'Hi, ladies. OK, I guess.' He and Fran shared a hug as well. 'What about you, Fran? You and Gretchen were really close. More like friends than co-workers.' He offered both ladies a pastille from a tin he pulled from his suit pocket. Both declined. He popped one in his mouth, and then tucked the tin away again.

Fran daubed at her eye with a tissue. 'I'm crushed. Gretchen was one of my best friends. Things won't be the same without her. You must feel the same way, David. The two of you were close once.'

'You and Gretchen?' Kitty looked wide-eyed.

David shrugged and looked at the ground.

'Not especially. We went out a few times, mostly with the gang from the studio. Working together long hours, people start feeling that tug of attraction. You know how it is. There's always a certain amount of hanky-panky around the set,' he said, making what Kitty could only interpret as amorous eyes at her. 'But it wasn't that way with me and Gretchen. There was quite an age difference, after all. Besides, she was more like a mother figure around the set.' He laughed. 'Maybe an evil step-mom would be more apt.'

'Maybe you should try her daughter,' Kitty quipped.

'Huh?' David's face darkened. 'Why do you say that?'

'I'm only joking.' She pointed to his suit pocket. 'I noticed you both have a sweet tooth, that's all.'

David still looked puzzled.

'I noticed a tin of pastilles on the table when we went to Cindy's place.'

'You went to Cindy's townhouse at the beach? What's it like?'

'Her house looks right out at the ocean,' Kitty replied. 'It's palatial.'

'I'll say,' added Fran.

'Did you learn anything?' David wanted to know.

'Not really. She wasn't very cooperative at all. She refused to even tell me who her father was.'

'That's no big secret,' answered David. 'It's that magician guy. He was here.'

Kitty nodded. 'Yes, Ernst Fandolfi. I know that now. In fact, he's one of my clients.'

'We learned one thing,' interjected Fran.

Kitty and David looked at her and waited.

'We learned that the woman lived like a queen.' Fran bit her lower lip. 'I can't believe Gretchen put up with that child. Nothing but a spoiled brat. Every time she came around the studio all they did was fight. And when Cindy went and took up with some guy that she absolutely disapproved of, I thought Gretchen was going to explode.'

David scowled. 'You know, she's never worked a day in her life. Yet there she sits, lording over the manor with a private gardener *and* a housekeeper. While mommy and daddy foot all the bills. No wonder she's such a . . .' His ears turned bright red.

Kitty nodded. 'I have to admit, I was snooping around, hoping to find out who'd killed Gretchen. Now, I hear that Teddy has confessed.'

'That's sick,' David replied. 'I wonder if dear old Cindy has an alibi. If either of her kids killed her, I'd put my money on Cindy.' He smiled. 'Not that I have any money to speak of.'

'Ditto that,' Fran said.

'If you want to poke around, you ought to poke around Cindy Corbett some more. See if she does have an alibi.'

Kitty nodded. David had a point. There was certainly no love lost between mother and daughter. She definitely needed to keep Cindy on her list of suspects, along with Steve and Bill Barnhard, Barbara Cartwright and possibly Mr Fandolfi. She wasn't certain she could rule out Sonny Sarkisian either. Gretchen had gotten him fired and now he was, almost magically, rehired. That could mean something, too.

'I hear you went to see Teddy this morning.' Kitty looked at her hand. Here she was standing around in public with a hundred grand in plain sight of everybody. Maybe even the killer.

She quietly stuffed the manila envelope deep into her purse. It barely fit. 'Did he say anything to you then about having murdered his mother?'

David shook his head. 'Not a word. But I only talked to him a minute or two, then Bill Barnhard showed up and the police were bending over backwards being obsequious to the guy. I wanted to see if there was anything I could do for Teddy, anything he needed.' He stuffed his hands in his pockets. 'It's got to be tough being stuck in lockup.'

Fran trembled. 'I would just die. It was sweet of you to pay him a visit.'

'I've always liked Teddy. I can't help it. Despite what he did, I feel sorry for him.'

Kitty and Fran agreed. There was something about the young man. Fran nudged Kitty. 'There she is now.'

'Who?'

'Cindy Corbett. She's just getting into that limo.'

'Rats,' Kitty said. 'We'll never catch her now.'

'That's okay. There's a wake being held at her place, remember? We can corner her there.'

'Are you coming?' Kitty asked David.

'No, I'm afraid I can't make it. I could use a lift into town though, if it's no trouble? My car broke down.'

'Sure, hop in.' Fran cranked up the Mini. Minutes later, they were dropping David off at his apartment. Fortunately, it wasn't too much out of their way. David lived in Park La Brea, a huge apartment community near Fairfax Avenue.

'Last chance,' said Fran, pulling up outside of David's building. 'Are you certain you don't want to hit the wake? I'm sure Cindy will have only the best liquor.'

'I hate to pass it up, but I really couldn't.' As David hopped out of the car, he said to Kitty, 'Hey, maybe you want to get together later? You'll never guess what I found.' He continued without waiting for her to guess. 'Our old high school yearbook – Newport Harbor High – from our senior year,' he finished, beaming from ear to ear.

'Oh, dear,' Kitty groaned. 'I'm not sure I could bear it. Besides, I'm afraid I'm swamped today. After the wake, I have to head straight home, prepare meals and then deliver.' Because she was missing lunch service for her clients' pets, Kitty had promised them each dinner.

'After that?' coaxed David. 'We'll have a laugh or two.'

'After that I have a meeting with Bill Barnhard.'

'Oh? What does he want?'

'I'm afraid he wants me to meet him at the studio tonight at eight o'clock.' Kitty sighed. 'I hope he's not going to fire me.' Kitty had made up her mind – if he did fire her, she was definitely going to ask him about Gretchen's murder. Who knew? Steve, Barbara and Mr Barnhard could all be alibiing each other. Wasn't that convenient?

'He did seem a bit testy at the cemetery,' added Fran. 'But don't sweat it, girl. I'm sure it's nothing serious.'

'Nothing serious? I accused his son of murdering Gretchen and then trying twice to murder me!'

David laughed. 'Somehow, I think you'll manage just fine, Kitty.' He thumped the car windowsill a couple of times. 'Somehow, you always do.'

Twenty-Four

'Look at him,' complained Kitty, her voice an angry whisper, 'sitting there looking so smug.' She was surreptitiously staring at Steve Barnhard, wishing the SWAT team would suddenly come bursting through the door of Cindy Corbett's beach house, wrestle his skinny body to the rug and haul his butt off to the clink.

'I mean, who wears white socks to a wake?' Kitty grumbled, as Steve crossed his legs on the sofa across from her.

Fran giggled inappropriately – this was a memorial service after all. Fran was on her second glass of white wine, or was it her third? Kitty wasn't really counting. Fran was a big girl and it really didn't matter, except that one of them had to remain sober enough to drive home afterward, though Kitty would prefer that neither of them did anything to embarrass themselves in this somber gathering.

Like Kitty had told David, she did have work to attend to afterward. She definitely needed to remain sober for that.

And she had a meeting with Bill Barnhard, the head of the entire network, to deal with after that. Somehow, showing up late and/or intoxicated to that meeting didn't seem like such a good idea. Though, after it was over and the dust had settled – and he'd kicked her off the show – getting drunk just might be worth the doing. She wasn't much of a drinker, no more than a social glass of wine here and there, but the events of today and the past several leading up to it might just have her rethinking that policy.

Kitty suddenly lurched forward, her hand squeezing Fran's knee.

'Ouch!'

'Sorry,' said Kitty, letting go. 'It's the socks!'

'Excuse me?' Fran reached for a handful of chips.

'It's the socks.' Kitty fell back into the cushion of the plump eggplant colored loveseat. It was about as comfortable as sitting on an eggplant, too. 'I remember now. Steve was wearing white socks when I met him.'

She grinned with satisfaction. 'And then, when I saw him later with his feet up on the desk in Sonny's empty office after the murder—'

'Yes,' Fran mumbled, her mouth stuffed with bits of potato chip.

'Steve wasn't wearing white socks.'

'Wasn't wearing white socks?' Fran's voice was thick with confusion. 'Where are you going with this?'

Kitty's eyes twinkled. 'He wasn't wearing any socks.' She clapped her hands. 'I remember it clearly. Steve wasn't wearing any socks.'

'And?'

'Don't you see?' Kitty whispered, one eye on Fran, the other on Steve. 'He stabbed Gretchen. Probably got blood all over his socks somehow.'

'He stabbed Gretch in the back and got blood on his socks?' Fran looked unconvinced.

A couple hovering nearby glanced their way. They'd been speaking too loudly.

Kitty sidled closer to Fran. 'Yes. Somehow. Don't ask me how. But somehow, in the heat of the moment, he must have spilled some blood on his shoes.' Kitty took a deep breath. 'Gretchen's blood. He probably threw them away afterward. Maybe he dumped them in the ocean or burned them in his fireplace or—'

'Steve lives in a condo. You saw it. I don't think he has a fireplace—' Fran leaned forward and hiccupped, sloshing white wine down the front of her dress. She frowned, gave the spot a quick wipe, and reached for another handful of chips.

'Then he threw them away, dumped them in a landfill.'

'Uh-oh.' Fran pursed her lips. 'Did you say *spilled*?' Fran giggled.

'What's so funny?'

'You're not going to like this.' Fran set her glass down on the coffee table, where it was no doubt going to leave a nasty ring. Kitty was going to warn her about this but, in the end, figured Cindy would get what she had coming.

'I'm not going to like what?'

'That was me.'

'What was you?'

'I remember, now that you bring it up. That day at the studio, the day Gretchen was killed?'

'Yes?'

'I spilled a cup of coffee all over Steve's shoes. His socks were a wet mess.' Fran shrugged helplessly. 'He must have taken them off.'

Kitty felt like screaming. She really, really wanted Steve to be guilty, if not of murdering Gretchen Corbett, then of something.

Kitty felt a bump against her knee and looked up. Cindy Corbett loomed over her, looking mad. Looking drunk. And not a tissue in sight. Had she noticed Fran's wet wine glass already?

Her eyes looked hard enough to pound nails, but they weren't all puffy around the edges and red through the middle to indicate that she had been crying. Apparently, Cindy wasn't about to shed a tear for the loss of her beloved mother, Gretchen.

In fact, now that she thought about it, Kitty hadn't seen her cry at the funeral ceremony either, though there had been several handkerchiefs sopping up the tears of other mourners, including Mr Fandolfi, Teddy, and even his father, gruff old Chevy Czinski.

'So, have you heard?' Cindy Corbett's below-the-knee, silky black dress swirled around her legs like it was alive, a devoted creature of the underworld wrapped around its mistress's legs. Her bare arms revealed marmoreal skin, no doubt an outward manifestation of her inner hardness.

Both Kitty and Fran shook their heads in the negative, but it was Kitty who asked. 'Heard what?'

'My attorney has released Mommy's will. It seems dear Mother has only left me a quarter of her estate.'

Gretchen Corbett was very well off. It seemed to Kitty that Cindy had been well provided for. Apparently, Cindy wasn't seeing it that way.

'Who gets the rest?' Kitty inquired. It was tacky to ask, but since Cindy had brought it up, why not?

Cindy's eyes narrowed and her lips puckered as she spoke. 'Teddy gets a quarter – though, I doubt he'll ever see it, seeing as how he murdered dear Mother. My attorney says he will not be entitled to profit by his crime.' Cindy managed a smile.

'What about the rest?' Fran said.

Cindy's countenance darkened. 'Her exes. My father. And Teddy's father.'

Ernst Fandolfi and Chevy Czinski. That gave both of them motives for murdering Gretchen. Not that Chevy didn't have a motive already. Gretchen had apparently stolen the entire idea for *The Pampered Pet* from Chevy. Was he mad enough or desperate enough for money to murder poor Gretchen?

And what about Fandolfi? Was he having any money problems? It didn't appear so on the surface, but one never knew. The rich had a way of keeping up appearances long after the money had gone. He was ambidextrous; that was just as good or better than being left-handed. He was at Bunny's Bakery the day Kitty received that threatening note that Jack said had been written by a leftie. Could that leftie be Fandolfi?

But how? He wouldn't have known she was coming and he hadn't left the table. Then again, he was an expert magician. An expert at sleight of hand.

Then Kitty remembered. She had left the table for a minute. He could have written the note himself when she had excused herself to go to the ladies room.

But what was his motive? Kitty was going to have to dig deeper.

She excused herself from the two women and threaded her way across the crowded room. Mr Fandolfi, his wife ever at his side, was speaking with Greg Clifton, *The Pampered Pet* director, off in the far corner of the living room. She put on a smile and wormed her way into the conversation in a not so subtle fashion. The director was one person that Kitty was pretty sure hadn't murdered Gretchen. He had been directing her show at the time.

The director was talking while Fandolfi made eye contact. '. . . Poor Gretchen was having a fit. And then I yelled for camera one, but cam—'

Kitty interjected, 'Good afternoon, Mr Clifton, Mr and Mrs Fandolfi.'

'Oh, hello, Kitty,' Greg said. 'I was just telling

Ernst a funny story about a show I was working on with his ex-wife.' He sighed. 'I can't tell you how much we are all going to miss dear Gretchen.'

'You and Mr Fandolfi know one another?'

'Oh, yeah,' replied Greg. 'I've known this old coot for as long as he and Gretchen were married. Funny, we don't see each other for years and then suddenly I see him twice in a handful of days, right Ernst?'

Fandolfi muttered ambivalently.

'Yeah, first Ernst shows up at the studio to catch the taping of your first show and now . . .' The director paused, apparently having realized the hole he'd dug himself into. 'Well . . . here.' He coughed nervously.

So, thought Kitty, Mr Fandolfi had been at Santa Monica Film Studios for the taping of *The Pampered Pet*. On the very day that Gretchen Corbett, his ex-wife with whom he shared the somewhat dubious honor of parenting the charming Cindy, was murdered. 'I didn't realize you and Gretchen went back that far, Mr Clifton.'

Greg shook his head vigorously up and down but it was Fandolfi who replied. 'Greg has been directing shows for Gretchen for many, many years.' He pressed Greg's arm. 'She will be sadly missed.'

Greg dittoed the magician's remarks then glanced at his empty glass. 'I'm gonna need a refill, anybody else?' Fandolfi and Kitty demurred, only Holly accepted his request.

She held out her own glass. 'If you wouldn't mind?'

The director grinned. 'Well, then it looks like

just the two of us. It isn't often I get to take the arm of a lovely young woman and show off in front of a room full of jealous and bewildered onlookers.'

'But I—'

'Come along, my dear. You don't mind, do you Ernst?'

'Of course not,' the magician replied. 'It will give Kitty and I a moment to talk.'

Holly stole a quick glance at her husband as Greg looped his arm through hers and hustled her off through the crowd toward the bar.

Kitty watched them leave. 'I didn't realize you were at Santa Monica Film Studios the day Gretchen was murdered, Mr Fandolfi. Your name wasn't on the register. Why didn't you tell me, or anyone else for that matter? Why haven't you told the police?'

Fandolfi smiled graciously and laid a long-fingered hand on Kitty's arm – his left hand, she noticed. 'I confess. I couldn't resist coming to see your first taping. I managed to slip in unnoticed.'

That didn't answer her question. 'But why didn't you tell me?'

'I did not want to make you uncomfortable,' he replied quickly. 'Nervous. Also,' he shrugged, 'I am somewhat of a celebrity. I thought it best to be low key, incognito, as they say.' He touched her chin with the tips of his fingers, 'I did not wish to distract others from your charms.'

Hmm. Kitty thought about his answer. That could all make sense. But still, there seemed to be something fishy going on and she was going to get to the bottom of this fish tank no matter how much it smelled. 'Did you see anything at all suspicious while you were there?'

He shook his head. 'No. If I had, I would have notified the police as soon as I had learned of Gretchen's murder.'

'Were you there for the entire taping?'

'Yes, but I left immediately afterward. You can ask Sonny Sarkisian.' Kitty noticed the magician had said the name of the once-fired marketing and promotions man with particular distaste. 'He saw me in the parking lot. I was going out as he was coming in. I did notice Gretchen speaking with you before the show and that was the last time that I saw her.'

He let go of Kitty's arm. 'It was nothing really. That's why I didn't say anything.' He winked. 'I thought you did a wonderful job by the way. How's your arm?'

'Thank you.' She rubbed her right arm. It was still a bit sore from that morning's mishap in Fandolfi's wicked magic box. 'It's fine.'

She hadn't seen Sonny's name on the guard's list either. Whoever had been on duty that day had done a bang-up job. She was going to have to find out whom that guard was and have a word with him. 'When did you learn that your ex-wife had been murdered?'

'The next morning.' He smiled and his eyes danced, much like those of a cat toying with a mouse, Kitty thought. 'I believe I already told you that, Kitty.'

She shot a quick glance Cindy's way. 'How's your daughter holding up?'

The magician blinked. 'Cindy has a way of managing. In fact, I've never known anyone so determined to get what she wants as Cindy. Except, perhaps, her mother.'

Cindy had certainly gotten her way with her parents. Now Kitty understood that crack Cindy had made the day she and Fran had visited, when she talked about her father sending her a big fat allowance and how every month she made it 'disappear'. She'd said it with a smirk that Kitty hadn't understood at the time, but now it all made sense. A little joke at her father the magician's expense.

Maybe Cindy's lifestyle was bleeding her father dry. Maybe he killed Gretchen for his share of her estate. She was beginning to wonder just how much money was at stake. She'd have to ask Jack about that. He may have some idea.

Kitty had an idea of her own. She unclasped her purse and pulled out the thick and crumpled manila envelope, carefully watching Fandolfi's eyes as she did.

He cocked his head. Was he taking the bait?

'What have you there, my dear?'

'Oh.' She waved the envelope in the air. 'This belonged to Gretchen. Fran picked it up for her from Gretchen's apartment the day she was murdered. Fran said she got the impression that it might be important.' She shrugged. 'And then Gretchen ended up dead. I was thinking that maybe I should turn it over to Cindy or Teddy. Maybe even the police . . .'

'Really? How interesting.' He fingered his moustache. 'I love secrets,' he said. 'Maybe it's the magician in me. What's inside?'

Kitty smothered a smile. She gently opened the end of the envelope, careful not to let the magician see all its contents. 'Oh, this and that.' She dug into the envelope and pulled out the silver ring. 'This ring for instance.' She held it out between her thumb and index finger.

'Exquisite,' muttered Fandolfi.

'Do you think so?' Though Kitty watched for some sort of sign, she couldn't tell if Fandolfi recognized the ring or not. Was it his? It looked like the sort of ornate jewelry he would wear. 'Why don't you try it on?'

He looked hesitant.

'Just for fun.'

Mr Fandolfi smiled. 'Just for fun.' He slid the ring over his right index finger. He could not get past the knuckle. He handed the silver ring back to Kitty and she dropped it back in the envelope.

Fandolfi glanced over his shoulder then gently pushed Kitty into the corner. He gripped her arm. Kitty felt a bit frightened, even though the room was filled with people. 'Listen, Kitty, we have to talk.' His face was dark and troubled.

'About what?'

He shook his head. 'Not here, not now.' He glanced over his shoulder once again. 'Meet me later.'

'Later?' Kitty hesitated. What on earth was this all about? And did she really want to meet Fandolfi later? Something about him was beginning to smell very fishy – especially since she'd learned he'd been at the studio around the time Gretchen was stabbed in the back.

'Yes,' he said. 'Come by the house this evening.'
'I have to go to Santa Monica Film Studios this evening. I'm meeting Bill Barnhard there.'
His black eyes flashed. 'Then come to the house afterward. I'll be waiting for you. It's important.'

Twenty-Five

'Hey, hey, what have we here?' Sonny Sarkisian suddenly appeared between them. Fandolfi took a step back as if he'd been exposed to the plague. Sonny greedily fingered the manila envelope Kitty was holding. 'What's in the envelope?'
Sonny grinned a lecherous grin. In his left hand, he clutched a half-filled glass of red wine. 'Not dear Gretchen's ashes, I hope? I thought we buried her corpse this morning!' He hiccupped loudly and put his hand to his mouth. 'Oops.'
Mr Fandolfi looked venomous. 'What do you want, Sonny?'
Sonny looked taken aback. 'Why, to pay my respects, of course.' He shrugged weakly. 'I mean, me and your ex may have had our differences but she was a heck of a producer. Made us all lots of loot.'
'Yes, and to hear Gretchen tell it, you'd been looting her for years,' retorted Fandolfi.
'Hey, what's that supposed to mean?' Sonny asked, belligerently.
'It means you've had too much to drink. And

I have had too much of you!' The magician turned on his heel. 'Tonight, Kitty.'

Kitty stood there with her mouth hanging open.

'Careful, something might just fly in there.' Sonny pointed a fat finger at her gaping mouth and Kitty snapped it shut. 'So, what is in the envelope?'

'Fran picked it up for Gretchen the day she was murdered. I thought I would give it to her children, Teddy and Cindy.' She gauged Sonny's eyes; bloodshot from the booze he'd obviously been swilling. 'Though, maybe I should turn it over to the police. What do you think?'

Sonny couldn't hide his interest. His hand reached for the envelope. 'I could take care of this for you.'

Kitty snatched the envelope away from him. For a moment, she thought he might attack her and try to snatch it back again. But apparently he thought better of it. He smiled. 'I'm sure you'll do what's best.'

Kitty dropped the envelope safely back in her bag. 'Yes, maybe I'll just hold on to it a little longer.' She asked Sonny what he'd been doing at Santa Monica Film Studios the day that Gretchen was murdered. 'Kind of odd, isn't it? Considering Gretchen had fired you some time before?'

Sonny said that he'd gone back to clear out his desk but Kitty wasn't buying it. 'I was in your office after Gretchen's body was discovered. The police questioned me there. Your old office was empty.'

'What? Did you peek in all my drawers?' He

wriggled a lascivious brow and his nose followed along. Kitty thought she was going to be sick. 'Because if you'd like to peek in my drawers, I wouldn't mind.'

'Oh, please. You do know my boyfriend is a cop, don't you? Should I call him over here and repeat to him what you just said?'

Sonny threw up his hands. 'OK, OK. Only joking. Sheesh.' He bounced from foot to foot. 'I went back to clear out a few things I'd forgotten in the breakroom and to say hi to some of my friends. I'd been working there for eight years. I've got friends.'

Kitty found that hard to imagine but refrained from saying so. If Sonny was going into Santa Monica Film Studios when Fandolfi was going out, then that meant he could have murdered Gretchen.

But what was his motive? Not money, surely. He wasn't going to inherit. She had fired him. Though, now that she was in the ground, Bill Barnhard had hired him back. That could be a motive for murder. 'Did you talk to Gretchen?'

Sonny barked out a laugh. 'Are you kidding? If Gretchen had seen me there, hell, she just might have stuck a knife in *my* back.' He let out a deep breath. 'No, like I said, I grabbed a few things from my desk. Said hi to some of the crew, you know, cameramen, stagehands.'

Kitty would have to ask Fran if she had seen Sonny milling about. She worked behind the scenes, maybe she saw Sonny at some point that day.

Sonny emptied his glass and looked at it

forlornly. 'The wine is gone, Gretchen is gone.' His frown turned to a smile. 'But life goes on!'

He half-turned. 'Just look at Cindy over there.' Kitty couldn't help but look. Cindy was still haranguing poor Fran, or so it appeared. 'Gretchen is only barely in the ground but I have yet to see her shed a tear over her mother's spilt blood.'

Kitty had to admit, though Sonny appeared more and more to be a major louse, he made a good point.

Sonny motioned for Kitty to come closer, then whispered in her face. 'Of course, you wouldn't expect a murderer to show remorse for their victim, would you?'

Kitty stiffened. 'Are you trying to say that Cindy murdered Gretchen? That's impossible. Teddy has already admitted to the murder. Besides, Cindy has an alibi.' Kitty's brow wrinkled up. At least she thought Cindy had an alibi. She was getting all her suspects and their alibis mixed up now. She shook her head but nothing got any clearer. Why couldn't her brain be more like an Etch A Sketch?

'Sure,' Sonny replied, in a devil-may-care fashion, 'that's because she got her halfwit brother, Teddy, to do it.' Sonny winked lewdly. 'That woman can talk a man into anything – like mother, like daughter. Of course, if you don't like her for the lead role, there's always your new roommate.'

'My new roommate?'

'Yeah, I hear you and Fran Earhart are roomies now. She had the backstage practically to herself.

Ample time and opportunity to stab somebody in the back, if you ask me.'

He leaned in closer and Kitty drew back. 'If I was you, I'd sleep with one eye open.' With that, he turned on his unsteady heels and cut through the mourners in his path.

Kitty stared at Sonny's broad back. Darn. Was Sonny correct? Could Cindy have talked her own brother, albeit half-brother, into murdering their mother? It was entirely possible. Cindy came across like a very cold, hard woman. From what Kitty had been told, Cindy and Gretchen barely tolerated one another. And from what she'd seen and heard, Teddy did seem like he might be easy to manipulate.

What he'd said about Fran was preposterous though. Fran was no killer. Of course, Fran did have Gretchen's envelope with a hundred grand in it. Maybe she'd looked inside and had known that all along. Could she have murdered Gretchen with the intent of keeping the money and then got cold feet afterward?

Kitty pushed the ugly thoughts from her mind as she sidled up to Fran. 'Sorry to leave you alone with that witch,' Kitty said.

'That's okay,' Fran exclaimed, pulling her friend closer. 'You'll never guess what Cinderella told me.'

Kitty said she had no clue. At this point, she hadn't a clue about anything and was getting quite annoyed with herself.

'Well, she asked me about David.' Fran's eyes twinkled.

'Our David? David Biggins?'

'That's right, Mr He's-so-sweet-on-you Biggins himself.'

'What was it Cindy wanted to know?' After all, what would Cindy Corbett have in common with David Biggins? Kitty was surprised that a woman of Cindy's nature even knew the guy existed. He was cute and all, and quite charming, but he was a cameraman. To a woman like Cindy, David was nothing but a common laborer.

'She asked me where he was. Acted all disappointed when I told her he wasn't coming.'

Kitty's face pinched into a frown. 'That's funny.'

'You're telling me.' Fran pulled Kitty down on the sofa. 'But that's not all.'

Kitty waited. What else could there be?

'Now,' began Fran, 'keep in mind, I think Miss Cinderella's smashed. I think she woke up swilling tequila with her orange juice and hasn't let up yet. But anyway, Cindy told me that she and David had been lovers.'

Kitty gasped, then blushed when she saw people looking at her. 'Cindy and David?' she said softly. Was that even possible? 'So, she dumped him and now she wants him back?'

Fran shook her head slowly. 'Nope. *He* dumped *her* and now *she* wants *him* back.' Fran beamed. 'She told me that now that everything is "over",' Fran made quote signs with her fingers, 'that there's no reason she and David can't get back together.'

Kitty was shocked. 'And you believe her?'

'Why not?' answered Fran. 'And Cindy believes it. She says they broke up once before and then got back together and so she sees no reason why that shouldn't be the case now.'

Kitty chewed her lower lip and stole a furtive look at Cindy who seemed to be accepting condolences from an elderly couple that she didn't recognize. Her heart beat to get out of her chest. This could be it!

Cindy had murdered her mother, or gotten her half-brother Teddy to do the terrible chore. What was her motive? To get her troublesome mother out of her way? Out of her life? And get the money she thought she deserved? So she could go live it up on the Riviera or somewhere with David Biggins? Cindy was cold, but was she that cunning? Had she ruthlessly murdered her mother or gotten her weak brother, Teddy, to do the deed? Kitty figured she was.

Was Cindy trying to implicate her father, Mr Fandolfi, as well? Was that what the magician so urgently wanted to talk to her about? Or was it because he had some information implicating his own daughter and didn't know what to do? The poor man . . . she felt for him if that was indeed the case.

Kitty leapt from the sofa. 'Come on,' she said, 'let's get out of here.'

Fran dropped her glass on the table, where it skittered and fell sideways on to an Architectural Digest magazine. 'Where are we going? The bar's still open.'

'You've had enough to drink. And I've had enough of Hollyweird for one day.'

Kitty slammed the door behind them, saving the startled liveried doorman the effort.

Twenty-Six

Kitty sat in her old friend, the Volvo 740 wagon. Jack had dropped it off at the apartment for her and she was glad to get it back. She was really going to have to do something extra nice for Jack to make up for having been at least somewhat responsible for his beloved Jeep Wrangler now being a hunk of twisted metal at the body shop. There was still no word on whether the patient was going to make it or be officially relegated to the scrap heap. Kitty hoped for Jack's sake that the Jeep was salvageable.

She raced through her meal deliveries – the ones she had promised her clients in lieu of their usual lunch deliveries. A glance at her watch told her what she already knew. She was running late. Again.

Sitting in the long brick drive at the Fandolfis' home, she took a moment to collect her thoughts. There were lots and lots of them scooting around in her brain and the task proved pretty much insurmountable.

The live-in housekeeper had informed Kitty that Mr and Mrs Fandolfi were out to dinner when she'd arrived at their pharaonic estate. That was a pity. He had seemed so desperate to talk to her, and she was anxious to find out what about. What secret was he keeping? Was he protecting himself? Cindy?

Looking back at the Fandolfi house, she wondered, for the first time, how much the upkeep on a place like that would cost. A bundle, no doubt. A big bundle. No matter how much the magician earned, keeping up with all his household expenses, and the added burden of supporting a shopaholic wife and money-leeching daughter, could have Fandolfi desperate for money. Kitty needed answers and nothing was adding up.

Kitty ground her teeth. Now she'd have to wait. Fandolfi wasn't home. She was due at Santa Monica Film Studios in less than twenty minutes and it would take her all of that twenty minutes to make it in city traffic. She couldn't afford to keep the president of CuisineTV waiting.

She stepped on the gas, even as she punched in the number that David had given her. 'Hello, David? It's me, Kitty.'

She was dying to know whatever it was that he might know about Cindy. Had they really been lovers? What dirt could he spill on her? Or was this hypothetical affair of hers with David something she had made up? Was Cindy delusional as well as greedy and homicidal?

Maybe David could shed some light on the mystery of Gretchen's death, after all. Would he agree that Cindy could have convinced Teddy to murder their mother, Gretchen?

'Hiya Kitty. What's up?'

Kitty swerved back to her side of the road as the car beside her honked and shot her a universally known hand gesture. Jack always complained that she shouldn't be using her cellphone while driving, and she wasn't particularly adept at it. But this was one of those times where she simply had no choice – at least there were no cliffs to go careening over at the moment. 'Hey, I'm glad you're there. I was hoping we could talk.'

'Sure,' David said, readily. 'Come on over, Kit.' Kitty remembered he used to call her that in high school.

Kitty reminded him that she was on her way up to the studio to see Bill Barnhard and promised to stop by after that. Then she'd go see Fandolfi.

'Cool,' said David. 'See you then.'

Kitty rang off and concentrated on driving – at least for a minute or two. Then she called Jack. 'Hi, Jack. Thanks again for getting the Volvo back to me today. You fixed the door handle.' The one Chevy Czinski had accidently broken when she'd innocently mentioned Gretchen's name in connection with her then impending interview for the pet cooking program.

'And for washing it. That was so sweet.' She still couldn't believe he'd done that. Why, he'd even vacuumed the interior, something she had never ever done though always meant to do. The floor before today had been more dog hair and food crumbs than carpet. She was dying to ask him if there was anything new on Gretchen's murder and whether Teddy had recanted his story or was sticking with it.

'No problem. What are you up to? Are you home? How about if I come pick you up and we go grab a bite?'

Kitty said she was sorry but she had an appointment with Bill Barnard. Jack sounded disappointed. 'He's the head of the studio, Jack, I can't say no.'

Jack said he understood though she could tell he didn't.

'So, what's up with Teddy Czinski?'

'He isn't saying much and frankly his story doesn't add up real good,' Jack answered.

'So you don't think he killed his mother?'

She could practically hear Jack shrug through the phone. 'He says he did.'

'He may have had help.'

'What do you mean?'

Kitty outlined her theories about Gretchen and even Gretchen's other ex, Ernst Fandolfi. She didn't leave out Chevy Czinski. She explained how Gretchen had stolen the idea for the pet cooking show from the retired actor and what his reaction had been when he'd found out about it. 'Fran even found some old love letters that we think were written by one of them.'

'Love letters? Where?'

'Oh, you know. Lying around the studio.'

'And you're only telling me this now?' Jack didn't like that she'd been holding out on him and he let her know it in no uncertain terms. He also didn't sound convinced regarding her theories and conjecture, but he didn't shoot her down completely. 'If Teddy does go to trial, I imagine he may be found not guilty by reason of insanity. I'm not so sure he's entirely aware of his own actions.'

Kitty agreed. 'I'll tell you what, how about if

I come by after my meeting? I'll whip something up for the two of us.'

Jack's laugh spilled through the phone. He agreed and said he'd pick up a bottle of wine and meet her later. 'Elin and I have some paperwork to finish up. I should be home by nine thirty.'

If Elin was with him in the car when he came to pick her up, she was going to clobber him with that bottle of wine. Kitty stifled a growl, rang off and called Fran, who answered on the first ring. 'Fran, I'm heading over to the studio for my meeting with Mr Barnhard. Do you think you could feed Fred and Barney for me?'

'Done and done,' quipped Fran. 'I not only fed them, I gave them each a good brushing.'

Kitty told her she was a real trooper.

'Trooper, nothing,' replied Fran. 'The way these two were looking at me, I figured if I didn't feed them soon, they'd start gnawing at my leg.'

Fran hung up after telling Kitty not to worry about getting fired. Kitty dropped her phone on to the passenger seat. The battery was nearly dead anyway. It was an old phone and the battery never did last for long. She looked at the clock on the dash. With a little luck, she wouldn't be more than ten minutes late to her appointment.

The studio was all but deserted when she arrived. She pulled up to the guardhouse and came to a stop. Brad was on duty again. She recognized him, of course; she'd spoken to him the other day. Not to mention, he'd found her crouched over Gretchen's dead body. She put on a smile. 'Good evening, Brad. Working late again, huh?'

The guard's lip turned down. 'Yeah, just little old me. I've been out here mostly working the night shift ever since, well, you know . . .'

Kitty knew.

Brad's skinny shoulders bobbed up and down. 'But that's OK by me. After what happened in there, well, I can't get the image out of my mind, you know?' He hugged himself. 'To tell you the truth, that place,' he said, with a nod to the soundstage, 'gives me the heebie-jeebies. That's why I asked to be on gate duty for a while.'

Again, Kitty knew. She told Brad that she understood completely. When she was finished talking to Mr Barnhard, she intended to ask Brad about all those names that had not appeared on the sign-in sheet the day of Gretchen's murder. He hadn't been working the gate, but he would remember who had and could hopefully put her in touch with him.

'You go ahead, cat lady.' He gave a friendly wink and punched a button in the guardhouse. The gate went up and Kitty went in.

Twenty-Seven

Kitty punched in the code at the soundstage door and entered the narrow hallway. A lone bulb at the juncture of two corridors provided the only illumination. She could perfectly understand Brad's concerns. This place was downright spooky at night, murder scene or no.

'Mr Barnhard?' She frowned. 'Where could he be?' She should have asked Brad. Then she realized that he was probably using his son, Steve's, office, which was down the hall from Gretchen's old office.

She padded off in that direction and soon came to Gretchen's door. It was ajar. Up ahead, she could see that there was no light on in Steve's office or any of the others along the hallway for that matter. Was she early? She glanced at her watch. Not if her watch was right.

So that meant that Mr Barnhard was late. Kitty smiled and rubbed her hands together. This meant she had some time – maybe no more than a few minutes, but time enough to get a look inside Gretchen's office. There was no police tape, nothing to indicate that she should keep out. So why shouldn't she go in and take a peek?

Kitty pushed the door open. Her heart was beating faster than usual. It had to be the eerie atmosphere. That and the fact that, the last time she was in this room, Gretchen's dead body was lying on the floor, not inches from where she was now standing, with one of Kitty's best knives in her back.

The blinds were up. The glow from a tall lamppost in the parking lot allowed a small amount of light to spill into the cramped office. A white studio van and a dark SUV with one of those ridiculous black vinyl car bras were the only vehicles on the lot other than her Volvo. Funny, had they been there when she parked? She couldn't remember. If so, where were their owners? Something tickled at her brain but slipped away before she could figure out what that tickle was trying to tell her.

Kitty pulled down the blinds; no point drawing attention to herself.

Kitty avoided the spot on the floor where Gretchen had been and gingerly stepped behind the desk. Maybe there was something the police had missed. Some clue as to what this was really all about.

She sat, flipped on the brass desk lamp and quietly slid open the drawers one by one. She found nothing out of the ordinary. Pencils, papers, rubber bands, tea bags.

From her purse, Kitty pulled the envelope she and Fran had taken turns holding and laid it atop the desk. She'd had a sudden and brilliant idea. She didn't have to tell Jack about the money and about how she and Fran had withheld possible evidence from the police.

All she had to do was slip the envelope into one of Gretchen's desk drawers, shove it way back where it might look like the police had simply missed it and presto! Or she could stuff it into one of those filing cabinets along the wall.

Yes, brilliant.

As her fingers went to the manila envelope, Kitty thought she heard the sound of steps coming up the hall. Her mouth framed an O, her heart froze, and she held her breath, straining to hear.

There were no other sounds. Still, what if Mr Barnhard came back and caught her spying in Gretchen's office, riffling through her papers? Totally embarrassing.

She glanced at her watch. Nearly eight fifteen. 'Where is that man?' she muttered.

Kitty used Gretchen's desk telephone to call the guardhouse. 'Hey, Brad. It's me, Kitty. I'm still waiting for Mr Barnhard. Has there been any sign of him? Has he shown up yet?'

'Oh, geez,' Brad said, 'is that what you're doing down here so late? Mr Barnhard came in over an hour ago. But he got a phone call and had to run right back out again.'

Kitty asked how long ago that had been. Brad said maybe twenty minutes or a half hour at the most. 'So it's just me, huh?' This certainly had been a waste of her time. Oh well, she could stick the envelope with the money and ring in it someplace not too obvious, yet easy enough for someone to *stumble* on when Gretchen's office got cleaned out. That way, she wouldn't be in trouble with Jack, and whoever was the rightful heir would get what was coming to them. It was the perfect plan.

'That's right,' Brad replied. 'The studio's pretty much empty, except for you and Biggins.'

Kitty twitched. 'David?'

'Yeah, that's right,' answered the security guard. 'He came in a few minutes after you arrived.'

'Hi, Kitty.'

'David!'

David stood blocking the doorway. He was wearing dark jeans and a black T-shirt. He wasn't looking nearly so charming as usual. In fact, in his right hand, he clutched a long-bladed knife. He motioned for Kitty to hang up and she carefully dropped the phone back in its cradle.

'I'll take that,' he said.

'What?'

'The envelope,' David said. His voice had a harsh quality to it that Kitty had never heard from him before. He wriggled his fingers. 'I said I'll take it.'

Kitty looked down at the envelope. Her hand was resting on it. David wanted the envelope? 'I–I don't understand.'

David's laugh came out like an ugly bark. He stepped nearer. 'I'm sorry it has to be this way, Kitty. Slide it over, *now*.' His voice was hard and, worst of all, ominous.

Suddenly everything made sense. David had been in the building right after Kitty discovered Gretchen. He said he'd come back, but he'd probably never left. And that SUV outside in the parking lot, the one wearing the ridiculous car bra. She remembered now that David drove an SUV – a silver one!

She'd seen it before, like when they met at the diner the night of Gretchen's murder. But it wasn't a Porsche like she thought – it was an Acura or something. She'd gotten them mixed up. Steve hadn't tried to run her off the road in the Hollywood Hills at all. It had been David.

The car bra that wasn't there originally had probably been stuck on to hide the damage to his own vehicle.

She blinked, as if seeing David Biggins for the

first time. 'You're Cam!' she exclaimed. Cam, as in *cameraman*.

David nodded. There had been an issue between Gretchen and David at the time of the taping. What was it? Kitty remembered now. David was nowhere to be found when the show started and Gretchen was furious. In fact, she'd said she could kill him.

Instead, he had murdered her. Kitty knew the *who*, but not the *why*. Kitty had a sick feeling in her stomach. If she didn't do something quickly, she was about to die.

Twenty-Eight

Her shaking hand played atop the envelope of cash. 'It's no use, David. What are you going to do after I give you the envelope? Murder me, too?'

He shrugged as if it was all too obvious. Maybe she should have kept her mouth shut.

'You'll never get away with it, David.' Kitty was shaking so bad, she was surprised that she could even get her mouth to operate, let alone manufacture words and then string them into sentences. She knew that she had to keep David talking if she was going to keep living. 'You're forgetting, Brad knows you're here.'

David's smile, that in other circumstances would have looked positively charming, now looked positively scary. 'Not to worry.'

He stepped closer. Kitty rolled back an inch in her chair. It was all the room she had as the chair bumped the wall behind her. She was cornered. 'You see, Kitty. I told Brad that you and I had a hot date tonight.'

'A date?'

He nodded. 'Yep. So you and I are going to leave here together. As we stop at the guard gate on our way out, you're going to smile and wave real big and friendly like. Let our pal Brad know that we are all happy-happy.

'Then later, when you disappear . . .' He paused and scratched his cheek with the sharp edge of the knife. 'Well, it won't matter. Because I'll have disappeared too. A guy can go a lot of places with a hundred thousand dollars in his pocket.'

Kitty felt queasy and cold inside. David was sick. He was a murderer to boot. 'What makes you think I'm going to cooperate?' If he was going to kill her, she certainly wasn't going to make it easy for him. How she wished now that she had asked Jack to meet her here instead of suggesting that she meet him at his house.

David never stopped grinning. He looked at the hand clutching the ugly knife. Up close, Kitty recognized it as a CuisineTV branded carving knife. The blade was only of middling quality but no doubt would suffice for the job David seemed to have in mind.

'This knife, for one thing.' He rested his free hand on the desk. 'And the fact that, if you don't cooperate, I'll go after your new roomie and your pets. Fred and Barney, that's their names, right?'

Kitty gasped. 'How do you know their names?'

'I've been to your apartment, remember?' Kitty did. She had been out. Her neighbor, Sylvester, had been pet-sitting and mentioned that David had stopped by.

'I don't understand why you're doing this, David. Why would you murder Gretchen?'

He clenched the knife so hard his knuckles turned white. 'I hated that woman. She was a manipulating cow.'

Kitty had been hearing a lot of that ever since Gretchen's death, but the woman had always been kind to her. And Gretchen and Fran had been close friends.

Mr Czinski had a lot of animosity toward his ex-wife. Kitty wasn't certain what Fandolfi thought of her. He couldn't have despised her too badly after all – he had done her the somewhat dubious favor of referring Kitty to his ex when she needed the right host for her cooking show. Now, with David hovering over her with murder on his mind, Kitty was pretty certain she could scratch Fandolfi off her list of suspects.

She swallowed hard. Sweat was building up in her palms. 'I still don't understand. What about the money? If you and Gretchen hated each other so much, why on earth would she give you one hundred thousand dollars – and a silver ring?'

'The ring's mine,' he said. 'My cousin made it for me. I gave it to Gretch.' He made a fist with his free hand. 'And I want it back.'

'You–you gave it to Gretchen? Why?' Kitty wasn't simply stalling for time – the stalling for time was definitely a good thing – but she really wanted to know what David's motivation was. And what was his relationship with Gretchen? Twisted, yes, but what else?

David's laughter filled the office. 'Don't you get it, yet, Kitty? You said it yourself. I'm Cam.' He was smirking. 'You found those stupid love letters, didn't you?' He said the word love with a healthy dose of mockery.

'You and Gretchen? It's true that you were lovers?' Kitty's eyes grew ever wider. 'I heard that you and Gretchen's daughter, Cindy, were lovers, too.'

'We were.' He folded his arms across his chest, though he never let go of his hold on the knife. He shook his head. 'Gretchen and I had an affair. Oh, we were hot and heavy for a time. I even gave her my ring. It was too large for her finger, of course. So, she wore it on a silver chain around her neck.'

He paced and, while he did, Kitty looked for some avenue of escape. He was between her and the door, so that was out. And the window was latched and the blinds were down.

'But she was such a pain. We broke up.' David explained how he'd then taken up with Gretchen's daughter, Cindy, partly out of spite. He knew Gretchen would hate it and he'd been right. Gretchen had become enraged.

'Gretchen didn't think I was good enough for her daughter. She tried threatening me, but I laughed in her face. She said she'd tell Cindy about our affair. I called her bluff and dared her to, but she chickened out.' His eyes flattened.

'But then she promised me money.' He used the knife to point to the envelope. 'That money.'

'She was paying you off to stay away from Cindy?' This was getting more and more bizarre. What sort of people had she gotten involved with?

'That's right.' He laughed again. Kitty was glad somebody was finding this whole situation funny, because she sure wasn't.

'And I didn't mind. To tell you the truth, Cindy's just as bad as her mother. A real pain in the butt. A spoiled cow herself. How I loathed that woman.'

'So what happened? If Gretchen was going to pay you, why kill her?' There really seemed no point.

David's jaw tightened. 'Because, dear Gretchen said she'd had a change of heart. It was the afternoon of your first taping. Gretchen was supposed to pay me. She'd sent Fran to pick up the money,' he explained. 'I couldn't wait to get my hands on all that loot.' His fingers wriggled. 'But Gretchen was full of herself. You know she told me that the idea for your cooking show wasn't even hers, like she'd told everyone?'

Kitty knew.

David shook his head. 'Turns out, that ape of an ex-husband of hers had come up with the idea – and she was bragging how she'd practically swindled him out of any share of the profits. Boy, she was convinced there were going to be huge profits for her and the network. What a piece of work.'

He waved the knife in the air. 'But that was

no skin off my nose. I mean, if she wanted to screw her ex that was her business. All I wanted was what was coming to me.'

He stopped and his voice grew cold. 'But then Gretchen said she wasn't going to pay me. The hag reneged on our deal. She laughed and said that since I'd already dumped Cindy, there was no reason to pay me. She laughed in my face, Kitty, and demanded that I leave her office.'

Kitty took a deep breath. David looked ready to pounce. She needed to calm him down again. 'That's terrible. I mean, you must have felt betrayed.'

He studied her face, and then spoke. 'I knew the set was hot – the show had already started. I saw your open bag backstage and grabbed the knife. It was handy, you know?

'I slipped the knife inside my shirt. I wanted to scare her. I went to Gretchen's office. Nobody saw me. Everybody was busy out front with *The Pampered Pet* show. I started digging around. Fran had come back to the studio so I knew the money had to be there someplace.'

But Kitty knew that it hadn't been. Fran had never given the envelope to Gretchen. It had remained in her bag.

'I knew Gretchen would come looking for me and she did. She found me looting her office and started screaming like a banshee on fire. She demanded that I leave and get back to my camera. I told her that she really should pay me.

'The cow yelled that I was fired and that she would insist that Bill Barnhard blackball me from ever working for CuisineTV again. She pointed at the door and then had the gall to turn her back on me.'

Kitty held her breath. The room seemed alive with negative energy and looming menace.

'So I gave her what she had coming. Dear Gretchen liked to stab others in the back.' He ran his tongue along his lower lip. 'So I gave her a taste of her own medicine.' His eyes dropped to the spot on the floor where Gretchen's body had lain only days before.

Kitty didn't think she'd get another chance. With one hand she tossed the envelope toward the ceiling. With her other hand, she threw the heavy brass desk lamp at the side of David's head.

He looked up reflexively at the rising envelope as the brass lamp hit him in the ear. He howled with rage and turned toward Kitty.

But Kitty was already halfway to the door and running as fast as she could. The lamp had come unplugged and the room had gone dark. Light from the hall beckoned and Kitty dove for the door. David's hand grabbed her ankle and she fell face first. He was pulling her back.

'Let. Me. Go!' Kitty lashed out with her free foot. David screamed in agony as her shoe made contact with something soft and squishy. His grip relaxed and Kitty surged out into the hall, yanking the door shut behind her to buy herself some time.

But would it be enough?

Twenty-Nine

Kitty stumbled down the dimly lit hall with no direction in mind and escape her only goal.

Think. Think. Think.

The words bounced through her mind as she ran noisily down the narrow hall. Each bang made her wish she had worn quieter shoes. Then again, the heels had served her well as a weapon. Kitty heard a scream that would have curled her blood if it hadn't all congealed the minute David had suddenly popped into Gretchen's doorway clutching that vicious-looking knife.

She'd scream herself but what would be the point? There was nobody else around. The studio was deserted but for her and David inside, and Brad the security guard outside. This was a soundstage. It was meant to protect those inside from the sounds of the outside world. She could scream at the top of her lungs, and though Brad was only fifty or so yards away, he'd never hear her.

Kitty turned at the nearest intersection even as she heard David's pounding feet pulling closer. It was nearly dark. Shadows were everywhere and each one gave her a start that she thought would stop her heart for sure.

Which way was the door? There had to be an exit around here somewhere. One of those fire exit doors that the law required. If she could find one of those, not only could she escape outdoors, but hopefully going out the door would set off some sort of alarm. That would bring down the fire department, the police department, and half a dozen news hounds and countless lookie-loos.

That would be her salvation.

If she could find a door.

'Come on, Kitty,' cajoled David. He didn't sound nearly as winded as Kitty was feeling. 'What are you running for? Let's talk about this. We can do a lot with a hundred thousand dollars. You can come with me to Central America. Start fresh. I've got a little place all picked out.'

Like she believed that. *I'm thirty years old, not some child!* she wanted to shout, but she wasn't about to give herself away. No point making this easy on him.

Kitty turned left again and banged face first into something hard and unforgiving. It shook and rattled loudly. She reached out to quiet it. Not that it mattered much. David would have heard the noise for sure. She ran her hands up and down the cold metal object, her eyes adjusting to the dark, and smiled. She knew where she was now. She was on the set of *The Pampered Pet*. What she'd slammed into had been one of those big spotlights the crew were always aiming at her during taping.

Kitty ran her tongue around her lower lip and tasted blood, bitter and metallic. She'd cut her lip on the light stand. Running to the pantry, she scanned the shelves. She grabbed a jar of virgin olive oil and clutched it to her chest. If anything, she'd clobber him with the thick glass bottle if he got too close.

Kitty was working her way around to the backside of the kitchen island when David suddenly appeared only a few yards away. He'd managed to pick up a flashlight. He shot its beam across the otherwise dark set like a pulsar.

Kitty ducked and held her breath, leaning against the island. There had to be something around here that she could use as a weapon that would be superior to a lousy jar of olive oil. This was a kitchen, after all.

'Here, Kitty, Kitty.' David chuckled.

Kitty shivered and twisted around on her hands and knees. There was a set of CuisineTV knives on the counter beside the sink. Did she dare stick her neck up and try to reach them?

Would she have the strength, both physical and mental, to use one if she did? That mental part was sketchier than the physical part. Kitty had never purposely hurt anyone before. Even at risk of her own death, she wasn't certain that she could do it now.

The light danced above her head. David was getting closer. Then she had an idea. She pulled the stopper from the jar of oil and quietly dumped the entire bottle out on the floor between the island and the counters. If anything, the oil slick would slow him down.

An open shelf on the rear of the island held pots and pans. Kitty studied the dark shapes, exploring them with her hands. She wrapped her fingers around a heavy cast iron skillet. She slid the skillet off the shelf. If she could hurl it at him or maybe in the direction she had come in from, she might be able to distract him long enough to make a run for it.

Of course, she'd have to be careful to avoid all that extra virgin olive oil she'd just spilled across the floor. If she remembered correctly, there was a fire exit off to her right, just beyond the bleachers where the audience sat the day of the taping. There was a chance that she could reach it. Slim, but worth taking. It wasn't like she had a lot of options.

Kitty eased herself up slowly, praying her movements didn't give her away. As she did, the beam of the light caught her in the face, momentarily blinding her. She screamed. David was only inches away and there was an ugly-looking knife tucked under his belt.

She swung the skillet at his head.

David knocked it away with his elbow. 'Not this time!' he snarled. He tossed the flashlight aside and clamped his fingers around her neck.

The skillet slipped from Kitty's hand and landed on David's foot. He howled with rage and pain. Sensing his weakness, Kitty drove her heel into his foot even as she felt her vision fading as his hands tightened around her throat.

The knife!

Kitty groped for the knife at David's belt but he beat her to it. 'Oh, no, you don't!' He knocked her hand away. But to do so, he'd had to release his death grip on her throat.

Kitty pushed free and turned. David grabbed her by her hair and spun her back around. Tears of pain flooded her eyes. She kicked him in the shin, broke free and ran.

'You want the knife?' David chuckled. 'Here!' he shouted. 'You can have it!'

Kitty screamed and twisted to one side. The knife whistled past her, clanged against the refrigerator and spun loudly on the floor. Kitty dove for it but she was too late.

David was already there. 'Get up!' He glared at her, flashlight in hand. Blood oozed from the side of his face. His clothes were a mess. Whether all that damage was the result of the skillet, her earlier beaning of him back in Gretchen's office with the brass desk lamp or her shoe, she didn't know. But he deserved every bit of it. And then some.

David slid the knife closer to himself with his shoe then bent to retrieve it. Kitty scrambled to her feet, mindful of the oil on the floor, and pushed up against the countertop. Somehow she had to squeeze past David, get to the fire door and safety. But how?

David stuffed the flashlight under his belt and bounced the knife in the palm of his hand. 'Think you're going to get away?'

'That was the idea.' She edged further behind the counter, careful to stick closer to the edge. There was a puddle of oil somewhere and it was meant for David, not her.

'Funny. Very funny.' David stepped in and slammed Kitty against a bookcase. A pair of the flimsy bookcases held books written by various CuisineTV hosts. 'Not so funny now, is it?'

Kitty grunted and bit down on her lip as she

thrust her arms back to keep her balance. The bookcase shook – it was only meant as set decoration after all and wasn't permanently attached to the wall – and went crashing down.

Kitty twisted to the left as it fell.

David jumped for her but he never had a chance. He slipped in the pool of oil. 'What the—' His feet flew from under him. Kitty heard his skull crack the ground. She pulled on the second bookcase and watched as it crashed down on top of him. Kitty threw herself across the bookcase. David lashed out, arms and legs swinging and kicking madly.

Kitty was wondering how long she could keep this up when several of the large klieg lamps suddenly snapped to life, filling the set with their bright, hot lights. Fran burst into the middle of the soundstage, her mouth hanging open. 'What is going on here?'

What she saw was Kitty straddling a fallen bookcase and riding it like it was a raging bull at the strangest rodeo on Earth. 'Quick!' Kitty cried. 'Don't just stand there – give me a hand!'

'I'll kill you,' David bellowed, grabbing Kitty's arm and yanking mercilessly. 'I'll kill you both!'

'Not if I can help it!' yelled Fran, racing over to come to her friend's aid even as Kitty grabbed the nearest thing at hand – a hardcover copy of *The Joy Of Cooking* – and brought it down on David's face. He raised a hand to fend her off. The thick book bounced off his fingers and crashed into his nose. After a moment, he stopped thrashing.

Kitty fell forward, out of breath. The book dropped from her hand. Her hair and clothes were wrecked and her brain was still trying to make up its mind what was real and what was not and whether it even cared one way or the other.

Fran leaned over her, hands on hips. 'So, tough day at the office?'

Thirty

Kitty weakly thrust out her right arm. 'Hand me your phone, would you?'

'What happened? Did this jerk make a pass at you?' Fran cast a suspicious eye on David. 'You calling the cops?'

Kitty nodded. She looked at her watch. Jack was probably still at the station. Perfect. She punched in his number.

'Hello, Jack?' she said, a look of supreme triumph on her face, that she sorely wished her fiancé could see but sadly could not. Her smile betrayed her extreme satisfaction. She had been praying for this moment for days but never thought it would come. 'Would you be a dear and put Elin on the line, please?'

Jack muttered some words of confusion then passed along his cellphone.

'Good evening, lieutenant. This is Kitty Karlyle.' She winked at Fran. 'I've got your killer here if you'd like to come pick him up.'

David started thrashing again but he wasn't

going anywhere. He was pinned down good. Fran planted her foot on the back of the bookcase, adding her weight to David's burden, just for good measure.

Nordstrom's bellowing forced Kitty to pull the phone some inches away from her ear. When the lieutenant calmed down, Kitty told her to head over to Santa Monica Film Studios.

'No hurry,' said Kitty, rubbing a little salt into the wound, 'everything's under control here.'

She hung up as Jack came back on the line demanding to know what was happening. Kitty said she would explain it to him when he got there.

'David killed Gretchen?' Fran looked incredulous.

Kitty nodded and explained the how and why. 'What are you doing here?'

Fran pulled a face. 'Two reasons. Number one, I thought you might need a friend to pick you up, figuratively that is, after your meeting with the big boss. I thought I'd buy you a drink and give you a shoulder to cry on after he canned you. I tried calling you but it went straight to voicemail.'

'My phone died.' Kitty frowned. She'd almost died, too. 'I thought you said I had nothing to worry about?'

Fran shrugged sheepishly. 'I could have been wrong.' She looked around. 'Where is Bill Barnhard anyway? What happened?' She looked at the bookcase. 'He's not under here too, is he?'

'He received a phone call and had to leave before we even had a chance to talk. He was gone before I arrived.' She jabbed her thumb in David's direction. 'I'm guessing that call came from this jerk.'

David's stony face and icy stare told her she was right.

'What was the second thing?'

Fran said, 'I finally remembered where I'd seen that silver ring we found with the money. For a while, Gretch was wearing it around her neck on a silver chain. When I asked her about it, she said it came from an admirer but she wouldn't say who.'

Fran snapped her fingers. 'Hey, David used to wear a ring like that on a chain around his neck, too.'

Kitty nodded weakly. She felt completely drained and her shoulders felt like she'd attempted to lift a five-hundred-pound dumbbell over her head. Instead, she had a two-hundred-pound dumbbell under a bookcase.

'That makes sense.' Kitty cocked a hand toward David, lying sullenly beneath her. 'Fran, meet Cam. As in cameraman.'

Fran gaped. 'Gretchen's lover? I knew it!' She paused. 'But, I thought he and Gretchen's daughter, Cindy, were lovers?'

Kitty coughed out a laugh. 'Oh, Fran. This is Hollyweird, remember?'

Fran pursed her lips and was about to reply, when the police suddenly appeared. Lieutenant Elin Nordstrom was in the lead, dressed in a navy dress suit, long legs practically dancing across the soundstage like it was opening night on Broadway. Jack was right behind her.

Nordstrom's flashing eyes went from Kitty to Fran to David Biggins' bruised and bloodied face protruding from the side of the bookcase. She yelled for several of her uniformed officers to pull him out. Kitty and Fran scooted off the bookcase and left them to it.

'What's going on?' demanded Nordstrom.

'Hi, Jack,' Kitty said, looking past the annoying long-legged lieutenant and giving her boyfriend a waist-high wave of the hand. Kitty couldn't stop smiling despite what she'd just been through. After all, this was one time she was actually happy – no, make that very happy – to see Elin Nordstrom.

'Kitty,' Jack seemed to be struggling to control his voice, 'what have you been up to?'

Thirty-One

The backyard party was a success. The sun was sinking slowly behind some wisps of cloud. There was a cool bite to the air that added a pleasant tingle. The smell coming from the grill of burgers, veggie burgers, corn on the husk and artichoke added an earthly pleasantry to the air.

Jack's black Lab, Libby, was running freely around the yard, begging for, and usually receiving, scraps of food and strokes of attention from everyone she could.

Kitty helped herself to a glass of white wine. It was her second. Not that she needed it. She was feeling great. David Biggins was behind bars – thanks in no small part to her efforts – and she'd been able to rub the ridiculously long-legged Elin Nordstrom's nose in that fact.

Speaking of which, Lieutenant Nordstrom was standing beneath the lone elm in the far corner of Jack's yard, chatting with Detective Richard Leitch. Both were dressed casually in jeans and clutching bottles of Spendrups, the imported Swedish beer that Nordstrom seemed to prefer – and she could have posed as a bikini-clad poster girl for in their ads.

Rick Leitch, to Kitty's relief, had come as Elin's date and apparently she was doing her best to make a Swede out of him.

Leitch had been one of the first on the scene the day of poor Gretchen's murder. He seemed like a nice enough fellow and he was an eligible bachelor. Kitty could only hope that the lieutenant didn't ruin him completely. Still, if she was honest with herself, she had to admit that she was glad that Nordstrom had found someone other than Jack to sink her claws into for a while.

Several other coworkers of Jack were also present, along with some of the crew from Santa Monica Film Studios – including her director, Greg Clifton, in tow with his assistant director, Julie McConnell, with whom Kitty had heard he was in a relationship. Julie was half Greg's age, but they were both single and consenting adults, so who cares?

Sonny Sarkisian was there, currently with a spatula wrapped up in his fist, lending a hand at the grill, which seemed to be addling Jack's nerves. If Sonny wasn't careful, Jack just might take out his police issue automatic and do some tenderizing of his own.

Kitty was planning to keep an eye on Sonny. She'd finally learned from Bill Barnhard that the reason Gretchen had fired Sonny was because she'd suspected he'd been collecting kickbacks from advertising clients. However, she'd been rash in her decision-making, something she was prone to doing – it seemed to be a flaw in her character – and had been unable to prove her allegations.

Sonny had gotten himself a good lawyer and was threatening a multimillion-dollar wrongful termination lawsuit against the studio and the network. Rather than face the trouble and expense of fighting the charges, Sonny had been given his job back.

Mr Barnhard explained that, this way, either Sonny would prove himself innocent or do something stupid – and unethical/illegal – and they could fire him for good. The company would be keeping an eye on him.

Kitty was determined to do the same. There was simply something – she couldn't put her finger on what exactly – but something innately suspicious about Sonny Sarkisian. Not the least of which was his apparent camaraderie with her nemesis, Steve Barnhard.

Speak of the devil, Steve was in attendance, too – with his boyfriend. Even though he was a pain in the butt, she couldn't exclude him from the invitation list. Kitty had to admit, she'd pegged Steve wrong in a lot of ways.

Looking at Steve and Roger cuddling on the patio, sharing a chaise longue, Kitty couldn't suppress a laugh at her own expense. How could she have been so wrong about him?

They made a cute couple. Each wore tight black jeans and equally tight black T-shirts. Steve hadn't been having an affair with Barbara Cartwright; he was in a relationship with her assistant, the ever-so-French Roger Matisse.

As it turned out, Steve hadn't been going behind her back trying to get her fired or sabotage her show either, though initially he admitted he had toyed with the idea. He, Roger and Barbara had come up with a concept for a show that they had secretly been developing for Barbara. They had pitched the idea to Steve's father the night that Kitty had been run off the road and thinking that Steve was to blame.

They had even produced a pilot, with Greg directing, that had apparently blown Bill Barnhard's socks off. So it looked like Barbara would be getting a new travel/cooking show of her own soon. Hopefully, both Barbara Cartwright and Steve would be hitting the road.

Gretchen's death had all been the result of a crazy love affair gone bad, mixed with greed. David had had an affair first with Cindy. But Gretchen quickly found out about it and didn't approve. She'd concocted a cockeyed plan to woo David away from her daughter by offering herself to him.

David and Gretchen had become lovers and all was well . . . for a time. With personalities like theirs, it was only a matter of time.

David had been writing her love letters, signing them Cam. That was her nickname for him. In a moment of passion, he'd also given her the silver ring he usually wore around his neck. The one his cousin had designed for him.

Eventually, however, David and Gretchen broke up, and apparently it was ugly. To make matters worse, David had started dating Cindy again. When Gretchen demanded that he stop, he laughed in her face. When she threatened to fire him, he laughed again. He had a union job. If she tried to fire him, she'd have a fight on her hands.

That was when she apparently decided to pay him off. And that was what the envelope full of money was all about. David was getting a hundred thousand dollars to dump Cindy and go away – and, to sweeten the pot, Gretchen was giving him back his precious ring.

Kitty wasn't sure what had made Gretchen change her mind at the last minute, but that decision had cost her her life. David wasn't about to see his prize – dangling like a winning lottery ticket before his greedy eyes – suddenly snatched away from him.

In a rage, he had stabbed her to death. The problem was he didn't know where the envelope was. He couldn't find it in the office anywhere, even though Gretchen had told him she had it there.

She didn't though, she only thought she did. Fran hadn't put it there. If Fran had done what she was supposed to, David would have found the innocent looking envelope in the top drawer of the producer's desk, which was where Gretchen had instructed Fran to stick it, and probably have disappeared for good.

Instead, the money was missing and David was desperate to find it. He had broken into Kitty's apartment and Gretchen's condo to no avail. When he learned that Fran and Kitty had what he wanted, he wasted no time in trying to retrieve it, either through devious means, or – when devious means failed – through deadly ones.

David had even been tailing Kitty. He'd seen her leave Jack's place in the Jeep and head into the mountains. He figured he'd run her off the road and snatch the envelope from the wreck if she had it with her or at least get her out of the way if she didn't.

Only good fortune and a jacaranda in just the right spot had saved her.

All this time, Kitty had thought David was completely charming and completely innocent. When David had espied Kitty and Brad hovering over Gretchen's corpse, he'd said he had come in with the security guard because he'd forgotten his jacket. What an idiot she had been to take that statement at face value. But then, she'd had no reason to suspect him of subterfuge.

Looking back on it, she remembered how Brad had looked at David sort of funny when'd he'd said it. On questioning, after David's arrest at the studio, Brad realized that he had forgotten to clarify that he had no idea where David had come from and that he, according to Brad's later statement, *just sort of came out of nowhere*. David had obviously never left the studio and had been lying in hiding for just the right moment to reappear.

If David had seen Fran backstage with the envelope and realized what was in it . . . Kitty shivered. There was no telling what he might have done. He might have grabbed another knife and stabbed her, too. Or maybe strangled her like he'd tried to the other night.

Of course, Fran was here at the dinner party, too, looking delightfully ravishing in a pale purple jump suit and navigating the lawn in gold tone heels, glass of merlot in hand. Fran had her old job back at the studio due to Kitty's insistence. Steve had kicked and screamed about it but in the end had caved. If Kitty was correct, Fran was now on course to connect with a civilian dressed pal of Jack's named Zeke. Fran being Fran, she'd probably spill half her glass on or in the immediate vicinity of the object of her current desires.

Zeke was standing off to one side, hands in the pockets of a faded denim jacket, looking lost. Kitty had spoken with him once or twice. He was very nice and very shy. Zeke wasn't going to stand a chance. Fran would bowl him right over; ply him like warm, wet potter's clay in her hands. He'd never know what hit him.

Kitty herself still barely knew what had hit her. It wasn't that long ago that she had parted ways with her longtime best friend. That was the first time she'd been involved in a murder, one involving a rock star client of hers. She hoped this would be the last. Then Fran had burst into her life and even into her apartment. They were roommates now, for goodness' sake.

Fran's job was secure for as long as Kitty had hers. Hopefully, that would be for a very long time to come. She could get used to having some money in her pocket for a change. Maybe she and Jack would finally set a date . . . and start thinking about having kids . . .?

Fran swerved around the picnic table and her smile locked on Zeke. She held out her free hand to introduce herself and Zeke responded by freeing one of his own pocketed hands. He smiled awkwardly.

Bingo! Direct hit.

Jack appeared out of nowhere and wrapped his arm around Kitty's waist. 'Having a good time?'

Kitty smiled up at him. She'd finally gotten over the trauma of being chased around Santa Monica Film Studios by David Biggins who'd been bent on killing her. Jack had finally gotten over being mad at her for taking so many crazy chances and risking her life the way she had – at least, he'd stopped complaining out loud about it.

But all's well that ends well, right?

She kissed him on the lips. 'Does that answer your question?'

He said it did. 'I heard from Greg and Julie that your show's going to continue.'

Kitty nodded her head vigorously. It had been touch and go there for a while. Bill Barnhard and the board of CuisineTV had been uncertain whether to continue or pull the plug on *The Pampered Pet* what with the murder and all the negative publicity and bad karma surrounding it.

In the end, public reaction to the pilot had been overwhelmingly positive and so the network had agreed to pick up a season's worth of shows. 'Isn't it wonderful? Mr Barnhard explained that the show only tapes two days a week. That means I can continue to run my pet chef business the rest of the week. I won't have to give it up at all. I didn't know what I was going to tell my clients.'

'Sounds like you're going to be extremely busy, Kitty. Too busy for me?'

She kissed him again. 'Never.'

Speaking of clients, it turned out that Mr Fandolfi's wife, Holly, had written the threatening note Kitty had found on her Volvo outside the bakery that day she'd met the magician in West Hollywood. That hadn't been Steve or David at all.

It seemed that Fandolfi's wife was insanely jealous and actually thought that she and her husband might be intimately involved. Holly had been following Kitty all over town, and had rigged her husband's new trick to *scare her off*. Holly had even disguised herself and come to the taping so she could spy on them.

Hollyweird, right?

That explained why Kitty had found the CuisineTV potholder at the Fandolfis' house. In fact, that explained the one at Mr Czinski's place, too. The potholders had been handed out to the audience at her taping as tokens of appreciation.

Kitty couldn't help but wonder how it was that the rich always liked getting something for free. Human nature, she supposed. Kitty very much doubted that Holly even spent any time in the kitchen let alone knew what to do with a potholder.

Kitty still had a hard time believing that the young and gorgeous Holly could ever have seen her as a threat to her marriage. Yet, that was exactly what Mr Fandolfi had wanted to see Kitty about the night that David had tried to kill her. He wanted to explain to Kitty about his wife's extreme jealousy in the face of any other competition for her husband.

He hadn't wanted to say anything before because he was embarrassed and also because he didn't want to say anything unkind about Holly. After seeing Kitty get hurt while assisting him with his new trick, well, he figured he just had to say something before things got out of hand.

Go figure.

Again, all's well that ends well. Kitty and Holly had had a long talk and Holly seemed to understand that there had never been anything more between Kitty and Holly's husband than business. There had certainly never been anything to be jealous about.

Fandolfi and Gretchen's daughter, Cindy, was nowhere in sight, but Thadeus – Teddy – Gretchen's other child, had come with his father, Kitty was glad to see.

'Poor Teddy,' Kitty said. He had been exonerated, of course, with sincere apologies from the police department.

'How's that?' Jack wanted to know. 'He stands to inherit a bundle.'

Kitty shrugged. 'I know, but I still feel bad for him. Money's not everything, Jack,' Kitty said. 'Finding his mother dead like that. Then actually starting to believe that he was guilty of the crime.' Kitty couldn't suppress a shiver. 'How could such a thing happen?'

Jack frowned. 'Yeah, you can thank your pal, David Biggins, for that. He's one slick character. When he came by to see Teddy at the station, acting like he was Teddy's friend there to solace and comfort him, he actually managed to talk him into confessing that he'd killed his mother.'

Jack cursed. 'Worse still, he had the poor guy believing it.' He hugged Kitty closer. 'It was sweet of you to give Teddy a job as an assistant on your show.'

Kitty smiled. 'It was the least I could do. I don't think working alone at night as a janitor with nobody around is good for him – maybe not good for anybody.'

She watched as Teddy, on his hands and knees on the lawn, wrestled with Libby. 'Besides, look at him, Jack. He's great with animals and it is a pet cooking program.'

Jack agreed.

Kitty cast a bemused look at Elin Nordstrom and Rick Leitch. 'It looks like the lieutenant has found someone to sink her claws into besides you.'

Jack turned to her with a big grin on his face. 'Oh, come on now, Kitty. You weren't jealous of me and the lieutenant, were you?'

'Of course not,' Kitty replied a little too quickly.

He squeezed her waist. 'You know you're the only woman for me.'

'I'd better be,' Kitty warned.

They kissed slowly, and then Jack looked into her eyes. 'And now that this case is solved and life is back to normal . . .' Jack sounded nervous.

'Yes, Jack?' Was this it? Was Jack about to set the date? Was a honeymoon in Mexico around the corner? After a smashing wedding in Newport Beach, of course. Oh. She'd have to call her mom!

Mom would definitely want to go bridal gown shopping with her, Aunt Gloria, too. Aunt Gloria was her mother's sister and head librarian in the City of San Diego Public Library system. Her mom already said she thought Kitty would look best in something empire style. Kitty leaned toward the mermaid silhouette, or even a more traditional ball gown.

Jack shuffled his feet against the dry grass. 'Well, what with your show being picked up and all . . .'

Kitty kept her eyes glued on Jack. Her hands were locked in his and her palms were growing sweaty. She would be very busy, maybe they should get married sooner, rather than later. She struggled to keep her smile under control.

'Well, I was wondering . . .'

'Yes, Jack?' Another minute of this suspense and she was going to explode all over the lawn. 'Yes,' everyone would say afterward, 'it was a lovely garden party. Until one of the guests exploded all over the lawn, that is . . .'

Jack opened his mouth. Here it comes, she thought.

'Could I borrow the down payment for a new Jeep?'

Kitty staggered and dug her nails into the palm of Jack's hand. 'Excuse me?'

Jack blushed. 'You see, I'm a little short right now. I've had some house repairs.' He cleared his throat. 'You totaled my Wrangler, remember? The insurance company said they wouldn't fix it – the damage was too much and so they've totaled it and given me a ridiculously paltry sum as recompense.' He was talking fast now. 'So I need a new car. But if I don't come up with some more cash, the monthly payments are going to be killer.'

Kitty frowned. 'David ran me off the road.'

'I know, I know,' he struggled to placate her. 'But you're okay now and since you're going to be making all that money with the show—'

He stepped back on seeing the flash in Kitty's eyes. 'It'd only be a loan. I'll pay you back as fast as I can.'

Kitty turned and marched toward the house.

'I'm expecting a raise at my next review!' he hollered to Kitty's fading back.

Though Jack couldn't see it, Kitty was grinning. It looked like the engagement wasn't about to end anytime soon. But that was OK, she could wait.

Oh, she'd let him suffer a little longer, but tomorrow she'd surprise him with a brand-new Jeep. She'd have to charge the down payment to one of her sorely overworked credit cards and would face the ridiculous interest charges that the banks were getting these days – at least until she got her first fat CuisineTV paycheck.

Kitty gave a mental shrug. Some things were just worth it, and Jack was one of them.